# DEATH ON THE CAROUSEL

A TWISTY AMATEUR SLEUTH MURDER MYSTERY

THE BREAKFAST CLUB DETECTIVES

HILARY PUGH

Housemouse Press

# 1

When Teddy Strang asked Jasmine Javadi if she would like a fun night out at the circus, a dead body landing at her feet was the last thing she expected. And yet here she was, staring a couple of feet in front of her at the body of a man. Jasmine was no expert but, on this occasion, she didn't need to be. The bruises around the man's neck, his bulging eyes and purple complexion as well as a complete lack of any sign of movement, even breathing, told her that he was decidedly dead. Not only was he dead now, he had been so for a while. She could tell even without touching the body, and that was the last thing she wanted to do. He lay bent stiffly in an awkward position, his knees drawn up under his chin as if he had been folded into a small space and left to set like a clay model. His hands and feet were tied together with rope, which had fixed him in a gruesome foetal position. She knew better than to touch the body, but she could tell it was stone cold. And as she stared, she could see that the rope was in two halves as if broken by the pressure of holding the body in position, until its limbs were stiff from rigor mortis, and it was no longer able to release itself.

At first, Jasmine thought this could be some bizarre ending to the show. A tableau of horror from which the man would miraculously spring back to life and proclaim the whole thing a joke. Circus performances were not immune from moments of dark melodrama. Like puppet shows, Jasmine had always found them unsettling. Clowns had never appealed to her. She had been seriously spooked when taken to the dentist as a child, by a huge mural of a clown on the wall in the surgery. She'd flatly refused to open her mouth in its presence and had to be taken into the adult surgery instead. There was a word for that. She searched her memory for it now. Coulrophobia, she remembered. Fear of clowns. So she wasn't the only one. But Quinn's Circus didn't have clowns, not in the traditional sense. They had a comedian dressed in tweed trousers and a trilby, who trotted round the ring between acts followed by a tame goose and handing out lollipops to children in the audience. But he wasn't at all frightening. It was as if those who ran the circus had deliberately decided not to include acts that might cause nightmares. And if that was the case, they'd hardly include a macabre tableau of a dead body to greet the audience on their way out.

The Quinn family spent the summer months touring the country with their selection of vintage circus acts and steam-driven fairground rides. They were extremely popular, with performances sold out months ahead. Jasmine had been lucky enough to have been offered a ticket by Teddy Strang. She'd met Teddy during the body in the Long Walk case. He had, in fact, been instrumental in solving it. Since then, they had kept in touch, meeting now and then for a drink or a meal. Teddy was a freelance journalist and had managed to obtain two tickets for that night's show, along with the promise of an interview with the founder of the circus, Cordelia Quinn. How this had come about, Jasmine didn't know and didn't enquire into. Teddy's contacts were mysterious and often dubious. And if Teddy occasionally strayed into questionable ethics to gather his stories, most of what he wrote was harmless and entertaining. Interviewing the founder of a circus was hardly akin to phone hacking and bribery. Not that Jasmine had any reason to suspect Teddy had ever been involved in either of those. He'd been invited to this interview, assured that a little mutual publicity would do neither Teddy nor the circus itself any harm and could even drum up lucrative results for both of them.

Until the body landed at Jasmine's feet, it had definitely been a fun evening; jugglers, fire eaters, some agile horses and dancing dogs. Even the man with the goose raised a lot of laughs by falling off the straw bales that separated the ring from the audience and throwing his hat in the air, pretending not to see where it landed and asking the children to help him spot it. The performance had ended with a spectacular finale; the horses with plumes now ridden by a young woman in a sparkling costume, who stood and even danced on their backs. Acrobats cartwheeled around the ring with some daredevil trapezing overhead, all accompanied by loud music supplied, so Jasmine read in her programme, by a Romanian Gypsy band. All of this was controlled by Cordelia Quinn herself, a woman in her sixties dressed in white breeches, red frock coat, black knee-high boots and a top hat, who stood in the middle of the ring cracking a whip.

After the performance the audience filed out to enjoy the fair; swing boats, a helter-skelter, and a carousel with horses and sleigh seats whirling around accompanied by a calliope which belted out fairground favourites such as *Oh I Do Like to Be Beside the Seaside* and *Daisy Daisy.* Probably not what the original Calliope, muse of eloquence and epic poetry had in mind, but enjoyable when chowing down hot dogs and getting a sugar rush on candy floss.

But Teddy and Jasmine arrived later than most to these delights. They remained behind in the big top after the rest of the audience left. Teddy to interview Cordelia Quinn, and Jasmine, not in any immediate need of either a hot dog or candy floss, staying inside the tent until he'd finished. While waiting for him she chatted to Caitlyn Quinn, Cordelia's granddaughter, a woman in her twenties who trained the horses and performed precarious feats, dancing on their backs as they galloped around the ring.

The interview finished, Teddy switched off his recorder and took a few photos on his phone. Then, followed by Cordelia Quinn, he crossed the ring to where Caitlyn and Jasmine were perched on hay bales, chatting. Cordelia stared at Jasmine and frowned. 'I thought you were the photographer,' she said. 'I was expecting decent professional photographs, not phone snaps.'

'Er, sorry, no,' said Jasmine. 'I'm sure Teddy knows what he's doing, though.'

'Granny,' said Caitlyn. 'Don't be so grumpy. The latest phones take very high quality pictures.'

'That's right,' said Teddy. 'It's what most of us pro journalists use these days.'

Cordelia ignored him. 'I'll give you grumpy,' she said to Caitlyn. 'Run and get changed now and see to the horses.'

'Sorry,' Caitlyn mouthed at Jasmine with a wink as she left the ring and headed, Jasmine assumed, for the stables.

'Well,' said Cordelia, turning back to Teddy. 'You'll send me a copy before it goes to press? Photographs as well.'

'Of course,' said Teddy. 'It's been commissioned by the local paper. I can send it to you as soon as their editor has looked it over.'

Cordelia nodded, shook Teddy's hand and disappeared through the artistes' entrance, ignoring Jasmine altogether.

'Bit of a diva,' said Jasmine as Teddy checked the recording he'd made of the interview along with the photos and emailed everything to himself.

'More of a despotic matriarch,' said Teddy, tucking his phone into the inside pocket of his jacket.

'You're not going to publish that, are you?'

'Of course not. I'll be tactful and admiring. I don't want her chasing after me with that whip, do I? How about a hot dog?'

By the time they emerged from the big top, most of the audience had left the fairground and things were winding down for the night. They managed to grab the last hot dogs before the stall closed and ate them while watching as the carousel came to a juddering halt after its final ride of the night.

And that was when it happened.

The body that at first appeared to have landed from the sky, had in fact been tossed from somewhere on the carousel, flying through the air, knocking into one of the horses and landing at Jasmine's feet.

Recovering from the shock, Jasmine began to notice the activity around her. Teddy, among others, had got out his phone to call for help and to take pictures. People were videoing the scene while a man dressed in an acrobat's leotard dragged a couple of hurdles between the body and a small crowd of people, who were staring open-mouthed. He gestured at them to move back. Gestures which were largely ignored by the crowd until Cordelia appeared with a megaphone. She was followed by Caitlyn and a couple of stocky men, who herded everyone towards the car park, instructing them to stay in their cars until the police arrived. Teddy was making the most of this sudden drama and was busy recording eyewitness comments and taking photos. Jasmine stood speechless, starting to shake from the shock until Caitlyn led her by the arm to an old-style caravan parked at the back of the circus tent. She sat her down on one of the bunks, wrapped her in a knitted shawl and poured her a drink from a flask. 'For the shock,' she said, handing it to her after taking a swig herself.

Jasmine swallowed a gulp and gasped as it stung the back of her throat. She felt as if she had swallowed a burning match. She screwed up her face and handed the flask back to Caitlyn. She looked around for Teddy but couldn't see him. 'He's getting eyewitness statements,' said Caitlyn.

*Should he be doing that?* Jasmine wondered. Weren't they supposed to leave it all to the police? But Teddy could never leave a story alone and Jasmine couldn't blame him. Journalism was his job, and he couldn't really have had a better view of the incident. And who knew, he might even have picked up something that would help the police. But she couldn't rid her mind of the sight of the body. 'Do you know who the dead man was?' she asked Caitlyn.

'Yeah, he was one of the mechanics, Badger Waites.' She screwed the top back onto the flask and put it down on a table.

'Badger?'

'I think his real name is Greg, but he's called Badger because of the white streak in his hair.'

'Did you know him well?'

'Not really. He's a friend of my cousin Joseph. He joined us a couple of weeks ago when we first set up here. An out-of-work mechanic, he helped with the rides. He lives locally, apparently. Joseph got him the job here after they'd met at some music thing.'

Jasmine was feeling better and thought she should go and look for Teddy. She hoped he hadn't forgotten her and driven away in a rush to file his story, and get it online before anyone else got wind of it. She wasn't far from home and on a nice sunny day she'd have enjoyed the walk along the riverbank into town. But after such a shocking event she didn't fancy setting out on her own in the dark. She'd stay here a while longer and if Teddy didn't turn up to look for her, she'd call a taxi.

There was a tap at the door. Jasmine stood up, hoping it was Teddy ready to take her home. But it wasn't Teddy. As Caitlyn opened the door, Jasmine recognised the detective sergeant standing on the step. Jasmine had known Flora Green for a few years and seeing her now brought back memories. Flora had been a newly qualified detective constable when they'd met after Jasmine had handed in some useful footage she'd filmed. Footage that Flora had passed on to the drugs squad, assuring Jasmine that it was going to be very useful and would lead to arrests. That was long before the Breakfast Club Detectives had even been a thought in her head. But it was when not only Jasmine, but Jonny and Ivo had solved their first crimes. At the same time as Jasmine's covert filming, Jonny Cardew, chairman of a cardboard packaging factory in Slough, had uncovered a case of people smuggling. And Ivo Dean, the handyman who'd worked for Jasmine's father, Karim, since he'd been at school and who Jasmine thought of as a younger brother, had, with his dog Harold, caught a juvenile burglar. Now Jonny was retired, and Ivo was happily settled as the caretaker of *Shady Willows,* a site for affordable homes upriver from the town centre. Harold's burglar-catching talents, Jonny's lifelong ambition to be a detective and Jasmine's general nosiness had all come together when they met Katya Roscoff, the fourth member of their quartet of amateur detectives. A meeting that gave birth to the Breakfast Club Detectives. And since then, Harold had added the detention of a murderer to his list of sleuthing skills. Katya Roscoff had also known Flora Green for a while. She was on the same team as Flora, working for Detective Inspector Lugs Lomax. And now, like Jonny Cardew, Katya had retired. At least, she'd retired from the police. She was, she told everyone, as active as a detective as she'd ever been and frequently with more interesting cases. After Katya retired, Flora had been promoted from constable to sergeant. Jasmine was pleased for her. She was also extremely pleased to see her right now in the doorway of Caitlyn's caravan. Never mind swigs of strong alcohol, what one really needed having been recently confronted with a dead body, was a down-to-earth detective sergeant.

'Jasmine,' said Flora, coming into the caravan and closing the door behind her. 'I didn't expect to see you here. I was told this was where I could find the woman who discovered the body.'

'That's me,' said Jasmine. 'Although he found me rather than the other way around.'

Flora looked puzzled. 'Like to tell me what happened?' she asked, clicking the record button on her phone.

'He was trapped somewhere on the carousel,' said Caitlyn.

'And then he fell onto the ground at my feet,' said Jasmine. 'But I'm sure he was already dead when he fell. He was stiff and kind of folded up.' The image in her head was making her feel a bit queasy and she sat back down suddenly. She could murder a cup of tea. *An unfortunate phrase,* she thought, relieved she hadn't said it out loud. In any case, Caitlyn was more interested in filling in details for Flora than putting the kettle on.

'He must have been hidden somewhere on the carousel and thrown off when it stopped,' said Caitlyn. 'It sometimes stops quite suddenly. People are warned to hang on tight, but if you're dead, well...'

'And you are?' Flora asked, turning towards her and holding the phone up for her to speak into.

'I'm Caitlyn Quinn.'

'You're related to the owner?'

'I'm Cordelia's granddaughter. Although she's not the sole owner now. She founded Quinn's fifteen years ago but she owns it jointly with my three uncles.'

Flora glanced at her phone to make sure it was still recording. 'And your uncles' names?' she asked, once she was satisfied that she was picking up every word.

'Patrick, known as Paddy, he's my dad, Aidan and Dara. All Quinns. Gran always told us she didn't believe in daughters.'

*An odd thing to say,* Jasmine thought. Did it just mean she hadn't got any daughters? And what about granddaughters? Caitlyn was a starring act with her horses and presumably Cordelia approved of that. But this wasn't the moment to ask.

'Right,' said Flora, clicking to end the recording and putting the phone in her pocket. 'You've had a shock. We'll get you home and take statements from both of you in the morning.'

'This is home for me,' said Caitlyn, waving her arms around the caravan.

'I'm afraid it's a crime scene,' said Flora. 'Do you have anywhere else to stay?'

'No,' said Caitlyn. 'There are six caravans. We live on site and don't know anyone in the area.'

Flora scratched her head. 'Everyone who works for the circus lives on site?' This was obviously about to become a huge headache for her.

'Or on the campsite in the other field, near the car park,' said Caitlyn. 'There are one or two people we employ locally who stay off site, but I don't know them well.'

'I'll need to take advice,' said Flora, getting out her phone again and heading for the door.

'I don't live far away,' said Jasmine. 'You could stay with us. But we don't have room for all of you.'

'It's just police fuss,' said Caitlyn. 'They can't keep us from the site. We've animals to care for.'

After a few minutes, Flora returned, putting her phone in her pocket. 'I've talked to my DI,' she said. 'He's sending a scene of crime team and they will cordon off the carousel. You can stay in your caravans but he's asking you not to leave the site or to breach the cordon.'

'Do you want me to pass that on?' Caitlyn asked.

'No, I've couple of PCs doing it. They'll check on who is where and post patrols on the gates. No one will be allowed to enter or leave until we've assessed the crime scene, which will probably be sometime tomorrow.'

'Does that mean Teddy and I have to stay?' Jasmine asked, thinking it could be fun to sleep in one of the caravans, although she wasn't sure Teddy would agree. He'd want to be off doing whatever he needed to do to get his story published.

'That's Mr Strang, is it?' said Flora. 'He's outside talking to my detective constable. You can both go home. Call me tomorrow and arrange to come in and make statements. I'll get someone to escort you both to the car park. The team are there taking contact details from everyone who was still here when the incident happened before they let them leave, but they should be through with that by now.'

'Well,' said Teddy as he drove out of the car park and headed for town and Jasmine's café. 'That turned out to be an interesting evening.'

'Interesting is one word, I suppose,' said Jasmine. 'That poor man. What do you think happened?'

'Murdered, wasn't he?'

'So you've got a good story to send?' A bit disrespectful, taking advantage of the poor man's death, but she assumed that's what journalism was all about.

'Already done,' said Teddy, shaking his phone at her. 'The wonders of modern technology.'

It was a short drive into town and a few moments later he

dropped Jasmine off at the back of the café. 'You won't be on your own, will you?'

Jasmine shook her head. 'Dad's there,' she said.

'Good,' said Teddy. 'Not nice to be on your own after coming face to face with a dead body.'

# 2

Sundays were usually quiet at *Jasmine's*. On weekdays commuters were in and out cramming in breakfast before hurrying off to work, often taking their coffee with them in disposable mugs. But on Sundays the café opened late for customers who had slept in and were in no hurry to get on with their day. People lingered over newspapers and regulars had time to gossip. Breakfast merged into brunch and the kitchen was as likely to serve up baked potatoes with cheese as bacon and egg with toast; even the occasional pre-midday slice of cake was not unknown. It was as if time ceased to matter. Mealtimes were ignored and customers ate whatever they fancied.

The day after the murder at the circus, the café was buzzing with chatter and speculation about what had happened. *Jasmine's*, although unconnected to Quinn's Circus, was known as the best place to pick up local gossip as well as the home of the Breakfast Club Detectives, who would surely take a keen interest in a murder on their patch. And once it was revealed that Jasmine herself had actually been there, had been the first to see the body as it flew out of the carousel, excitement grew even more. She was deluged with questions. Had anyone known the victim? Were there any clues? Was there a dangerous criminal still lurking in the area? A three-week-long visit by a well-known vintage circus was already an attraction, but one that provided the excitement of a murder doubled its appeal. The Wi-Fi at *Jasmine's* became clogged with customers trying to discover more online. The Quinn's Circus website had gone down from the weight of people wanting tickets for the show, even though there was no guarantee that there would actually be a show until the police had finished their enquiries into the death.

Teddy Strang's eyewitness account had appeared on local news websites within hours of the event and had instantly gone viral on social media. Teddy himself was currently sitting in *Jasmine's,* tucking into one of their extra large full English breakfasts and looking pleased with himself. He was waiting for Katya Roscoff, whom he had called at what she complained to him was an unnecessarily early hour that morning. Seven a.m., Teddy had told her, was not that early, but Katya had moaned and growled at him about having her lazy Sunday routine disrupted until she caught the word murder, at which point she pricked up her ears and promised to hotfoot it round to the police station to glean what she could of the enquiry.

Jasmine approached with a jug of freshly brewed coffee and yawned as she topped up Teddy's cup. She'd not slept well. But who would after a shock like that? She'd get over it, and in hindsight, it had all been quite exciting. She'd watched the police at work and seen the inside of a real old-style Gypsy caravan. She'd even talked to actual circus performers. Well, she'd not really talked to Cordelia Quinn, who'd turned against her at the outset for not being a professional photographer – hardly Jasmine's fault. But Caitlyn had been friendly. Jasmine, as her father's partner in the café, was, of course, familiar with family-run businesses. But a family-run circus was very different. A much larger family to start with. And a lot more exotic and exciting.

'Recovered from the excitement?' Teddy asked as she finished pouring his coffee.

'I'm fine,' said Jasmine.

'I called Katya,' said Teddy.

'I was wondering about that,' said Jasmine. 'She'd never have forgiven us if one of us hadn't told her about it.'

'She's gone round the police station.'

'Good. There's no one as good at getting inside information from the local detective squad as Katya.' Katya had been one of them before she retired, and was still on their list of go-to civilian investigators, having been a long-term friend of Inspector Ludwig Lomax, who would no doubt be heading the case of the man flung unceremoniously from the carousel the previous night.

Her customers not needing her immediate attention, Jasmine put the jug down on the table, pulled up a chair and sat down, pleased to rest her feet for a moment, her sleeplessness catching up with her. 'To be honest,' she confessed, 'I was quite envious of Ivo finding the body in the river.'

'Ah, your last case,' said Teddy. 'The man who died twice. And you feel that after last night, you and Ivo are now equals in the finding of bodies. That could be seen as rather bloodthirsty of you.'

Jasmine laughed. 'No more than you getting your story into every possible news outlet within hours.'

'Fair enough,' said Teddy. 'Think you'll be called upon to help the police again?'

'I doubt it,' said Jasmine. 'The body in the river looked like an accident at first. We were just asked to find out about the man's background. Last night's body was definitely the victim of murder. That's not the kind of thing the police hand out to civilians.'

'Even in these cash-strapped times?'

'Even then. The police need convictions and there's nothing like a high-profile murder to keep their arrest rate looking good. And this was definitely a murder, so they'll pour all they've got into solving it.'

Teddy finished his plate of food and reached for a piece of toast, which he spread liberally with butter and marmalade. 'I agree. The poor guy might have killed himself, but he could hardly have trussed himself up like that. I imagine the police have already opened up a murder file.'

Katya breezed in. She'd obviously jumped out of bed the moment she got Teddy's call and rushed off to the police station without giving a thought to what she was wearing, or even running a comb through her hair. Although, Jasmine reflected, that was what Katya looked like most of the time. Today, as a concession to the warm weather, she was wearing a pair of cotton combat trousers, a shirt bedecked with pineapples, and orange Crocs.

She plonked herself down between Teddy and Jasmine and grinned at them.

'We were just saying that the police will be throwing everything they've got at the circus murder,' said Jasmine.

'Not only that,' said Katya, studying the menu she already knew by heart. 'They've already arrested someone.' She left them to order her breakfast at the counter while Teddy and Jasmine stared at each other in surprise.

'Did you get the details?' Teddy asked as Katya returned a moment later carrying a set of cutlery wrapped in a paper table napkin. Teddy had his phone out ready to record everything he hoped Katya was about to tell him.

'There will be a press conference later today,' said Katya. 'You can go to that. I need to eat my breakfast undisturbed by your questions.'

Teddy sighed. 'You know what pressers are like,' he said. 'Just a scramble of irrelevant questions then everyone coming out with the same story.'

'It wouldn't hurt to give us some details, would it?' Jasmine asked, wondering if she still needed to go and make a statement if it was all sorted. 'Not if it's all going public in a few hours, anyway.' And Katya, Jasmine thought, was itching to tell them what she knew, however much she was pretending otherwise.

'Well,' said Katya. 'I suppose not.'

'We already know the victim was Badger Waites,' said Teddy. 'And that he was working as a mechanic on the fairground.'

Katya nodded. 'Actual name Greg Waites. Known as Badger because of a condition called poliosis which is an absence of melanin and causes white streaks in the hair. Nothing to do with the cause of death, except perhaps that it made him easy to spot in a crowd. He was twenty-five years old, worked at an engineering plant in Slough until recently when he was laid off. The circus gave him a job two weeks ago.'

'And the person who was arrested?'

Jasmine's assistant arrived with Katya's breakfast, and she shovelled in half a plateful before she answered the question.

'Jeremy Quinn,' she said, taking her time with her coffee, spooning in sugar and stirring it with deliberate care before continuing. 'He's the son of Aidan Quinn, one of the co-owners of the circus.'

*A family feud of some kind?* Jasmine wondered. The victim had been a friend of one of the Quinns, hadn't he? She was having trouble remembering who was who in the family but she thought Caitlyn had mentioned a cousin. If they were all as aggressive as the matriarchal Cordelia Quinn, it wouldn't surprise her if there had been a falling out among cousins. But why the drama? Why tie him up in the carousel where sooner or later he would be discovered in a dramatic fashion? Suspicion would obviously fall on someone close by. 'So this Jeremy Quinn,' she said. 'He allegedly killed the victim and strung him up somewhere inside the carousel. How come no one saw the body? Was he hanging up in the roof?'

'There's no forensics report yet,' said Katya. 'But they seem to think he didn't die from hanging. He was strangled and then hidden, possibly at the top of the carousel tied to the struts. Trussed up by his wrists and ankles, which would explain the rope. But you can't print any of that.' She gave Teddy a warning look. 'Quinn hasn't been charged yet. They can hold him for twenty-four hours for questioning. You can only publish what gets released at the press conference.'

'You think I don't know that?' Teddy asked. 'Don't you trust me to do my job properly?'

Katya didn't answer. She just gave him a look that suggested *trust* and *Teddy Strang* were not words that usually appeared in the same sentence without the addition of *lack of* before the word *trust*.

'Did Lugs suggest you might get a role in the enquiry?' Jasmine asked hopefully.

'Unlikely this time,' said Katya. 'It looks like a cut and dried case of murder and Quinn is a suspect because the two of them were heard quarrelling earlier in the week.'

*So what?* Jasmine wondered. People squabbled all the time. It didn't usually lead to murder. Unless it was over a lover, a crime of passion. Perhaps they'd fallen out over a woman and the murderer had left the body in a prominent place as a lesson to the lady involved. A message to say she would be next. Jasmine shuddered. 'Did he say what they were quarrelling about?' she asked, hoping it might reveal a clue.

'That's not been released,' said Katya. 'They'd be worried it might stir up a media frenzy of speculation.' She raised an eyebrow in Teddy's direction.

Teddy adopted an expression of hurt innocence. 'More likely to do that if they *don't* release the information.'

'You'll just have to go to the press conference and ask.'

Teddy finished his toast and swallowed the last of his coffee. 'I'd better be on my way,' he said as he stood up. 'I'll dig up what I can about Jeremy Quinn.'

'Let us know if you find anything interesting,' said Katya.

Several customers had finished their meals and were looking around for assistance. 'I'd better get back to work,' said Jasmine. 'Would you like another coffee, Katya, or are you going up to the office?'

'Another coffee would be nice,' she said, holding up her empty cup. 'There's not much going on in the office right now.'

'Okay,' said Jasmine, picking up the jug and noticing the coffee was now cold. 'I'll just get a refill.' *Katya was right,* she thought as she headed for the kitchen. The office wasn't getting a lot of use at the moment. Nothing, in fact, since the end of the body in the river case. Her hopes had been raised after last night's incident, but if it was a straightforward case the Breakfast Club Detectives were not going to be needed. And it made her wonder if that was going to be the end of it all. She hoped not. They'd all miss it.

# 3

Jasmine was relieved that by four o'clock the café had become quiet again. It had been unusually busy for a Sunday, and after her sleepless night she'd been tired even before they opened that morning. Once Katya and Teddy had left, it was back to work for her, and she'd been kept busy for the rest of the day. She supposed there was a limit to how much speculation one could do about a murder when it had only just happened, and with the exception of Katya there was no one they could ask. There was also a limit to how much food could be eaten in a single sitting and at last things slowed down and Jasmine was able to turn the door sign to *Closed.* She went into the kitchen to finish the washing up, relieved to be on her own. Her father, Karim, had slipped out as soon as the café closed. He'd gone to visit an old friend from Iran, a regular Sunday afternoon visit, and Jasmine knew the two of them would sit chatting over sweet, gritty cups of coffee for hours. Anyone who said it was women who did all the gossiping hadn't heard her father and his friend once they got going.

She quite enjoyed being in the kitchen on her own. She could take her time and arrange things the way she liked. She put everything away in its correct place, tidied the kitchen and hung up the tea towels. Then she wondered how to spend the rest of her day. She was too tired to be sociable and after the previous evening at the circus, she really didn't want any more excitement. A quiet time at home seemed like a good idea. There was paperwork she could get on with and food orders to see to. Or she could do some pampering; paint her nails, sit in front of a movie with her face covered in an exfoliating pack, or browse some favourite sites for new clothes. But the weather had been warm and humid since early morning and by the time she'd finished clearing up, she felt hot and sweaty. She decided on a cool shower followed by an hour or two with a good book and a glass of lemonade with ice and mint. It was a drink she served often enough to customers, particularly in the summer, but one she rarely had time for herself. She looked into the fridge and found a nearly full jug, the last of several she'd made that morning. It didn't keep well so she'd be doing herself a favour if she finished it off, ready for a new batch the next morning. She poured some into a tall glass and cut herself a piece of the apple pie they'd served to customers with their afternoon tea. She'd not had time to eat since early morning, so she made it a large slice and, adding a piece of cheddar cheese, carried it all upstairs to the flat she shared with her dad.

She settled in a comfortable chair with her Kindle, feet up on a footstool and her cool drink within easy reach on the table at her side. She'd have been asleep in minutes if her phone hadn't chosen that moment to ring and keep her awake. She should have been pleased really – sleep now and she probably wouldn't tonight.

She glanced at the caller ID and saw Caitlyn Quinn's name on the screen. They'd exchanged numbers the night before while they were in Caitlyn's caravan. They were now friends and calling each other for a chat was what friends did. But all the same, Jasmine was surprised that Caitlyn had called, particularly right now. She'd supposed the Quinns' lives would be all over the place, with a family member accused of murder and a business disrupted by a grisly event that was likely to attract not only visits from the press, but every rubbernecker for miles around.

She picked up the phone and tapped to answer the call.

'Are you busy?' Caitlyn asked.

'Not right now. I've finished work for the day.'

'I just called to ask how you are,' said Caitlyn.

'I'm fine,' said Jasmine. 'But more to the point, how are you? I heard about your cousin. How are you coping?' She couldn't begin to imagine how Caitlyn must be feeling. Were they a close family? She assumed they must be, living and working together the way they did. Was her cousin still being held by the police? They could keep him for twenty-four hours and then they would either have to charge him or let him go. The worry for the waiting family must be horrendous. Or did they all assume he was guilty and that he was getting what he deserved? But even if they did think that, the resulting publicity wouldn't do the circus any good. They'd be worried that audiences would die away to nothing, and they'd be left with all the expense of, well, she wasn't sure what their expenses would be but she couldn't imagine touring with a circus would be cheap.

'It's grim,' said Caitlyn, sounding surprisingly cheerful about it. 'We're not doing the show tonight, which means we've all the hassle of refunding tickets and turning people away. The carousel is still cordoned off, although the police have gone. They took a load of photos so we should get it back soon. Not that anyone will want to use it after what happened.'

'You never know,' said Jasmine, hoping to sound encouraging. 'It might have a macabre fascination.' How could she have said something so stupid? It must be tiredness making her blurt out the first thing to come into her head. 'Sorry, that was tactless.'

'It's fine,' said Caitlyn. 'You're probably right. But we're waiting to see if Jeremy will be released soon or if the police will ask for an extension while they gather more evidence. He's got the duty solicitor with him, but Granny's trying to get hold of a guy she knew in Dublin who's good with criminal stuff apparently.'

'That's good,' said Jasmine, not sure what to say and not wanting to put her foot in it again.

'The thing is,' Caitlyn continued, 'Granny asked me to call you.

She says you're in some detective club and she's read about a murder you solved.'

*How did she know that?* Last night Cordelia Quinn had barely noticed she was there. And when she did it was to accuse her of not being a photographer. 'We call ourselves the Breakfast Club Detectives. There are four of us led by an ex-copper.' Jasmine should have been flattered that a well-known circus owner had heard of them. It was probably thanks to Teddy Strang and the follow up pieces he'd written about them after the Long Walk case. Perhaps he'd told her about his role in it when he was interviewing her. But whatever the reason, it was nice that failure to be a photographer wasn't the only thing that had stuck in Cordelia Quinn's mind when Jasmine's name was mentioned.

'The thing is,' said Caitlyn, 'none of the family think Jeremy did it. In fact, we know he couldn't have. He's simply not the murdering type. He's a bit of a rebel but he would never hurt anyone. And he's a vegan.'

Jasmine didn't think being a vegan was actually a character reference or an indication of blamelessness. She wasn't aware of any research that showed not eating animals made one less likely to commit murder. It might be an interesting topic for an academic criminologist, though.

'Anyway,' Caitlyn continued, 'if they do charge Jeremy, Granny wants you to prove he's innocent.'

*Wow,* thought Jasmine. Did that mean the Breakfast Club Detectives might have a new case? Not that she wanted Jeremy to be charged with murder, unless of course he really had done it. But if he was innocent, it would be great to be involved with clearing his name. 'I'll need to discuss it with the team,' said Jasmine, trying to be sensible and to keep the excitement out of her voice. 'You can let me know if the police release him within twenty-four hours. But if he's still being held after that and the others agree, how about we fix a meeting for tomorrow morning?'

'Sounds great,' said Caitlyn. 'But it should be away from the showground.'

'No problem. We have an office here. I'll text you the details.'

'Thanks so much. I'll pass that on to Granny. You're a real star, Jasmine.'

Jasmine ended the call buzzing with the excitement of a possible new case, her tiredness forgotten. She scrolled through the numbers in her contacts. Katya should be the first to know. She tapped in the number to call her and explained everything she and Caitlyn had discussed. 'But, of course, Jeremy Quinn might have been released by then.'

'Lugs was pretty sure he'd be charged when I spoke to him earlier.'

'But a lot can happen in a few hours. They might have new evidence, or someone else might have confessed.'

'Unlikely, I think. We should plan to meet as soon as possible. We can always cancel if things turn out differently.'

'I suggested a meeting in our office tomorrow morning.'

'Good work,' said Katya. 'Office nine o'clock tomorrow it is.' She sounded almost as excited as Jasmine felt. 'Can you get cover? You should be there.'

'Mondays are quiet after the first breakfast rush,' said Jasmine. 'I can set it all up and get Stevie to come in and take over for an hour or two.'

'I'll let Jonny know,' said Katya. 'Can you call Ivo?'

JASMINE, always an early riser on working days, woke up to a text from Caitlyn. Jeremy Quinn had been formally charged with the murder of Greg Waites AKA Badger in the small hours of Monday morning. He would appear in court at two o'clock that afternoon and, as travelling with a circus meant he had no fixed address, he would be unlikely to get bail.

So the meeting was on. Jasmine had already called Stevie, who arrived at seven while she was preparing the tables for breakfast ready for a seven-thirty opening. The kitchen staff were at work, and everything seemed to be humming along nicely. There was no need for her to hang around, so she went up to tidy the office. The death in the river case had ended back in early April and it was now June, so the office had been unused for two months and had a musty, shut up feel to it. She opened the windows and cleaned the whiteboard. Then she vacuumed and dusted, sharpened pencils and made sure there was plenty of paper to make notes on. Cordelia and Caitlyn were coming so they'd need two more chairs. She went back downstairs and borrowed a couple of the dining room ones, which she placed at the far end of the table.

She stood back and looked approvingly at her work. It was businesslike again. The last thing she wanted was for Cordelia to think they were untidy and disorganised. But having cleaned and dusted to her satisfaction, Jasmine was left to wonder how on earth they'd begin to prove Jeremy Quinn's innocence. She just hoped Mrs Quinn and her granddaughter had more than just the fact of Jeremy being a vegan to support the claim that no way could he be a murderer. Hopefully Katya would have some ideas. Katya could be demanding but Jasmine found she was looking forward to her giving out orders again. Ivo had sounded keen as well when she'd called him. And Jonny was always up for a new challenge.

# 4

'You want to join a circus?' Belinda stared at Jonny over the top of her glasses.

Well, at least that had caught her attention. She'd been distracted since losing her seat on the council. She was currently wading through a mass of papers; requests from people who ran charities and were in need of volunteers, pamphlets about worthy causes, and a couple of letters from the chairman of a local political party, inviting her to fill in an application to become a parliamentary candidate at the next general election.

Belinda was sorting things into two piles; one that she might consider and one that she'd definitely reject. Right now, the reject pile was winning by a big margin. In fact, there was only one thing in the *maybe* heap. Jonny surreptitiously glanced across the table to try to see what it was and read something about homes for donkeys. Well, that would be a change from council work. He'd not been aware that Belinda was fond of donkeys. It had never really come up in conversations. But if it was what she wanted, who was he to object? Perhaps they could keep one in the garden. He didn't suppose donkeys did much harm to garden plants, and their grandson would love it. But would it really keep Belinda busy?

Jonny understood, he really did. He'd always supported Belinda and never begrudged the time she spent on her council work, but now she had a big gaping hole in her life, and he knew she worried about how she was going to fill it. He'd no idea how he could help her, so as usual he did nothing, just jogged along in his customary aimless way, telling himself something would turn up and Belinda would soon be back to her old energetic self; rushing off to meetings and getting dressed up for formal events. 'I don't want to join a circus,' he said. 'You haven't been listening. What I said was that we have a meeting this morning with a woman called Cordelia Quinn, founder of Quinn's Circus.'

Belinda shuffled some of her papers to one side of the table and removed her glasses before looking up at him. 'There was a murder at the circus a couple of days ago, wasn't there?'

She was still keeping up with local news, Jonny was pleased to note. He'd not known anything about the murder until Katya called him, summoning him to a meeting first thing that morning.

Belinda looked at him with an amused expression. 'Are you going to solve the case?' she asked.

He ignored the look on her face. He was used to not being taken seriously. 'Not exactly. Someone has already been charged.'

'Then what is there for you to do?'

'The man in custody is Cordelia Quinn's grandson. She's convinced he didn't do it. I think she's going to ask us to look for evidence that will clear his name.'

'Her grandson? Well, she would think he was innocent, wouldn't she? It's what grandmothers do. Won't you just be giving her false hope if you let her think you can prove it?'

'I'm assuming she has her reasons. But we haven't accepted the case yet. That's why we're meeting her.'

'At the circus?'

'No, at the office.' Jonny looked at his watch. Eight o'clock. Belinda had been up for hours and it didn't look like she was about to take a breakfast break. Jonny made toast and coffee and put it on the desk in front of her.

'Thanks, love,' she said. 'Aren't you having anything?'

'I'll grab something at *Jasmine's* before the meeting.' He kissed the top of her head and looked at the pile of papers on the desk still waiting for her attention. 'Make sure you take a break from all of this, won't you?'

'I will,' she promised. 'I might find time to do a bit of gardening.' Belinda loved gardening. She said it was therapeutic, but Jonny had never understood that. As far as he was concerned, gardening involved doing stuff that would need doing all over again a week later. But then, his role in the garden was weed control. Belinda's was to nurture plants. A subtle but significant difference.

KATYA WAS ALREADY TUCKING into a plate of bacon and eggs when Jonny arrived at *Jasmine's*. He ordered the same and sat down next to her.

'Great idea, this breakfast club of yours,' she said.

Jonny smiled. Katya was fond of her food and strapped for cash. Strictly she didn't qualify for breakfast club membership. She wasn't on benefits or entitled to use the food bank. She certainly couldn't afford the paid membership. But as uncrowned head of the Breakfast Club Detectives, he and Jasmine had made her an honorary member and she took full advantage of it. 'It was Jasmine's idea,' he said. 'I just arranged the sponsorship. I keep an eye on the books and sometimes help with the washing up.'

'Bloody good idea whatever,' said Katya, scooping up some remaining egg yolk with a piece of toast.

She was right. It had been very successful with people queuing up to join. They might start something similar in another town, if they could find someone with Jasmine's talents to run the place, and of course someone with his own connections to woo sponsors. *Could that be something for Belinda?* he wondered. She'd reject the idea if he suggested it, but she might come round to it on her own. But although he was pleased with the breakfast club and his hand in it, he was more pleased with the spin-off detectives, which had allowed him to fulfil a lifelong ambition to be a detective and solve crimes. And if they were about to embark on a new case, so much the better.

'What do you know so far about the murder at the circus?' he asked, keen to get going as soon as possible.

Katya removed a folder from her bag. 'I've got info from Lugs,' she said, waving it in his direction. 'It looks like a cut and dried case, but this Quinn woman seems convinced they've got it wrong. The least we can do is hear her out. There might be nothing in it, but...'

'But we just might have a new case,' said Jonny. 'How did she know about us?'

'Teddy Strang was at the circus the night of the murder. He was there interviewing Ms Quinn for the local paper. He took Jasmine with him.'

'Oh, yeah?' Jonny said with a grin. 'Something going on there?' He couldn't see them as a match made in heaven, but opposites attract, he supposed. And Jasmine deserved to have someone in her life with a bit of zing. Ivo, he thought, was far too young for her, and in any case seemed to be involved with a young man called Brian who worked for BA as cabin crew. No, Ivo and Jasmine were more like brother and sister. There was Stevie, of course, but that didn't strike him as an exciting partnership. Jasmine ran rings around him and Stevie followed her like a puppy dog. Teddy would definitely be exciting, but quite possibly dangerous as well, and almost certainly a stranger to long lasting relationships. No, he should keep away from speculation and meddling. He was almost as fond of Jasmine as her own father was. She would make her own way when she was ready.

'Jasmine was hanging around while Teddy interviewed Ms Quinn. She got chatting to the granddaughter.' Katya looked at her notes. 'Caitlyn Quinn. She does stuff with the horses. I suppose our cases came up in the conversation.'

'Bit of a coincidence.'

'Just a case of being in the right place at the right time.'

'Are they both coming this morning?'

'As far as I know.' She pushed her now-empty plate to one side and stood up. 'I'll be up in the office. Could you wait down here for them and bring them up? Jasmine's already there tidying up.'

So that's why Stevie was serving breakfast this morning. 'Be happy to,' he said. 'I assume Ivo's coming in as well?'

'And Harold, no doubt. Couldn't leave him out of a possible case, could we?'

Jonny wasn't sure if she was referring to Ivo or Harold. They definitely couldn't leave Ivo out, and where Ivo went Harold followed.

JONNY HAD JUST FINISHED his own breakfast when he noticed a crowd around the door. Ivo and Harold came in first. Harold wandered over to where Jonny was sitting and wagged his tail. *Still friends then.* Jonny patted his head and Harold gazed up at his empty plate with an appealing expression. He knew Jonny was a soft touch from when he'd lodged with him and Belinda while Ivo waited for a solution to their housing problem. Harold had missed Ivo, and had greeted him with excessive energy whenever they were reunited. But, Jonny was convinced, he had also enjoyed the luxuries he and Belinda showered him with; expensive dog food, a warm blanket to sleep on and plentiful grooming.

Jonny and Harold watched as Ivo held the door open for what seemed to be a sizeable group of people. First through the door was a tall woman with well-cut white hair and a dogged expression. Cordelia Quinn, he assumed. She was dressed in a dark red suit with brass buttons. *Bespoke,* he thought, doubting there had been much change from a grand. Jonny was well acquainted with Belinda's wardrobe, which held a number of pricey outfits. He knew high-end ladies' tailoring when he saw it. There must be money to be made in circuses. She was followed by a young woman wearing skinny jeans and a sparkly pink top, unruly dark curls escaping from a hair clip shaped like a horse's head. That would be Caitlyn, the granddaughter, a younger but equally confident version of Cordelia Quinn herself. If one danced around on the backs of galloping horses, Jonny supposed, one would need to be confident. Looked like it carried over into day-to-day life as well.

After the women came three men. Two forty-somethings, sturdy with dark curly hair. One wearing a suit, and once again with an air of affable confidence. The other looked in need of a shower, a good night's sleep and a suggestion that he had grabbed the first clothes that came to hand before he was dragged out to this meeting. The third was a much younger man. The same dark hair but slim and dark eyed, appearing more sensitive than the other two.

Jonny, remembering his role as host, stood up and approached them. He held out his hand to the older woman. 'Mrs Quinn, I assume.' He adopted the air of breezy charm that had carried him a long way in matters of business. 'I'm Jonny Cardew,' he said as they shook hands. 'I'm very pleased to meet you. If you'd like to follow me, I'll show you up to the office. DS Roscoff will meet you there. All of you,' he added, shepherding them through the café, where a number of customers stared at them open-mouthed as their food cooled on their plates. When they reached the staircase that led up to the office, he turned to Ivo, who looked bemused by the crowd of Quinns. Even Harold lacked his usual tail-wagging welcome. 'You'd better find some more chairs,' said Jonny, wondering if there would be room for all of them in the office.

'Okay,' said Ivo, leaping into action, no doubt glad of something to do that didn't involve staring at strangers. 'I'll get some of the folding ones.'

Jonny led them upstairs, noticing with relief that someone had done some dusting and hoping the office wasn't too untidy. He couldn't remember how they'd left it at the end of their last case, some weeks ago.

KATYA AND JASMINE stood up as they came into the room and Jonny looked around, checking that it all seemed orderly, professional and free of cobwebs and clutter.

'Ah, my dear,' said Cordelia Quinn, stepping forward and taking Jasmine in her arms. 'It's good to see you again. And so good of you to see us all. Caitlyn has told me all about you.'

Katya cleared her throat and Jasmine freed herself from Cordelia Quinn's embrace. 'May I introduce Katya Roscoff?' she said. 'She founded the Breakfast Club Detectives and she's in charge of all of us.'

Cordelia nodded at Katya and gave her an appraising look. 'I just hope you are able to help us,' she said coldly, eyeing Katya's usual array of mismatched apparel.

The two groups stood and stared at each other until Ivo arrived with the chairs and relieved the tension by opening them up and arranging them around the table. Harold studied the group of strangers with his head on one side. Having seemingly selected Caitlyn as the most dog-friendly of them, he wandered up to her and wagged his tail. 'Oh, hi,' said Caitlyn, bending down to stroke him. 'You look like a very clever dog.'

'His name's Harold,' said Ivo. 'And he is very clever. He caught a burglar once and detained a murderer.'

Caitlyn smiled up at Ivo. 'We have a dog act in the circus,' she said. 'It's very popular.'

'They must be clever dogs to do that,' said Ivo. 'Do you train them yourself?'

Caitlyn nodded. 'You'll have to come and see them perform sometime.'

'Why don't you all sit down,' said Katya, not wanting to be upstaged by dogs. One dog was distraction enough. She didn't need a whole team of circus dogs encroaching onto her territory. Best establish her authority from the get-go. 'We should all introduce ourselves,' she said, seating herself at the head of the table.

They'd never dealt with a group of clients before, and it felt crowded in the office. Katya removed her cardigan and hung it over the back of her chair. She should probably have offered to hang up Cordelia Quinn's jacket for her, but decided against it. She didn't want to look like a cloakroom assistant. She was in charge and intended to leave no one in any doubt about it. The Quinns might own a circus, but the Breakfast Club Detective group was all hers, and right now, the Quinns needed her more than she needed them.

After some shuffling around, the Quinn family sat at one end of the table, the detectives at the other. Harold crawled underneath it and settled down between Jasmine and Caitlyn. There was not a lot of spare space.

'As I was saying,' Katya raised her voice to be heard above the chatter and tapped her pen on the table, 'we should start by introducing ourselves. I'm Katya Roscoff, detective sergeant. Retired but still contracted as a civilian investigator. I worked with the detective team locally and we had an excellent clean-up record.' She gave them one of her *I was potential inspector material* looks.

'Have you solved murder cases before?' one of the men, the middle-aged, smartly dressed one asked.

'We have indeed,' said Katya. 'One of the team can furnish you with the details after this meeting if you wish.'

'I already have some facts from the journalist who interviewed me,' said Cordelia Quinn with a note of impatience in her voice. 'Mr Strong.'

'Strang,' Jasmine corrected.

'No matter. We have other things to see to today. I suggest we get on with discussing my grandson.'

'Of course,' said Katya, turning towards Jonny, who was sitting next to her. 'Jonny? Like to tell everyone who you are?'

Jonny smiled across the table at the Quinns. 'Good cop, bad cop?' he suggested with a nervous laugh. Katya frowned at him. 'I already introduced myself downstairs, but for those of you who didn't hear, I'm Jonny Cardew.' He paused as if not sure how to describe his detecting credentials.

'Jonny's really good at networking,' said Ivo, taking advantage of an awkward silence. 'And admin stuff. I'm Ivo Dean. I'm more of an ideas person.'

'Not always good ones,' Katya muttered under her breath.

'And Harold's your bloodhound?' asked Caitlyn with a laugh.

'He caught a—'

'Yes,' said Katya. 'They already know he caught a burglar and detained a murderer.' She held up a hand to stop Ivo saying anything more and turned to Jasmine. 'I believe you've already met Jasmine. She and her father own the café and provided us with our office.'

'Mrs Quinn and Caitlyn already know me,' said Jasmine. 'I'm good at research and IT stuff.'

'Thank you, that's all very helpful,' said the man Katya took to be the eldest Quinn son. He'd been writing everything down in a reporter's notebook. 'My name is Patrick Quinn – Paddy. I'm the finance manager and producer.' He indicated Caitlyn, who was sitting on his left. 'This young lady is my daughter. She runs the horse and dog acts. And this,' he said, pointing to the young man sitting at the far end of the table, 'is my nephew Joseph. He is our musical director and son of my youngest brother, Dara, who we left at the showground as we couldn't leave it unattended.'

'I take it you all know who I am,' said Cordelia Quinn, looking around as if she dared anyone to suggest they didn't.

They all nodded. Which left one more person. Another Quinn brother, Katya assumed. His likeness to Patrick Quinn was striking, although while Patrick was jovial and outgoing, this man was quiet and surly. 'Aidan Quinn,' he growled. 'Backstage manager. My son, Jeremy, has been charged with murder.'

As good a reason as any for surliness, Katya supposed. Perhaps if they could clear Jeremy of the charge, his father would be as cheerful as his brother. Although, maybe not. The sour expression looked like one that would be hard to change.

'It would be helpful if you could give us a bit of background,' said Katya. 'Mrs Quinn, I believe you founded the circus?'

'You may call me Cordelia. And yes, it was an ambition since childhood to run a circus. My late husband was in business in Dublin, and when he died fifteen years ago, he left me enough money to carry it out. Patrick works in finance in Dublin and Aidan manages a logistics company. They have been involved in the circus since the start and they both join me for our summer tours. My youngest son, Dara, worked abroad and joined us five years later. He was in a band,' she said, with a slightly lowered voice and a disapproving curl of her lip.

'And your grandchildren work with you as well?'

'Caitlyn trained as a dancer and has always loved working with animals. She has been with the circus since she left college two years ago. Joseph joined us after working as a rehearsal pianist in Dublin.'

Katya wrote it all down, then looked up at the gathering of Quinns in front of her. There was one who had yet to be mentioned. 'And Jeremy?' she asked, looking directly at Aidan, who shrugged and looked towards his mother for help.

Cordelia was silent for a moment. Jeremy was clearly the elephant in the room. 'Jeremy manages the fairground when we are on tour,' said Cordelia, 'and he works for Aidan when we are back in Dublin.'

Katya noticed her use of the present tense. 'And what does managing the fairground involve?'

'Maintenance of the equipment and health and safety on the rides,' said Aidan.

*A bit vague,* Katya thought, but let it pass.

'There are others involved,' Patrick butted in. 'Every year we engage acts from abroad who travel with us. This year we have a Romanian Gypsy band and a troupe of Hungarian acrobats. We also contract caterers, people we've known for years who have stalls selling street food, real ale and the like. And short contract maintenance staff, cleaners and mechanics mostly.'

'They all travel with you?'

'Our guest acts do. The short contract staff we employ locally according where we are.'

'I understand Waites was a mechanic,' said Katya. 'How long had he worked for you?'

'Just a couple of weeks,' said Patrick. 'He lived locally.'

'He was a friend of mine,' said Joseph, speaking for the first time. 'Known as Badger because of his hair. I knew him a few years back. He'd tried to join a band I was involved with.'

'In Dublin?' Katya asked. That could be an interesting lead. If Waites had lived in Ireland at some time in the past, perhaps he had made an enemy of one of the Quinns, who had caught up with him when they arrived in Windsor. But that could well have been Jeremy Quinn, so it wouldn't help to clear his name. In fact, it would make him look even more guilty. What they needed was to discover if someone else had taken against Waites in Dublin and followed him here to extract revenge.

'No,' said Joseph. 'It was when I lived in London. I was working with a band.'

*That knocks that theory on the head.* Katya reluctantly put it out of her mind. 'Waites was a musician?' she asked.

'He played keyboards but not very well. I bumped into him when we were preparing the site here and he picked up one of the flyers we'd scattered around the town. He recognised my name. He'd been laid off from an engineering company and was picking up casual work as a motor mechanic, but he said he hated it. He asked if I could give him a job. He'd hoped I might be able to use him in the band, but we're sorted for this season with the Romanians. Anyway, he'd never have been good enough. Playing for shows needs more skill than you might expect. But we did need help with the fairground stuff and Jeremy said he could use him.'

'Had he met Jeremy before he started work?'

'Not as far as I know,' said Joseph. 'It's not very likely.'

Katya agreed. Jeremy worked in haulage with his father in Dublin. Waites was a mechanic working in Windsor. So unless Jeremy just happened to be driving a lorry through Windsor that had broken down, it was unlikely their paths would have crossed. Until Waites started working for Jeremy at the circus. And that was odd. Two weeks didn't seem long enough to develop such hatred for an employee that murder was the only solution. Sacking would have done the job just as well. And in Katya's experience, strangling wasn't an act of sudden anger. This was premeditated. Unless, of course, the murderer just happened to go around with a length of wire and some rope in their pocket. Katya thought about the usual contents of her own pockets and had to admit this was a possibility.

'And was he living on site?' she asked. That would make opportunity less of an issue.

'We have tents for the casual workers,' said Paddy. 'He could have had the use of one of those, but he said he preferred to go home every night.'

*Another theory bites the dust.*

'The band and the acrobats are all staying in the tents,' Caitlyn added. 'The rest of us have caravans.'

'They're lovely,' said Jasmine. 'Real old-style Gypsy ones.'

'We've collected them over the years,' said Cordelia proudly. 'Picked them up at horse fairs in Ireland and had them renovated and painted in the circus livery colours.'

'I like the sound of the circus,' said Jonny in a whisper to Jasmine. 'Perhaps when we get all of this sorted out, they'd give us tickets to one of their shows and I could take Belinda to see it. It might take her mind off losing the election.'

'That's a nice idea,' Jasmine whispered back.

'And what were Badger's working hours?' Katya asked, trying to get them back on track. Her team had an annoying habit of wandering off-topic.

'Jeremy's team works from midday until the fairground closes at around eleven. It's their job to check the machinery and make sure it's safe before and after the show every night.'

'The police seem to think Jeremy had a motive for killing Badger,' said Katya, reading the notes she had made after her visit to the police station. 'Do you know anything about that?'

Cordelia shook her head and remained tight-lipped.

'They were heard arguing earlier in week,' said Patrick.

Cordelia frowned at him. 'Means nothing,' she said. 'People argue all the time.'

'Granny's right,' said Caitlyn. 'There's a lot of tension on show nights. People get heated and shout at each other.'

'Any idea what this particular argument was about?' Katya asked, looking around at the blank faces. 'And how did Badger get on with the rest of the team?' she asked.

Again, no one had an answer.

'Jeremy is easy-going to work for,' said Aidan, speaking for the first time since his growled introduction. 'I've not heard any complaints about him.'

Did that mean he was a slacker? Katya wondered. It was possible to be too easy-going. Easy-going enough to let a murderer wander around unnoticed? 'Did anyone have a grudge against Badger?' she asked.

'I don't think any of the family knew him well,' said Cordelia impatiently before anyone else could answer. 'Apart from Joseph,' she admitted grudgingly. 'And I don't hear anyone accusing him of murder.'

'He's got an alibi, Granny,' said Caitlyn. 'He was in London from Friday morning until last night.'

'Yes, yes,' she said irritably. 'I'm not accusing him of anything. That would be as ridiculous as trying to pin it on Jeremy.'

More so, probably. There was a sweetness about Joseph that suggested he was an unlikely candidate for cold-blooded murderer. But Katya could be wrong. One never knew with murderers. They could turn out to be the most unlikely people. And she'd no idea what Jeremy was like. He could be even sweeter than his cousin. But she was allowing her mind to wander. She made more notes and then looked Cordelia in the eye and said, 'What is it exactly that you want us to do?'

'I told you. I want you to prove my grandson's innocence.'

Katya shook her head. 'I can't make any promises,' she said. 'The local police team tend not to bring charges unless they are certain they will get a conviction. From what I can see reading their notes, your grandson had a motive, admittedly not a strong one, and he certainly had the opportunity and the means.'

Cordelia stood up with a furious expression on her face.

'But,' Katya continued, remaining seated and meeting her gaze, 'we will look into it for you. I hope I will be able to discuss it with your grandson's legal representative. Better if we work with the defence rather than against them. And we will need to interview you all individually and talk to the rest of your employees.'

Cordelia, still on her feet, looked at them mutinously. Katya expected her to gather up her family and storm out. But Cordelia nodded curtly. 'You will let me know your fee?'

Had Katya expected a fee? She had certainly expected to be paid expenses, as she had when working for the police. That time she had a contract that paid her a small amount. But they'd not been together as detectives for long and hadn't been in a position to charge a fee before. She should have thought about possible payment the moment she heard that Cordelia Quinn needed their services. She should have been prepared. She hoped she was managing not to show this had taken her by surprise and arranged her expression into a suitably poker-faced countenance. 'We'll draw up a contract,' she said. 'Once we have an action plan in place, I will email you when we have assessed the number of hours we can give to this and the expenses we expect to incur. Jasmine will collect contact details from all of you before you leave. Jonny, perhaps you would escort our clients down to the café. I'm sure they would appreciate coffee.' She reached out to shake Cordelia's hand. 'You will find Jasmine's prices very reasonable, and I can recommend the pastries.'

'I don't doubt it,' said Cordelia, shaking Katya's hand with no sign of warmth.

~

*Cordelia Quinn and Katya Roscoff are going to make an interesting pair,* Jonny thought after he had said goodbye to the Quinns and was climbing the stairs, clutching a bag of pastries. They'd reminded him of a couple of cats prowling around each other before diving in for a fight to the death. Interesting that Katya had not offered them coffee at the meeting. He had himself provided the office with a top of the range coffee machine, from which she was pouring herself a cup as Jonny re-entered the office with Jasmine close behind him, carrying her laptop.

'I've got all their details,' she said, putting the laptop down on the table and opening it. 'I'll copy them across to the desktop contacts.'

'That was quick,' said Katya.

'They decided not to stop for coffee. They said they had things to do.'

'I think Katya scared them,' said Ivo.

'Rubbish,' said Katya. 'I was charm itself. Firm but charming. More likely they were scared of Harold.'

'They have dog acts at the circus,' said Ivo. 'There's no way they'd be scared of Harold.'

'No one's scared,' said Jasmine. 'They have a circus to run in difficult circumstances. They needed to get back.'

Jonny poured Jasmine a cup of coffee. She had a future as a peacemaker, he decided. Perhaps she should stand for election as a councillor. But probably not. He doubted her politics were the same as Belinda's and she was worried enough about whether she'd ever be re-elected after losing her seat. It would be extremely awkward if Jasmine were to compete with his wife for the role that she loved. Anyway, it was nearly four years until the next election and besides, if Jasmine became a councillor, she wouldn't have time to run a café and be a detective. It could mean the end of the detectives and that would be a pity, Jonny's life having taken a turn for the better since he'd been detecting.

'Stop daydreaming, Jonny,' said Katya sharply. 'Come and sit down. I want to know what you all thought of our new clients. None of you had much to say for yourselves at the meeting.'

'We were awed by your impressive handling of Cordelia Quinn,' said Jonny. 'I don't suppose she's used to people standing up to her the way you did.'

'I was confused,' said Ivo. 'There were so many of them. I wasn't sure who was who.'

'We'll start there,' said Katya. 'We need a family tree and then we can start thinking about what happened the other night.'

'Do you think Jeremy is innocent?' Jasmine asked.

'I think we should assume he is for now,' said Katya. 'The police case looks secure, but I don't think it's watertight. It's all political. They are under pressure at the moment to secure more convictions. I'll take Lugs out for a drink and get his opinion, but first we'll draw up a who's who in the Quinn family.' She picked up a pen and walked over to the board. At the top she wrote Cordelia Quinn's name and next to that she made a note that Cordelia had founded the circus fifteen years earlier using a legacy from her husband. 'Three sons,' she said. 'Can you remember which was which?'

'The smart one, Patrick, is the eldest,' said Jasmine. 'He likes to be called Paddy. He works in finance but joins his mother in the circus for the touring season. He's the producer.'

'What does that involve?' asked Ivo. 'All the acts are set up before the tour even starts.'

'I should think it means organising who goes on when, how long they have in the ring, what music they need, that sort of thing,' Jonny suggested. 'But who am I to say? I've never run a circus. It's probably very different from organising a cardboard factory.'

'Not that different,' said Ivo. 'It's all about who does what, where and when, isn't it?'

'Okay,' said Katya, writing it down. 'Who's next?'

'Aidan,' said Jonny. 'The bad-tempered one. He was also in at the beginning. Runs a logistics company in Dublin and works as back-stage manager when they're on tour.'

'That must be quite complicated,' said Ivo. 'With all those props and stuff. And making sure everyone's ready to go on when they should be.'

'I suppose his son being arrested didn't do a lot for his temper,' said Jasmine.

'You think he's a ray of sunshine the rest of the time?' Jonny asked. 'Can't see it myself.'

'You could be right,' said Katya. 'But there's one more son. Dara, who was working abroad but joined the family five years after the circus started.' She wrote his name on the board. 'We don't know much more about him at the moment. I'll leave a space so we can add anything we find out. Which brings us to the grandchildren.'

'Caitlyn is Paddy's daughter,' said Jasmine. 'Trained as a dancer and now organises the animal acts, dogs and horses.'

'Jeremy Quinn, the man charged with the murder, is Aidan's son. He's in charge of the fairground equipment,' Ivo chipped in. 'And he works for his father in Dublin in the off season. And there was Joseph. Paddy and Aidan's nephew, I think.'

The list was growing, and Katya was getting a clearer picture of the family who'd sat in front of them that morning. They now knew who they were but still knew nothing about the family dynamic. They worked together but did they get on? They appeared to, but perhaps they were on their best behaviour that morning. Was there much infighting and jealousy when they were on their home turf and no one was watching them? Did Cordelia rule them with a rod of iron or did they ignore her and do as they pleased?

'Jeremy interests me,' said Katya. 'Waites was working for him, but he'd only been doing it for a couple of weeks. Before that, as far as we know, they'd never met. A workplace argument is a very weak motive for murder. What about Dara, do we know what he does?' she asked.

'I don't think they told us,' said Jasmine. 'But he was left behind to see to the circus and it was his son, Joseph, who came to the meeting. He's the musical director.'

*Interesting,* Katya thought, adding Joseph's name to the list. Why leave Dara behind? Why not Joseph? But staring at his name didn't help. She'd think about that and come back to it later. And why were Cordelia and Caitlyn the only women? More dark family secrets, or just brothers who were not good at staying married? 'Do none of these guys have wives?' she asked. 'I assume three grandkids didn't spring from seashells.'

'And does Cordelia have any daughters?' Ivo asked.

'I don't think so,' said Jasmine. 'Caitlyn told me she didn't approve of daughters.'

Jonny laughed. 'Doesn't mean she doesn't have any. She just hasn't given them roles in the business.'

'We're getting sidetracked,' said Katya. 'We need to get going with this case. There's a lot to find out.' She picked up the pen again and made a list.

*Greg (Badger) Waites – who was he?*

*Talk to Lugs – get details of evidence.*

*Look into Quinn business interests.*

*Find out more about family, circus and employees. Any wives on the scene?*

'Four tasks for starters,' she said. 'Ivo, you take the first. Badger was local and working as a jobbing mechanic. He was in a band so might also have been busking in the area. You know local people. See if any of them have come across Badger and know any more about him than we've gathered so far.'

'Okay,' said Ivo. 'I've not much on this afternoon and it's a nice day. People will be out and about in town.'

'Good lad,' said Katya, pointing to the next item on the list. 'I'll do Lugs. See what evidence they've got against Jeremy Quinn. And they'll have done a background check on Badger Waites. That might throw up something interesting. Jonny, the next one has your name all over it. Think you can find anything about these Dublin companies?'

'I don't see why not. I'll start with Aidan and his logistics business. That usually means travel, so they might be known to some of our drivers.'

'And Jasmine,' said Katya. 'You've already struck up a friendship with Caitlyn Quinn, so go and chat to her and see if you can dig deeper into the family background. If any of you find out anything you think is urgent, email me. Otherwise, how about we meet back here tomorrow afternoon?'

# 5

Another day, another pub. And one thing Katya liked about Lugs was his ability to find pubs they'd not been to before. This one was in a village she'd not been to before either. Not that she got out of town so much since she'd retired, but even as a working cop she hadn't got to explore many of the out-of-town areas. Not a lot of crime in villages like this one, she supposed. Houses either built for or converted by the well-heeled commuter who, for all Katya knew, might be involved in crime, but probably not of the type dealt with by your average local plod. These would be more Interpol or fraud squad types. Traditional villagers, those who might in the past have done a spot of poaching or set fire to the odd haystack or two, were long gone. Driven away by the cost of housing and lack of employment opportunities.

Lugs had done well this time. The Green Man was what Katya had always considered a country pub should be. It had a comfortable lounge bar with an open fireplace flanked by horse brasses, an elderly sheepdog dozing in a sunny spot by a window and a jovial barman currently engaged in a heated discussion with, Katya assumed, one of the regulars about the likelihood of an imminent general election.

'Grab a seat over there,' said Lugs, nodding towards a wide window seat in front of a gateleg table. 'I'll get the drinks in and order some lunch. What do you fancy?'

Katya studied a blackboard fixed to the wall near the bar, chose steak and mushroom pie with carrots and mashed potato, and headed for the seat Lugs had chosen.

She sat looking out of the window at the quiet village. *Too quiet,* she thought. Devoid of any kind of life at all. A dormitory village occupied by commuters who caught early trains into the city having driven the kids to school in people carriers. Across the road from the pub, she saw what had once been a police house. She recognised the style, but now it had been extended and turned into a desirable family home. Further along, she could see what might once have been the village shop, also now converted into upmarket housing. No need for a shop now, when you could order from Ocado and have fresh veg delivered out of season.

A car pulled into the car park, a rakish red convertible. A couple climbed out and ran into the pub hand in hand. A middle-aged man with an air of confident entitlement, silver streaks in his still ample head of hair. His companion, a woman in a short summer dress and fake tan. They snuggled into a corner well away from prying eyes and giggled like teenagers. Not, Katya assumed, a happily married couple celebrating an anniversary. But a pub like this probably needed the extramarital trade to boost their lunch time numbers. One regular propping up the bar wasn't going to keep the bank manager happy. She wondered briefly what they made of her and Lugs, but then thought, probably nothing. They were too wrapped up in themselves to have noticed anyone else.

'I assumed you'd be drinking pints,' said Lugs, as he arrived carrying two pints and putting them down on the table. 'The food won't be long.'

'It's a nice pub,' said Katya. 'Have you been here before?'

'It's my go-to place when I want to be well away from the nick and anyone who might have an interest in my current cases. There's never much of a crowd here at lunchtime, not during the week anyway. It's more of a family pub at weekends.' He nodded towards a small garden at the side of the car park, where there was a playhouse and a yellow dinosaur with a slide on its back. He downed half of his pint and grinned at Katya. 'I'm guessing you're about to tell me our Jeremy Quinn is innocent.'

'Can't get anything past you, can I? But yes. His family think he is.'

'Families tend to,' said Lugs. 'Usually wrongly.'

'I haven't decided what I think yet, but I agreed to make some enquiries that could assist the defence team.'

Lugs took another draught of his beer and set the glass carefully down on the table. 'We were under pressure from upstairs to go ahead with this. There was enough evidence to charge the guy.'

'You sound as if you're not convinced,' said Katya, taking a long drink from her own glass.

'It seems like a cut and dried case. The evidence is all there. Quinn had a motive, he was in charge of the fairground equipment so he knew exactly where to conceal the body and we assume he and Badger Waites were the only two on site that morning.'

'So Badger was killed in the morning?'

'The autopsy report concludes the time of death was between six and eight am.'

'Jeremy lives on site, but why would Badger have been there that early? They don't usually start work until midday?'

'Jeremy might have asked him to come in early. Perhaps there was work that needed doing on one of the rides.'

Why would he have done that? Get him in to do a bit of work on the rides and then kill him? It didn't make sense. There were more questions to be asked about that, Katya thought, making a mental note of it. 'How was he killed?' she asked.

'He was strangled using electrical cable and then hidden somewhere in the carousel. Up in the roof, probably, or he would have been spotted during the day. He was tied by the feet and around the wrists using hemp rope, and we assume he was then hoisted up into the metal struts at the top of the carousel.'

'And why did he fall out?'

'The scene of crime team think the body could have been dislodged by a pole that one of the horses was attached to. Someone might have knocked against one of them and loosened it.'

'There are a lot of *might haves,*' said Katya. 'Is there forensic evidence for any of this?'

'Forensics did a thorough examination of the carousel and Jeremy Quinn's fingerprints were found all over it.'

That wasn't a surprise. 'Any rope fibres found up in the roof?'

'We don't have the full report yet.'

'Motive?'

'Quinn and Badger were heard arguing the previous night.'

Katya stared thoughtfully into her beer glass. 'An argument doesn't make sense for two reasons. If you're angry with someone, you'd strike out there and then. Not wait until the next day and strangle them. This seems premeditated to me.'

'Well, as I said, there's enough evidence for them upstairs to insist on a charge of murder.'

'But?'

'Well, first, Jeremy Quinn worked every day on the fairground equipment. You'd expect his fingerprints to be there.'

'Good point,' said Katya. She'd thought the same. In fact, it would be suspicious if they weren't. It would mean he'd tried to cover up the fact that he'd been there. 'Could he have had another motive?'

'He may have done, and I'm sure the prosecution will be looking into it. I just feel it all happened too fast. Too many assumptions were made, and it could all be torn apart in court.'

'Then your team would look very foolish,' said Katya, not without a note of relish. Not that she wanted Lugs to look stupid, but it wouldn't do all those stuffed shirts upstairs any harm.

'We would indeed. And guess who'd get the blame for the whole wretched business?'

He was right and Katya didn't envy them, but then their meal arrived and she was momentarily distracted. The food was delicious, and they ate in silence.

'Another thing,' said Katya as she scraped up the last mushroom.

'If it was premeditated, wouldn't Quinn have chosen somewhere well away from the showground? At some point the body was going to be found in the carousel and he would be the obvious suspect. He could have lured Badger way out of town and done it there. Concealed the body or buried it.'

'And even if he did kill him there, he was a circus mechanic and must know the insides of the carousel like the back of his hand as well as how to secure ropes.' Lugs sighed. 'But we've been told to leave it there. I'll be in deep hot water if I start to question the evidence now. But...'

'But there's nothing to stop me making enquiries, is there?'

'What I've told you today is off the record, although none of it is classified information. But I wouldn't want it known that I'd discussed the case with you.'

'Of course not,' said Katya. 'Any enquires I make will be to help the defence, but if evidence comes to light that could exonerate Quinn, it would be my duty to pass it on to you.'

Lugs raised his glass. 'You're a good egg, Katya. I've always said that. Now I'd better drive you back into town and get back to work myself.'

# 6

Ivo clipped Harold onto his lead and picked up a bag of Eccles cakes, a new recipe Karim was trying out. He ambled down the stone steps from *Jasmine's* towards the riverside park with Harold trotting along at his side. At the bottom of the steps Harold, anticipating a walk in the park, tugged at his lead, expecting to head off to the right, but Ivo pulled him back and led him towards the arches. They crossed a road and turned left under the railway bridge, a train rattling overhead on its way into the Royal Station from Slough. Harold and Ivo emerged from the bridge and turned into a narrow lane, home to a row of workshops and lock-ups tucked into arches below the railway track. Ivo knew many of the occupants: sellers of cheap car tyres; bodywork patchers; windscreen replacement services and cycle repairs. He headed for the final lock-up at the end of the lane to a door that bore the sign *Wilf's Car Repairs and MOT.* Wilf was no longer in charge, having died in an accident four years earlier. The business was now the property of his daughter Rosa, who, when asked why she had not changed the sign, said, 'Would you go to a car mechanic called Rosa?'

Personally, Ivo thought he would go to anyone who could keep his van on the road, but he could see her point. Customers of scruffy repair establishments were probably not born-again feminists and would definitely steer clear of anything *woke* even if they didn't actually know what the word meant.

As they approached, Ivo could see a pair of legs clad in navy blue overalls and heavy-duty boots sticking out from under a battered Toyota Yaris that had once been dark blue but now was faded to more of a denim blue, with some green and yellow side panels and mismatched blue areas that were obviously poor attempts at covering up dents and scratches.

'Morning,' Ivo shouted, crouching down to peer under the car. A figure trundled out on a wheeled creeper, clutching a socket wrench. She sat up as Harold bounded forward and started licking her face.

'Want an Eccles cake?' Ivo asked, holding out the bag.

Rosa put the wrench down, picked up a roll of paper hand towel and wiped her oily fingers. She reached into the bag for an Eccles cake and took a bite. 'Delicious,' she said. 'Hot from the oven?'

'Yeah, Karim's trying a new recipe.'

'Well, tell him he's got a winner.'

'Will do,' said Ivo, perching on a small wall at the side of the arch and watching Rosa tidy her tools.

'Does the van need attention?' she asked, looking around and not seeing it.

'No,' said Ivo. 'We walked here. The van's fine. I just wanted to ask you some questions.'

'Sounds interesting. Come inside. I'll clean up a bit and put the kettle on.' She led them into the workroom, which was a model of cleanliness and organisation with tools lining the walls on hooks, all arranged according to size. In one corner was a desk, which looked equally well-organised with orderly piles of paper held down with a glass paperweight, and job details pinned to a corkboard. Rosa crossed the room to a small kitchen, where she scrubbed her hands with Swarfega and then washed them in perfumed soap and dried them on a pink hand towel. She filled an electric kettle and plugged it in. She opened up a cupboard above the sink and took out two mugs. 'Tea or coffee?' she asked. 'I've only got instant coffee.'

'Tea then,' said Ivo.

'Builders' or Earl Grey?'

'Builders' is fine,' said Ivo, taking a bite of Eccles cake and breaking off a bit for Harold.

Rosa made the tea and reached into the small fridge for a carton of milk. 'Grab a seat,' she said, indicating a plastic folding chair and passing Ivo a mug of tea, seating herself on an upturned oil drum. 'What can I do for you?'

Ivo took a sip of his tea. 'Do you know a guy called Badger Waites?'

'Badger, yeah, I know him. He's worked for me a couple of times. Haven't seen him recently, though. What's he been up to?'

'Have you heard of Quinn's Circus?' Ivo asked, avoiding the question.

'Out on the meadow? I've noticed them, but they're way too pricey for me. What have they got to do with Badger?'

'He's been working for them as a mechanic on the fairground rides.'

'Makes sense, I suppose. He's not had a steady job recently.'

'One of the Quinns knew him and gave him the job when they set up here. It's part of their summer tour.'

'So when the circus leaves town he'll be out of a job and back here looking for work again?'

'He won't,' said Ivo. 'He's dead.'

'Really?' said Rosa, spluttering into her tea. 'How? Was he in an accident?'

'He was murdered.'

'Wow,' said Rosa. 'I wasn't expecting that. Who'd want to murder poor old Badger? I can't believe he had any enemies. Did he upset someone at the circus?'

'Looks like it. He got into an argument, and someone has been arrested,' said Ivo. 'One of the Quinns.'

Rosa looked puzzled. 'That doesn't make sense. If he'd got on the wrong side of one of the family, why not just sack him?'

'That's a good question. The Quinns think he's innocent, of course. And we're trying to prove it for them.'

'Oh yeah, your detective club. With ex police sergeant Katya thingy. I've read about you all in the local paper.'

'Nice to know we're famous,' said Ivo. 'I've been asked to look into Badger's background. So what can you tell me about him?'

Rosa thought for a moment. 'He seemed a nice enough bloke, but a bit of a drifter. He worked here a few times and for one or two of the others along here, just day-to-day, cash-in-hand stuff. He was quite a good mechanic. He could have found something more permanent if he'd wanted to.'

'He didn't work long hours, then? Do you know what he got up to when he wasn't working?

Rosa shrugged. 'Not sure. All he was interested in was his music. He played in a band, but I don't think they were very good.'

That supported what Joseph had told them. 'Can you give me any details? Others in the band, perhaps?'

'I might have a flyer somewhere.' She sifted through some papers on her desk and then shook her head. 'I know I've seen something, but that's all work stuff. Tell you what, I can look at home and WhatsApp a copy of anything I find to you.'

'Thanks.' That would be useful and he hoped she wouldn't forget. But there must be more she could tell him. 'Do you know where he lived?'

'He used to come on the train. He had a flat in Slough, but I don't know the address.'

That made sense. Rents in Slough were a lot cheaper than Windsor and only ten minutes away on the train. 'What about his family?' Ivo asked. There must be a next of kin somewhere. The police would need to inform them that Badger had died. He visualised a sad woman in an apron answering the door to a couple of police officers, who would tell her to sit down and ask if there was anyone they could call to be with her. Ivo wondered if Katya had more information about that. She'd know the process, having no doubt done it herself. Would Lugs tell her who Badger's next of kin was? He couldn't think of any reason why not.

'He never mentioned any family,' said Rosa. 'He always seemed a bit of a loner apart from the band. He was a gentle type. Not one to get caught up in violence, I shouldn't think. Want me to ask around?'

'Just listen out for any gossip about him. People are bound to talk about it once word gets round. It'll be all over the local paper.'

'Will do,' said Rosa. 'But right now, I should get back to work.'

'I'd better get back too. I've got people coming to empty the septic tank.'

'Sounds fun.'

'About as much fun as grubbing around under people's oily cars.'

Rosa laughed. 'Each to their own, I suppose.'

They went back outside together, and Ivo watched as she trundled herself back under the Yaris. He and Harold headed for the river path and the walk back to *Shady Willows*. Had he discovered much about Badger Waites? Most of what Rosa told him just confirmed what he already knew, but there were one or two things he could follow up. Did Badger live alone, and where? Did he have any close relatives? A girlfriend or boyfriend perhaps. He hoped Rosa would remember to look for flyers about the band. He'd drop her a message later to remind her. But if she couldn't find anything, he might be able to find them on his own. Where did not-very-good bands perform? He could wander around looking out for buskers or seek out pubs that went in for live music. And then he remembered they would be short of a keyboard player and wondered if they would be advertising somewhere. Local music shops, perhaps, although the only one he knew in town had closed down a year or so before lockdown. Social media might be worth a try. He'd go home and trawl round Facebook and Twitter, type in *band in search of keyboard player* and see what came up.

# 7

Jonny stood up and walked twice round the room, stretching his back. Too much sitting made it ache. He needed to get out more, join a gym perhaps, or a rambling club, but he didn't feel particularly excited about either of those. Gardening? No, he'd probably dig up some of Belinda's favourite plants. He looked out of the window at the perfect June evening; sunshine, a clear blue sky and a gentle breeze sending white cotton wool clouds across the sun, just enough to keep the temperature pleasant. He'd go for a walk along the river where there would be boats to watch, swans to feed, people fishing and dog walkers he could chat to. And when he wasn't doing one of those, he'd mull over what he'd discovered earlier today. A couple of hours searching the internet had thrown up some interesting facts about the Quinn family, and a couple of phone calls to ex-colleagues had revealed a few more.

Cordelia Quinn came from a background of Irish travellers and horse dealers. Who'd have thought it? She came across as a model of matriarchal respectability, although investing all she had in a circus should have given him a clue that she wasn't the upper crust committee type she first appeared to be. She also had political experience, having run unsuccessfully as a Fianna Fáil candidate for the

Dáil in the nineteen-eighties. Jonny's knowledge of Irish politics was vague, but after some googling he worked out that the party she'd stood for was middle-of-the-road right wing. That would probably work well in support of a businessman husband. *Not unlike Belinda,* he thought. Although the middle ground was a difficult place to be right now. Belinda was muttering about standing as an independent candidate next time around. But it was probably very different in Ireland. No Brexit, for one thing.

Jonny wondered about the nature of Mr Quinn's business. Oliver Quinn must have been successful if it had raised enough for his wife to start a circus after his death in 2008, but it hadn't been well documented. Jonny found a short obituary in a Dublin newspaper, but it was scant on detail and told him only that Quinn had left a widow and three sons and that he had been interred after a short ceremony in a Dublin cemetery. 2008 was the year of the global financial crash, in which Irish businesses had suffered more than most. But there was no record of Quinn having been in any kind of financial difficulty, so whatever he did must have been well insulated, either because it was highly respectable or dodgy to the extent that no one knew anything about it. Further internet searches discovered a copy of his will, in which he left everything he had, a substantial amount, to his widow, Cordelia. And according to a short article in an Irish newspaper he'd died of natural causes, so nothing suspect there, although Jonny supposed his death might have come about as the result of stress. However, he could find no evidence to support that.

Paddy Quinn, the financial manager, proved easier to track. He'd been in trouble several times having been suspected of tax fraud, money laundering and short selling. But he'd never been charged. Jonny called his own accountant, an old friend, and asked how that could happen. Either fake news, his rivals spreading gossip in the financial press, or friends in high places, Jonny was told. Whichever it was, spending time away from Ireland running a circus with his mother was probably a good move. Jonny suspected he still dabbled in a few dubious financial enterprises but that he covered his tracks well and operated them at a distance. Offshore accounts and tax havens came to mind. A little more digging into press records told him that Paddy's ex-wife, Cathy, had remarried. She was running pony trekking holidays near Galway and had been for the last fifteen years. So they must have been divorced for at least as long as the circus had been in operation. The divorce had not attracted any publicity and Jonny was unable to find any mention of a divorce settlement. Enterprises that involved horses didn't come cheap, so either she'd remarried someone rich, or Paddy had come to an out-of-court arrangement. Jonny favoured the latter, which suggested tax avoidance and fitted in with the image he was building of Paddy Quinn. Cathy might, of course, have been a woman of substance in her own right. And good luck to her if it meant she'd been able to turn her back on an unhappy marriage and set up on her own. Caitlyn, it appeared, had spent equal amounts of time with both parents. Jonny found a 2009 magazine article about Quinn's Circus with a picture of Caitlyn and Paddy with a pair of horses that had been purchased for the circus from a stud farm in Saudi Arabia. Another search turned up a photograph of Caitlyn in an advert for one of her mother's trekking holidays. She appeared to be in her late teens, so this was well after the divorce, which suggested her parents were still on speaking terms.

The year 2008 had been pivotal for the Quinn family. Jonny turned to Aidan Quinn to see if there was a similar connection. In 2008, Aidan had been running a fleet of lorries transporting goods to Northern Ireland and mainland Europe. He specialised in horse transport, among other things, having been responsible for getting elite horses belonging to the Irish Olympic team to Beijing and back. Nothing suspect there; nothing Jonny could find about possible smuggling or any other irregularities. Aidan still ran a thriving business as well as joining his mother and brother in the circus, where his logistics skills were probably needed as much as anywhere. Particularly if it involved horses.

His son Jeremy, the suspected murderer, had a very chequered history. He'd narrowly avoided time in juvenile detention, having been thrown out of a smart boarding school for dealing in drugs.

Family string-pulling, Jonny suspected, had kept him out of custody. At university, Jeremy had been involved in a number of fights and had also been viciously attacked by a jealous boyfriend who accused him of *trying it on with my girlfriend*. How had he even been able to go to university if he'd been expelled from school? Family connections again, perhaps. He didn't seem to have any career worth noting. Had he perhaps worked with his father as well as his not-very-spectacular role in the circus? Fairground manager sounded contrived. Had they created the role for him just to keep him occupied and out of everyone's way? Jonny couldn't help feeling little surprise that the police considered him a likely murder suspect. He might as well have been wearing a t-shirt with *prime suspect* emblazoned across the front. What Jonny hadn't been able to find was any trace of his mother. There was no marriage record for Aidan, although Irish records were notoriously difficult to access. He didn't even know how to find an Irish birth certificate. Had Jeremy been packed off to boarding school after a messy parental break-up? That could account for a lot of his bad behaviour. He'd have to ask Jasmine if she could find out anything from Caitlyn.

And that left Dara and his son, Joseph. Cordelia had told them that Dara had worked abroad until joining the rest of the family five years after the circus started. That would be 2013, and after a few searches on social media, Jonny tracked Dara to the Facebook page of a band called Feathers of Flight, who led a nomadic, hand-to-mouth existence busking their way around India and uploading recordings of their gigs, which sold quite successfully on Spotify. Jonny even found a photograph taken on a beach in Goa of Dara with his arm around a woman of extraordinary beauty, who the caption told him was called Safiya, and a young boy of around eight. Joseph, Jonny assumed. After searching further, he also found a heartbreaking account in an Indian newspaper of an accident involving two lorries and a camel cart. One of the trucks had plunged off a road near Fatehpur Sikri. Safiya, described as a singer, and two other members of the band were killed. After that, Dara and Joseph, then twelve years old, had returned to Ireland, where the family were still based when not touring with the now well-established Quinn's Circus. Joseph, presumably with a lot of help from his grandmother in the form of extra coaching and music lessons, won a scholarship to a well-known boarding school for musical children, while his father worked for the circus.

Jonny mulled all of this over as he walked, eventually reaching the river and finding an unoccupied bench. He sat down and opened his notebook, a new moleskin one with a dark green cover. New case, new moleskin, Jonny had decided. He fished a pen out of his jacket pocket and started making notes. He was beginning to agree with Cordelia Quinn that Jeremy was innocent. Well, clearly not innocent, he'd done a lot of bad stuff, some of which verged on the criminal. But had he murdered Badger Waites? Jonny thought not. Why would he? This was a cold-blooded, premeditated killing. From what Jonny knew of Jeremy, he was a hot-headed, knee-jerk reaction type. Killing someone in a drunken brawl, he'd believe. Planning a cold-blooded murder and setting up a gruesome tableau of a discovery just didn't fit the kind of personality that got thrown out of posh schools and dealt in drugs.

Could it be a set up? Someone with a grudge against the circus or the Quinn family? They'd probably upset a few people over the years. And maybe Badger Waites had inadvertently been caught up in it. The wrong person in the wrong place at the wrong time. Jonny couldn't imagine how they'd begin to untangle that. It was going to be a headache for the Breakfast Club Detectives. Not to mention a tragedy for Badger Waites.

# 8

Jasmine turned the sign on the door to *Closed*. She and her father had said goodbye to the kitchen staff, and Karim settled down in front of the TV for an evening of cricket. 'Nothing you wanted to watch, love?' he asked.

Jasmine was not a lover of cricket, well, not in the obsessive way her father was. She supposed Iran had a national team, although Karim never spoke about it. But he never talked about his life in Iran either. He'd been true blue British since he'd first become a UK national many years ago. He was an avid supporter of the English team, with a strong conviction that they could and should win back the Ashes this year. Jasmine supposed that if Karim had gone in the other direction and claimed asylum in Australia all those years ago, things would be very different now and her father would be cheering on the other side. But that was a really strange thought. If Karim had settled in Australia, Jasmine wouldn't exist. Unless Karim had met up with an Antipodean doppelgänger of her mother. On a Sydney beach, perhaps. But that was way too complicated to get her head around.

She bent and kissed Karim on the top of his head. 'No, Dad. You enjoy your cricket. I'm going out for a walk.'

It was a nice walk to the meadow where the circus had set up two weeks ago. The river path was at its best in June with wildflowers and butterflies, and a view of people in boats. She walked away from *Jasmine's,* across the park to the river path, and headed out of town. Half a mile on, she skirted *Shady Willows*, wondering if Ivo was in and might like to join her. She looked over the gate in the direction of his cabin but there was no sign of him, or of Harold, who could usually be found snoozing on the doorstep. She'd not seen so much of Ivo recently. He still came to do repair jobs for her and her father, and he was still a keen member of the detectives. But he had a social life of his own now. Of course, in a way it was the detectives that had led to that. If it hadn't been for the body in the river, Ivo wouldn't have met Poppy Cookson. And more to the point, he wouldn't have met Poppy's brother Brian, who had nothing whatever to do with their case, but their paths had crossed. Were still crossing. And Jasmine was pleased that Ivo now had someone who wasn't only interested in his sink-clearing expertise, or his skill with cross-headed screwdrivers and the like. Although it had been Brian's squeaky wardrobe doors that had brought them together in the first place.

Ivo was obviously busy this evening, so Jasmine walked on, leaving *Shady Willows* behind and heading to where she could see the flags fluttering on the top of the red and yellow circus tent half a mile ahead.

'Drop in any time,' Caitlyn had said when Jasmine called her and said she had a few questions to ask. 'We're not able to open again yet. It'll be good to have someone to chat to.'

Caitlyn was good company; even in the shadow of the murder, Jasmine sensed that they could be friends. And to make it seem more of a social occasion and less like an interrogation, Jasmine had packed up a few of Karim's cakes and some smoked salmon sandwiches that had been left over from lunch.

Arriving at the gate, she could see a queue of people waiting at the ticket office. They would be there to claim refunds for cancelled performances, she supposed. But as she grew closer, she could see they were actually buying tickets. She also noticed that the police crime tape had been removed and someone had put up a blackboard on a stand near the gate that said *Performances starting again tomorrow. Two shows a day for our final week.* She walked to the front of the queue and asked where she could find Caitlyn. 'She's in the ring with the dogs,' she was told.

Assuming the woman meant the circus ring, she walked up to the tent, pulled aside a canvas flap and squeezed inside. She walked past the tiers of seats and sat down on one of the straw bales that formed a barrier between the audience and the performers. In the ring, Caitlyn and a girl of about fourteen were working with a team of four dogs; three small terriers and a larger dog that looked like a more athletic, brown version of Harold. Jasmine watched for a while unnoticed. The terriers were impressive, agile and lively, and judging by the amount of tail-wagging, clearly enjoying every minute of what they were doing. The larger dog sat to one side and yawned. Less enthusiastic about show business, perhaps. A moment later, Caitlyn noticed Jasmine and waved to her before strolling across the sawdust ring to sit down next to her. The dogs carried on with their performance with the younger girl.

'Hi,' she said to Jasmine. 'It's nice to see you.'

'I hope I'm not interrupting your session. You did say drop in any time.'

'Absolutely. It's fine. We're just putting the finishing touches to a new act.'

'Who's the girl? I don't remember her at the show the other night.'

'That's my little sister, Keavy. She just arrived on Friday night. She joins us every year for her school holidays.'

'Already?' Jasmine didn't think school finished until mid-July.

'Term ends at the end of June in Ireland. Mum took her out a few days early because she has to go to some horse breeding conference with Keavy's dad.'

'So Paddy Quinn isn't her father?'

'No, we're half-sisters.'

Jasmine watched as Keavy and the dogs ran through their act. 'She's very good. The dogs as well.'

'This is the first time we've let her perform, but Keavy's grown up working with dogs and horses and she's been longing for an act of her own. Since the show was closed yesterday and today, we've been working up a new act for her and the dogs. She'll be performing in the shows from tomorrow.'

The act wound up with Keavy turning a series of cartwheels, the smaller dogs diving between her legs as she turned and then taking it in turns to jump on the larger dog's back. The dog had stopped yawning and was trotting along in Keavy's wake, finally standing still, forming a pyramid with the three small dogs on its back while Keavy took a bow.

Jasmine and Caitlyn applauded enthusiastically, and Keavy clicked her fingers, which seemed to be the signal for the dogs to relax as they bounded up to Caitlyn for their reward of treats and then scampered off, playfully chasing each other and jumping on and off the straw bales.

'They really enjoy it, don't they?' Jasmine wondered if they were smiling. It looked as if they were. People said dogs couldn't smile but Ivo had persuaded her they could. Harold's smile was a bit on the sinister side because of his dental misalignment, but Ivo assured Jasmine it was a smile of pleasure, and she was inclined to believe him since his half-tail would also be wagging joyfully.

'They love it,' said Caitlyn. 'They've missed the show too. You should have seen them when we let them into the ring this morning.'

'Do they have kennels?' Jasmine asked.

'They do, because the animal health people insist on inspecting them. But they sometimes sleep with me in my caravan. It's been a bit crowded since Keavy arrived, but she'd never forgive me if I banished them to the kennels every night, so I let them stay occasionally.'

Jasmine laughed. 'I don't suppose the horses join you as well?'

'No,' said Caitlyn. 'They have very posh stable tents.'

'Glamping for horses?'

'Something like that.'

Keavy had stopped playing chase with the dogs and came over to sit next to her sister. 'I need to take a shower after that,' she said. 'Ooh, food,' she added, spotting Jasmine's paper bag. 'I'm starving.'

'Help yourself,' said Jasmine, holding the bag out to her.

Keavy chose a chocolate doughnut and took a bite. 'Yummy,' she said.

'Thanks, I'll tell my dad.'

'Your dad can make doughnuts?'

'He's a bit of an expert at cakes and pastries.'

'And Keavy's a greedy little pig,' said Caitlyn.

'I'm a growing girl with a healthy appetite. And I've just spent all day training the dogs. I deserve to eat, don't I?'

Caitlyn laughed. 'And now you are all hot and sweaty. Did you mention a shower?'

Keavy swallowed the last of the doughnut and licked the sugar off her fingers. 'And Norah said I could go and try on my costume.'

'Okay,' said Caitlyn. 'I think Jasmine is here to talk to me, so off you go. I'll take the dogs to the caravan with us.'

'A doughnut to take with you?' Jasmine offered.

'Wouldn't say no,' said Keavy, plunging her hand into the bag again and then running off across the ring while Caitlyn restrained the dogs, who were trying to follow her.

'It must be nice to have a sister,' said Jasmine wistfully. 'I'm the only one in my family. Although Ivo is practically a brother.'

'It has its moments, I suppose,' said Caitlyn. 'Keavy's great, but I'm not sure I'd want her here all the time.'

Once in the caravan, Caitlyn put on the kettle and the dogs jumped up onto one of the bunks and settled down on a blue blanket with a design of dog paw prints. 'Mint tea okay?' she asked.

'Mint tea's fine. Have you got a plate? There are a few more doughnuts and some sandwiches.'

Caitlyn passed her a plate with a blue flower design and a gold edge, and Jasmine arranged the food she had brought. 'It's quiet here this evening,' she said.

'Nothing to keep anyone here until we start the shows again. The band and the acrobats teamed up for a tour of the castle followed by a meal somewhere. Dad and Granny have gone to talk to the lawyers and Aidan's gone off in a strop because although the police have okayed us to reopen, the fairground rides are still off limits. I think it reminds him that Jeremy's not going to be back for a while and he'll have to do all the work himself. He's probably in a pub somewhere and will stagger in drunk at closing time.'

Jasmine hadn't warmed to Aidan at the meeting, and she liked him even less now. Shouldn't he be the one to visit the lawyers? It was his son in trouble, wasn't it? 'Is he usually morose like he was at the meeting?'

'Always,' said Caitlyn. 'His partner went off with someone when Jeremy was ten. And Aidan was left holding the not-so-small baby. He's never forgiven her.'

'What's her name?'

'Rosemarie Farrell,' said Caitlyn. 'Is that relevant?'

'I don't know,' said Jasmine. 'I've been asked to get as much background as possible.'

'I don't remember Rosemarie very well. She was a contortionist and escapologist. She could bend herself into weird shapes and escape from a sack while fastened with chains.'

'Not a lot of career opportunities there, I don't suppose.'

'You'd be surprised. They're big in Mongolia, apparently.'

'Is that where she went?'

'No idea. She's a name we don't mention.'

Jasmine couldn't image Rosemarie had anything to do with Badger's death if she'd done a runner when Jeremy was ten. That would be soon after the circus started. It could hardly be an act of revenge after all these years. And she'd probably never heard of Badger, unless there was a lot they didn't know about him and his background. But she couldn't leave anything unexplored. 'You've no idea where she is now?'

'Nope, and I doubt that anyone else has either.'

'You mentioned someone called Norah. Is she family?'

'No, well, not yet. She and Dara are close, although it's probably rather one-sided. I can't see anyone replacing Safiya. Norah's the daughter of an old friend of Granny's. She joined us for last year's tour and she came back again this year.'

'What does she do?'

'She helps with costumes. Visiting acts bring their own, but there's still laundering and running repairs. She made the dog's outfits and one for Keavy.'

'The dogs wear costumes?'

'They have frilly collars with sparkles.'

*That I must see,* Jasmine thought. Perhaps Ivo would enjoy it too. 'Are there any tickets left?' Jasmine asked. 'I know you're moving on in few days. But I'd love to see Keavy and the dogs in action.'

'I can get you a couple for tomorrow evening,' said Caitlyn. 'We're sold out until the end of the week but we keep a few tickets back for friends. Then we're moving to Blackbushe. We've got two weeks there and it's only about fifteen miles from here. I just hope we get all this Jeremy stuff sorted before we have to leave there.'

Jasmine hoped so too. They weren't really set up for long distance detective work. 'Where will you be after that?'

'We're going to Brighton and then a hop over to the Isle of Wight. It's our usual summer tour.'

That wasn't too bad. There was always Jonny and his car if they needed it. 'I'm sure Katya will have it all sorted by then, and anyway the south coast isn't far.'

'Katya seems like a forceful lady,' said Caitlyn. 'Does she really believe us when we say Jeremy is innocent?'

'She's reserving judgement,' said Jasmine. 'But she's prepared to consider it.'

'It's the police we need to persuade.'

'Katya's ex police and she still has contacts.' Jasmine didn't mention the fact that Lugs, too, was not one hundred percent sure of Jeremy's guilt. She didn't want to raise Caitlyn's hopes. 'Katya has asked me to make sure we know who's who in the circus. I think I've got the family sorted so just talk me through other people who work here.'

'All of them?' Caitlyn raised an eyebrow.

A good point. There must be dozens of people working there. 'Start with those who would have been in regular contact with Badger Waites.'

'There's a bit of rivalry between the circus team and the fairground guys. Apart from Badger, there are only two others. Tony Black, who sells tickets at the box office and oversees the carousel when it's actually running. He just has to keep an eye on it because it works on a timer. He's a regular, been travelling with us for years.'

*A timer?* Jasmine wondered. Was that usual? 'You mean he doesn't watch it all the time?'

'It's his job to make sure everyone is safely on their horse or in one of the seats, but Jeremy's not all that strict about it and Tony sometimes gets distracted.'

'So what happens if there's a problem while it's working?'

Caitlyn shrugged. 'There never has been, but it's got all kinds of safety things which trip the mechanism if someone falls off a horse or starts mucking about. It's regularly inspected for safety.'

'And it's set to run for a specific amount of time?'

'Ten minutes, usually, although it can be adjusted.'

'You said there were two others apart from Jeremy and Badger, so who was the other one?'

'Mike Stone, who is usually on the kiddie roundabout. He's been with us for years as well. Longer than Jeremy, I think.'

'Does he resent that? The fact that Jeremy is his boss?'

Caitlyn shrugged. 'Not as far as I know. Both guys are very loyal to Granny and the circus. I don't suppose they really think of Jeremy as a boss. They probably see themselves as his caretaker. He's been in trouble, you know. I think Granny gave him the job because that's where he could do the least damage. Tony and Mike are very conscientious. The fairground could run just as well without Jeremy.'

That was interesting. Cordelia Quinn apparently didn't think a lot of her grandson. But that didn't mean she thought he was capable of murder. Obviously she didn't or she wouldn't have come to them for help.

'They're going to miss Badger, though. There's always mechanical stuff to see to, and Mike is fully occupied with the small roundabout because there are very young children riding on it. He's there all the time. Tony and Jeremy see to the helter-skelter and the swing boats. That's it really. The fairground is only a tiny part of the show. Granny got interested in it when she was offered the carousel for a knock-down price. She's picked up the other rides at auctions over the years.'

'And the rides only operate once the circus show has finished?'

'Before it starts as well. Not during performances, though.'

'And you say there is rivalry between the circus and the fairground?'

'Good-natured banter usually, although it can get a bit more heated after a night in the pub.'

'Any particular occasions you can think of?'

Caitlyn shook her head. 'Not really. Granny and Dad are pretty strict. Any problem and they wouldn't think twice about chucking troublemakers out.'

But not family. Jeremy could be as lazy and irresponsible as he liked and keep his job. Jasmine was beginning to think he wasn't very likeable and wouldn't take kindly to taking on someone else's work because they'd been sacked. 'So your dad and gran have to keep replacing people?'

'Yes, but that's not a problem. It's unskilled work and we get youngsters queuing up for jobs here.'

Jasmine was not surprised. There was something romantic about working for a circus. None of what Caitlyn had told Jasmine so far explained what had happened to Badger. He didn't live on site. He shouldn't even have been there when he was killed. 'The post-mortem suggested the time of Badger's death was between six and eight am on Saturday morning. Who would have been up and about then?'

'Hardly anyone,' said Caitlyn, laughing. 'We work until late every night. No one is up and about until mid-morning. I'm usually the first out of my caravan because I have to feed and water the horses. They start to kick up a fuss if they're not fed by nine-thirtyish.'

'Did you see anyone that morning?'

Caitlyn was slow to reply. 'Not really.'

She was holding something back. 'Not really? But you did see someone?'

'Not someone, something,' Caitlyn sighed. 'Probably nothing.'

'We can't help you unless we know everything,' said Jasmine. 'Even something you think was unimportant.'

'Well, I suppose I'd better tell you. Jeremy has this very distinctive leather jacket; mahogany brown with kind of stud things up the sleeves. He wears it all the time. That morning I passed the carousel as I always do to get hay for the stable tents. There's a small shed we use near the gate. I noticed Jeremy's jacket hanging from one of the guy ropes that hold the carousel cover in place overnight. On my way back with the barrow of hay, it had gone.'

Jasmine could understand why Caitlyn had been reluctant to tell her that. 'Like you said, it's probably nothing. Perhaps Jeremy had left it there all night and just went to pick it up. It doesn't mean he knew what was inside the carousel.'

'I hope you're right. I wouldn't want to get him into worse trouble than he's in already. Even if he is a waste of space.'

No, that wouldn't do much for family harmony. 'Don't worry,' said Jasmine. 'If Jeremy was guilty, he'd probably not have done anything as incriminating as leaving his jacket at the scene.' She hoped she sounded rather more convincing about this than she felt. 'Anyway,' she said, jumping up. 'Thanks for all the info and for letting me see the dogs in action. And wish Keavy good luck for the show.'

'Thanks,' said Caitlyn glumly. But then she smiled at Jasmine. 'I'll leave two tickets at the box office for tomorrow night.'

Jasmine walked away from the circus and headed back into town. From what Caitlyn had told her, the family was rather less united and respectable than they led them to believe at the meeting. And Katya was going to be interested in the jacket.

# 9

Jonny put down the cloth he'd been using to clean the coffee machine. He stood back and admired its sleek, shiny and now spotlessly clean surface. It had been wasted in his office at CPS. Much better that it was here where it was appreciated. That was one of the advantages of being a major shareholder. He didn't make a lot of decisions about the business any longer, but he got to choose the important stuff, like where to keep the coffee machine. He turned the machine on and waited for it to start its brew. 'Won't be long,' he said.

'It's fine,' said Jasmine, who was sifting through some notes Katya had printed for their meeting. 'It'll taste all the better once I've finished this lot.'

'No hurry for me either,' said Ivo, who was perched on a stepladder fixing some loose screws on the incident board.

'Pass me a glass of water, would you?' said Katya.

Jonny poured some water from an insulated jug, also provided courtesy of CPS, and handed it to Katya, who popped a couple of paracetamol tablets out of a blister pack and washed them down with the ice-cold water. She held the cold glass against her cheek and groaned.

'Problem?' Jonny asked. She wasn't looking too good this morning. She was no oil painting at the best of times, but today she looked wan and tired. And she was usually nagging for coffee as soon as she arrived.

'Bloody toothache,' she muttered. 'I'm seeing the dentist as soon as we finish here. But we've stuff to do first.' She clicked on an email Lugs had sent her and read it twice. Jonny sat next to her, pen poised to make notes.

'What does it say?' he asked. 'Is it helpful?'

'It's a summary of the post-mortem report. I can't tell right now if it's helpful or not. I'll list each point in turn and let you all comment.' Ivo jumped down from his stepladder and headed for the coffee. Katya picked up a pen and turned to the board. She wrote:

*The report suggests the time of death was between 6 and 8 am.*

'That confirms what Lugs already told me. I won't go into details, but rigor mortis completes within twelve hours of death and eases again after twenty-four. The body was still stiff when it fell to the ground at around ten-thirty that night, and skin discolouration suggests it had been there for between twelve and fourteen hours before it fell.'

Jasmine was counting on her fingers and making notes. 'That seems right. If the body was hidden in the roof, it would have been difficult to lift it into position once rigor was complete, so he was probably concealed quite soon after death, early in the morning when no one was about, so no witnesses. The site is usually deserted until midday and the killer would have wanted it out of sight before anyone else was up and about.'

'That's right,' said Katya. 'My guess is that he was tied up there very soon after his death. Around seven am?'

'Do we know for sure that he was in the roof?' Jonny asked. 'Couldn't he have been concealed somewhere else on the carousel?'

'There's not much room anywhere else,' said Jasmine. 'Unless he was strapped to one of the horses, but then he would have been spotted as soon as they took the cover off.'

The others nodded. 'How did he die?' asked Ivo.

Katya ran her finger down the items on the report. 'He was strangled from behind by someone of approximately the same height as himself, with three-core vintage electrical cable.'

'Vintage?' Jonny asked. 'How do they know?'

'It's braided,' said Katya. 'They could tell by the pattern of bruising around the neck. There were also some loose fibres, which tell us it was brown.'

Jonny remembered plaited wire on table lamps that his grandmother used. 'Is there any use for it now?' he asked.

'You can buy it on Amazon,' said Ivo. 'I bought some in dark blue for a friend who wanted to match his pendant lights to his curtains. It's a hipster thing.'

*A bit niche,* Jonny thought. 'Would there be uses for it in a vintage circus?' he asked.

'A good point,' said Katya, writing it down. 'We need to follow that up.'

'What about the rope used to tie him up?' Jasmine asked.

'That was hemp rope. Plenty of that kicking around, I'd imagine, but we should check with whoever is in charge of supplies.'

'How did the murderer get the body into the carousel?' Jasmine asked. 'Could one person have done that alone?'

'I wondered that,' said Katya. 'And yes, it could have been a single-handed job as long as whoever did it was familiar with the layout of the carousel. That's probably why the victim was tied by his wrists and ankles. That happened after death, so it wasn't to prevent him from escaping, but it would make it easier to haul him up onto the carousel, another reason why they think he was in the roof.'

'And the rope had been cut by something,' said Jonny. 'There are metal struts up in the roof that might have done that.'

'That doesn't make sense,' said Ivo, shaking his head.

Katya frowned at him. 'Want to explain?'

'It means the murderer was someone who knew the inside of the carousel very well but not well enough to know that the moving mechanism could weaken and cut through the rope.'

Katya read through the report again. 'There's nothing about how the rope was cut. It could have been done with a knife, even before Badger was tied up with it.'

'So if it wasn't to tie him into the roof, what was it for?' Ivo asked. 'It wasn't like he was going anywhere.'

'No idea,' said Katya.

'Anything there that would let Jeremy off the hook?' Jasmine asked.

'Not really,' said Katya. 'As fairground manager he would need to know about the equipment itself, but that might not include knowing a lot about rope.'

'He'd have known it was strong enough to hold the trapeze acts,' said Jonny. 'But presumably anyone who worked at the circus would know that.' Things were not looking good for Jeremy. If only he had an alibi, or they could find someone else who had a grudge against Badger. Then he had a thought. 'Have we got a description of Jeremy?'

'I know what you're thinking,' said Katya. 'And yes, he was the same height as Badger.'

'A pity,' said Jonny. 'If only he'd been a five-foot-two weakling there'd not be a case against him.'

'And there's the jacket,' said Jasmine. 'If he's innocent, Jeremy's not making it easy for us, is he?'

'Do you really think Jeremy is innocent?' asked Jonny. 'Or are we wasting our time?'

'I'm not committing myself one way or the other yet,' said Katya. 'Cordelia Quinn has contracted us to find out what happened and that's what we will do.'

'Where do we go from here?' Jasmine asked.

Katya tapped her pen against her teeth. 'Cordelia will be visiting Jeremy in jail as soon as a visiting order can be organised. I've given her some specific questions to ask him, including how he explains the jacket. She is going to report back to me after the visit.'

'Can we trust her?' asked Ivo. 'She might be selective about what she tells us.'

'It's something to be aware of. Evidence and interviews have to be disclosed to both prosecution and defence lawyers, which is why police interviews are all recorded. Visits from relatives and solicitors are not, so we need to take what we glean from those with a pinch of salt.'

'How do we decide what's true?' Ivo asked.

'With difficulty,' said Katya. 'I'm hoping we may be able to work with the defence team, but that might be a problem because Cordelia's lawyer is based in Dublin. The family are working with them to find someone who is trained in UK law.'

'That could take ages,' said Jasmine. 'The circus is moving on at the end of the week.'

'The case will still be based locally. Jeremy was interviewed with the duty solicitor present when he was arrested and charged. Further questioning is suspended until the family have appointed someone. And that could work in our favour.'

'How?' asked Jonny.

'It will give us time to collect evidence of our own and if we have something to offer, the defence team are more likely to work with us and tell us what *they've* got. The alternative being that we take what we find direct to the police.'

'But if it all has to be disclosed to both...?' Jonny wondered.

Katya interrupted him. 'It's a matter of timing,' she said, without explaining any further. 'It means we have our work cut out over the next couple of days to get as far ahead as we can.' She reached into her bag and pulled out a sheaf of papers. 'I've made a plan,' she said. 'I hope you all have time to spare right now.'

'I've always got time to spare,' said Jonny.

'I've nothing I can't put off,' said Ivo. 'Unless there's an emergency at *Shady Willows.*'

'I need to be here for breakfast,' said Jasmine. 'But I can get cover for the rest of the day.'

'Good,' said Katya. 'Ivo, I'd like you to take a good look at security around both the circus and the funfair. I assume they keep the place locked up at night so at the moment the assumption is that it was an inside job. That's one reason why Jeremy is the prime suspect. We need to know if there was any way in for an outsider. This could have been someone unconnected with either the family or the circus.'

'Someone who knew the inner workings of the carousel?' said Jonny. 'Wouldn't that have to be someone on the inside?'

'It might seem obvious, but we can't rely on it. It could be exactly what the murderer wanted everyone to think. Point the finger at someone in the circus.'

'And it worked,' said Ivo. 'The police don't even seem to have considered an outsider.'

'We need to know much more about carousels and that's where you come in, Jonny. Do some research on them. This one came from a steam fair that was closing down.' She shuffled through some of her papers and handed Jonny an advert that had been cut from a magazine for fairground enthusiasts. 'These are the people Cordelia bought it from. That would be a good place to start.'

Jonny took the paper from her. 'There will be websites about repairing vintage equipment,' he said. 'And lists of fairs that have gone out of business, and books by people who used to work in them.'

'That's the spirit,' said Katya. 'You just need to find someone who knows about funfair equipment and who might have had a grudge against the circus or Badger.'

*Not much of an ask, then,* Jonny thought. At least he had plenty of spare time, with Belinda obsessively looking for something to replace the council and him no longer having much of a role at the factory.

'Jasmine,' Katya continued, 'I'd like you to go back and chat to your friend Caitlyn again. See who was working when and what they were doing. Ask about these two blokes.' She shuffled some more papers. 'Here we are,' she said. 'Tony Black, who oversaw the carousel when it was in operation. And Mike Stone, who is in charge of kiddie rides.'

'Tony Black might have had the opportunity,' said Jonny. 'He'd worked on the carousel since the Quinns bought it. Presumably he would have had plenty of time to study its insides.'

'A good point,' said Katya. 'But once again, we mustn't make assumptions.'

'I already talked to Caitlyn about those two. They are long-term employees and trusted by the family. But I suppose either of them might have witnessed something,' Jasmine suggested. 'Do we know if they were questioned by the police?'

'I'll ask Lugs. But even if they were, there's no harm getting them to repeat their accounts and check for inconsistencies.'

'The circus is reopening this evening,' said Jasmine. 'Caitlyn has got two tickets for me so I can see her sister perform her act with the dogs. I'm hoping Ivo will come with me.'

'I'm up for it,' said Ivo. 'I can leave Harold with Bill.'

'Who's Bill?' Jasmine asked.

'One of my residents,' said Ivo. 'He gets a bit lonely, well, a lot of them do, but I can trust Bill not to stuff Harold full of biscuits.'

Katya winced, possibly for the first time in her life, at the thought of biscuits. The paracetamol hadn't really kicked in, but she'd got through the meeting. Nothing like a murder to distract one from pain. But it was time to get going. She didn't care what the dentist did. He could extract all her teeth if it stopped them hurting. She gathered up her papers and stuffed them into her bag. 'I need to get going,' she said. 'Date with a dentist.'

'Will you be okay?' Jasmine asked. 'Would you like me to come with you?'

'No, love. I'll be fine.' She was a kind girl, Katya thought. She'd never had that kind of consideration from the police team; even Lugs was impatient with their aches and pains. 'You've all got plenty to get on with. How about we meet again on Thursday. Late morning suit you all?'

# 10

They were meeting at *Shady Willows* and walking upstream to the circus together. Ivo thought they might take the van in case it rained, but Jasmine laughed and said the walk would do them both good and no rain was forecast. Even if it was, it wouldn't do them any harm. She'd have expected Ivo to be less bothered about a bit of rain, having lived on the streets, but perhaps that made him more sensitive. Being out in all weathers was probably a part of his life he wanted to forget, and she supposed getting soaked wouldn't help much with that.

Jasmine was intrigued by the life of a travelling circus. She didn't suppose you could drive onto any bit of empty land and set up shop. There would be regulations and fees to pay, and someone must own the land. She'd spent the previous evening on Google and had discovered that the meadow the circus was camped on was owned by an oil billionaire from one of the Gulf states who owned a mansion close by. The land that surrounded it, many hundreds of acres, was rented out. Most to farming companies for grazing, but there were two adjoining meadows that were hired out for events. In the last few years, they had been the venue for car boot sales, a funfair, an exhibition of vintage farm vehicles, an agricultural show, and for the last two years, Quinn's Circus. The first year was for a week, but the event was so popular that this year they were there for three weeks.

It would be interesting to catch a glimpse of a multi-millionaire. She couldn't imagine what anyone would do with all that money. There must be a limit to the number of yachts and mansions one needed. But she didn't suppose the owner was often in residence. He probably had multiple houses dotted around the world and didn't have much interest in circuses anyway. And he was unlikely to be involved in renting out his fields himself; he'd have people who did it for him. The house was probably surrounded by high fences topped with razor wire and monitored by CCTV cameras. But she smiled at the idea of someone peeping over the razor wire to catch a glimpse of the circus. It must be quite exciting to have all that going on at the end of one's garden.

Arriving at the gate to *Shady Willows,* she knocked on Ivo's cabin door. There was no reply and no barking. Had Ivo forgotten she was coming? She was just tapping his number on her phone to call him when he appeared from the door of one of the other cabins. He waved and trotted towards her. 'Sorry. I was just settling Harold with my neighbour.'

'Your dog sitter?'

'Yeah, they enjoy each other's company. In Harold's case it's pure cupboard love, but like I said Bill gets a bit lonely and enjoys having him there. Didn't mean to keep you waiting, though.'

'No problem. I'm quite early.'

'That's good. It'll give us time to look round a bit. Check up on their security, like Katya said.'

'I'd forgotten about that,' said Jasmine. 'Too excited about seeing the dogs in action. But you're right, we should take some pictures of the fences and gates so Katya will know we've not been slacking.'

They set out along the river path. Ivo was so lucky living here. Jasmine liked being in the town centre, but sometimes it would be nice to look out of the window and watch the river. It was a warm, sunny evening and the riverside was busy with dog walkers and picnickers; the river itself busy with boat traffic, the big tourist boats that chugged up and down, loaded with sightseers, small motorboats rented out by the hour, and privately owned cabin cruisers. Jasmine always hoped she might see a double sculling skiff of the type used in *Three Men in a Boat,* but they seemed to have gone out of fashion. Too uncomfortable, probably; people liked boats with proper cabins and soft bunks these days.

They could see the flags on top of the circus tent and followed the path to a gate, outside of which was a queue of people hoping for tickets. *They'll be disappointed,* Jasmine thought. Tickets sold out weeks in advance and even with the extra afternoon performances, Caitlyn told her, they were having trouble fitting in everyone who'd had tickets cancelled. News of the murder must have tempted people to come and have a look at where it had happened, maybe with the over-optimistic hope of returned tickets.

There was a sign on the gate that told them it would be unlocked to admit ticket holders only at six-thirty. They were half an hour early. 'That's good,' said Ivo. 'We can walk around the perimeter and look at their security.'

'It doesn't look very secure, does it?' said Jasmine as they strolled away from the entrance. The gate itself was an imposing six feet high, wrought iron with spikes on top and an impressive lock. But the field was surrounded only by a chain-link fence through which they could see the box office and a boardwalk leading to the entrance to the big top.

'We need to work out how Badger got in early in the morning when there was no one about,' said Jasmine.

Ivo walked up to the fence for a closer look. 'It's not easy to climb over a chain-link fence. There's nowhere to get a foothold and this one is too high to jump over. He might have had something to stand on, I suppose.'

'And he'd have been seen,' said Jasmine. 'Even very early in the morning there could have been people around who would have noticed.'

Ivo looked along the fence in both directions. After a few yards the fence curved around out of sight. 'There must be another way in for deliveries and people who work here,' he said. 'The main entrance was obviously for paying visitors who needed to negotiate the box office before being admitted to any attractions.'

'We'll walk all the way around,' said Jasmine. 'There might be stretches of the fence that are less easily seen from inside, where someone could climb over without being noticed. But we still don't know why Badger would want to get in early if he didn't start work until midday.'

'Maybe he camped inside overnight.'

'Why would he do that?'

Ivo shrugged. 'Dunno. Perhaps he missed the last bus home.'

'I think he came on his bike.'

'Has anyone found a bike?'

'That's a good question, but I don't see how it would help to know where he left it.'

'There might be clues. Or it might have been stolen by the murderer.'

'Killed for his bike? That's one of your dafter ideas.'

'It could have been an accident.'

Sometimes, Jasmine thought, Katya had a point about the stupidity of Ivo's theories. 'You think he was accidentally strangled and then accidentally tied up with rope?'

'Yeah, you're right. I didn't think it through.'

'Never mind, Ivo. You're right to consider everything possible even if you have to drop one or two of your theories. Don't reject anything, Katya's always saying.'

As they followed the fence away from the gate, they had a view of the backs of the caravans, which were huddled together in a group, rather like the covered wagons in old cowboy films, and further round they came to the stable and kennel tents. No sign of dogs but a couple of horses stared at them through the flaps of the tent. At the halfway point there was a service gate. It was similar to the one at the main entrance, but without the spikes. Nevertheless, it was stout and secure, possibly climbable, but without anyone noticing? Not very likely; it was too close to the caravans and even if the inhabitants were sound asleep, wouldn't the dogs bark at any kind of intrusion? On the far side of the gate was a man sitting in a deckchair, reading a newspaper. Jasmine cleared her throat, hoping he might answer some of their questions about people coming and going. He looked up from his paper and frowned at her. 'Bugger off,' he said. 'Bloody murder tourists.'

'That's a pity,' said Ivo as they moved away from the gate and continued their walk. 'He'd have been able to tell us how easy it would be for someone to get in and out unnoticed.'

'I don't suppose he would, though,' said Jasmine, trying not to feel guilty about her lack of questioning. 'He'd never admit that anyone could have got in without him noticing. Anyway, we can ask Caitlyn about him. I don't think he was a Quinn, do you?'

'He didn't look like any of the ones we've met so far. It could have been Dara, I suppose. We don't know if he looks like his brothers, do we?'

'That bloke certainly doesn't have the dark-haired, blue-eyed Irish charm that Paddy has.'

'And Aidan has the same looks but without the charm.'

'We met them all except Dara, didn't we?' said Ivo. 'And Jeremy, of course.'

'I've forgotten what Dara does,' Jasmine admitted.

'Helps backstage, I think.'

'Then he's probably backstage right now. The hour before the show starts must be a busy time for him. And you're right, that guy at the gate didn't look like the other Quinns. Even Caitlyn has dark hair and blue eyes. And Cordelia was probably dark-haired before she went that dramatic white.'

They walked on, past a storage shed just inside the gate, and a campsite in another field outside the fence. Beyond that was a car park. 'Those tents must be where visiting acts and seasonal staff sleep,' said Jasmine, nodding towards the campsite. 'How easy do you think it would be for one of them to slip in and out?'

'I don't think it would be hard to climb over the service gate when it was unmanned. I don't suppose deckchair bloke stays there all night or gets up very early. And it would be easy enough to slip in or out when something's being delivered.'

'What do you suppose gets delivered?' Jasmine wondered.

'Animal feed, straw, food for the refreshment stalls. Maybe milk and stuff for the people in the caravans, for their early morning tea.'

'I don't suppose they go in for early morning tea,' said Jasmine, laughing. 'As far as I can make out, they're all sound asleep until mid-morning. Except Caitlyn, who has to feed the horses.'

'You don't think she killed Badger, do you?'

Jasmine considered that for a moment, all kinds of unpleasant images floating through her head. Could Ivo be on to something? Self-defence during an attack? Then she rejected the idea. 'No, remember the post-mortem report said he was strangled by someone the same height as himself.'

'How tall was he?'

That was a good question. She thought it had been in the report, but it might be worth checking again. Her memory of the night he fell at her feet was that he was average height, but she hadn't been in the best position to say for sure. In any case, she was reassured by knowing that Caitlyn was small. She'd need to be for dancing around on the backs of horses. She was very agile but hardly strong enough to strangle a man of average build.

'What about the rope?'

'What about it?'

'Would that have been delivered?'

'I doubt it. There must be plenty of it kept here. We should find out how often that gets replaced and if anyone would know if some went missing.'

'Has anyone explained the plaited flex yet?'

'I don't think so. I'll check with Katya. It might help us establish if it was an inside job or not.'

'And if it was, that wouldn't help Jeremy, would it?'

'Quite the opposite. But remember, it's the truth we're after. We shouldn't ignore any evidence just because it makes Jeremy look bad.'

FIVE MINUTES LATER, they had completed their perimeter walk and were back at the main gate. 'So we think it's possible that someone got in early that morning,' said Jasmine. 'This gate would have been locked and it's well patrolled. But the service gate's a possibility, isn't it?'

'Jeremy could have let Badger in early in the morning,' said Ivo. 'But if the killer was someone from outside, both of them would have needed to get in.'

He was right, and it seemed even more likely that the murderer must be someone inside the circus. 'We'd need more than that to get Jeremy off the hook. One of Katya's tasks should be to look into Badger's past and see if anyone's got reason to want to hurt him.'

'We can bring it up at the next meeting. She may have info from Lugs about him.'

'Would he tell her if he had?'

'I'm not sure. We might need to do some digging of our own.'

They walked up to the ticket booth, where there was now only a handful of people waiting. The man dispensing the tickets was wearing a badge with his name – Mike Stone. Jasmine told him Caitlyn had two tickets waiting for them and he handed her an envelope with her name on it. 'Enjoy the show,' he said. 'Sorry there's no funfair tonight, although it means I can knock off early. Get to the pub before closing time.'

*Kiddie rides,* Jasmine thought, remembering where she'd heard his name before. 'Do you travel with the circus?' she asked.

'Yeah, been with the Quinns since they started. I used to be Mrs Quinn's gardener when she lived full time in Ireland and before she sold the big house.'

A loyal retainer, then. 'That must have been quite a change for you?'

'It was. I still get home for the winter, though.'

'And Mrs Quinn. Does she spend the winters in Ireland?'

'She's got a posh flat in Dublin now. No garden. But I'm kept busy with all the maintenance and repairs.'

'And you work for Aidan Quinn?'

'Only on the summer tours. In the winter I work with the engineering company we have a contract with to service all our stuff. You know Aidan, do you?'

'We've met him,' Jasmine said, and Ivo nodded his agreement. 'He seems a bit surly. Is he difficult to work for?'

'Not really. He's a lot on his mind at the moment, though.'

'You mean his son being arrested?'

'Yeah, although that wasn't really a surprise. A bit of a tearaway, young Jeremy. Always has been.'

'So you think he did it?'

He paused as if unsure how to answer. 'Wouldn't want to comment.'

*Evasive,* Jasmine thought. Wouldn't a loyal employee leap to Jeremy's defence? Not for the first time, she was sensing some tension and not just within the family.

'You'd better be taking your seats,' said Mike. 'You don't want to miss the start of the show.'

He wasn't going to say any more to them, so Jasmine picked up the tickets and they headed into the auditorium, where they found seats in a tiered stand just as the band started to play. Ivo put his hands over his ears. Twelve men armed with battered brass instruments, and dressed in what Jasmine assumed was traditional Gypsy attire, were giving it all they'd got. After a few minutes Ivo, getting used to the volume, lowered his hands from his ears and started to tap his feet. The music was lively and rhythmic. A long way from *Brassed Off,* which was Jasmine's only experience of brass band music. These Romanians may have lacked finesse, but no one could fault their enthusiasm. She assumed they were staying on the campsite so they might have seen someone entering or leaving on the morning of the murder. Could one of them have done it? She doubted it. They had travelled from Romania a few days before Easter at the start of the Quinns' tour, and even if any of them spoke perfect English, could they have taken a murderous dislike to Badger in so few weeks?

The show was almost exactly the same as the one she'd seen with Teddy a few evenings ago and it was every bit as enjoyable. There was plenty worth seeing again and a few things she had missed the first time. Once again, Cordelia wound up the finale in spectacular style. The only addition was Keavy's dog act, which kept Ivo on the edge of his seat and received enthusiastic applause from him. Jasmine was amazed by Keavy's agility and her control over the dogs, who were every bit as obedient with an audience of a couple of hundred as they had been training in the empty ring. And Keavy looked amazing. Norah – was that the woman's name – had done her proud with a scarlet leotard decorated with yellow flowers under a flimsy frill of a skirt, her hair held back in a yellow clip and her feet bare. She was agile in a way Jasmine could only imagine. She'd been a bit of a gymnast at school, but nothing like Keavy, who must have been in training since she started walking or possibly since she'd started to crawl. Part of the act involved the dogs rolling a barrel with Keavy curled up inside. Leaping out to the delight of the dogs, who had been pretending to search for her. How do you even begin to train a dog to do that? Wasn't Keavy's mother a contortionist? No, that was Jeremy's mother, who had escaped from a sack fastened with chains. Keavy was not even related to her, but the skills were very similar and Jasmine imagined there'd be very little Keavy couldn't escape from. She applauded loudly as Keavy and the dogs took a bow. All the dogs, even the large Harold-type dog, stretched their front paws in front of them and bowed to the audience while Keavy held her arms in the air and performed a deep bow. *Where does she get her energy?* Jasmine wondered. She didn't even look out of breath.

'Harold could do that,' Ivo said as they filed out at the end of the show. 'The little dogs were clever but that big one didn't do very much. He just bowed at the end. I could teach Harold to do that.'

'He'd rather be with you catching criminals,' said Jasmine. 'Why would he need to bow?'

'I wasn't offering his services, just saying...'

'Let's go and find Caitlyn,' said Jasmine. 'She told me she'd be in the stables at the end of the show.' She led the way past the artistes' entrance to the ring and followed the unmistakable odour of horse. Backstage it was busy; equipment being put away, the band packing up, a team sweeping the sawdust in the ring. But no one asked them what they were doing there, which surprised Jasmine. If anyone could just wander in a few days after a murder, what must it have been like before? Had one of the audience calmly strolled behind the scenes, camped out somewhere for the night and then sought out Badger Waites and killed him early the next morning? But unless they could find a member of the public who hated Badger that much, there'd be no motive or suspect. They could hardly track down and interview everyone who had been in the audience that evening. She supposed the police could trace people who had bought tickets online, but why would they? They already had their man. And it would be no good trying to interview current audiences because the murderer wasn't likely to return. Unless he wanted to kill someone else. A maniac who had it in for circus people? An idea that made Jasmine shudder. It was a stupid idea, anyway. She was as bad as Ivo.

The stables were deserted apart from the horses, who stared at them over the railing at the front of their tent while munching from the troughs placed on the grass outside. A reward for their performance, perhaps. She wondered if horses enjoyed trotting round the ring with Caitlyn dancing on their backs and jumping from one to another as much as Keavy's dogs obviously loved their own performance. She reached out and patted one of the horses on its nose. 'Do you like being a circus horse?' she asked, but it was too busy munching to answer. Jasmine would probably never know. She led Ivo to Caitlyn's caravan, where they found Caitlyn and Keavy sitting on the steps drinking cans of Sprite. They had both changed out of their sparkly costumes into tiny shorts and skimpy tank tops. Caitlyn looked up and waved at them as they approached. Keavy reached into a cool bag and handed them a can each.

'Your dog act was brilliant, Keavy,' said Jasmine.

'Cool,' said Keavy modestly, staring at Ivo.

'This is Ivo,' said Jasmine. 'He's got a dog that looks a bit like one of yours. The big one.'

'That's Brody,' said Keavy. 'He's not very bright so he gets to do the easy stuff.'

'Harold's very clever,' said Ivo, showing her a picture on his phone. 'He couldn't be in a circus, though. He likes catching burglars and murderers.'

Keavy looked at the photo. 'Catching criminals is so cool. Brody would be useless at that. He's too easily distracted by food and the burglars would probably know that and fill their pockets with sausages.'

'Are you just here to talk about dogs?' Caitlyn asked. 'Or are you working on getting my cousin off his murder charge?'

'Both,' said Ivo, winking at Keavy.

'We've been checking out your security,' said Jasmine. 'We were wondering how easy it would have been for someone not connected to the circus to get in and out.'

'Dad and a couple of people who work for him do a walk round at eleven-thirty every night to check that everyone apart from people with caravans have left.'

That was what she'd been afraid of. But at least it knocked her most recent theory on the head, and she wouldn't have to track down and start interviewing everyone who'd been at the circus on Friday night. 'I thought the caravans were only occupied by family?'

'There are a couple of others. Mike Stone's been with the family for years and has his own caravan. Norah sometimes stays with Dara and Joseph.'

'What happens if one of you wants to stay out late?'

'We've all got keys to the back gate.'

'Could anyone have come in with the audience that evening and hidden somewhere overnight?'

'Dad's pretty thorough with his checks, but it's not impossible. There are probably places people can hide.'

That was the first glimmer of hope for Jeremy. Everything else they'd discovered just seemed to stack up the evidence against him.

'Paddy takes his dog with him,' said Keavy. 'A big German pointer called Boyo. They are sometimes used by the military as sniffer dogs, so he'd probably have found anyone who was hiding.'

But Jasmine guessed any intruder would not have his pockets stuffed with sausages. Hidden somewhere smelly, like the stables, they might not have been discovered. 'And what time do the gates open up in the morning?'

'Not very early. You saw Bertie at the back gate?'

'Bad-tempered bloke?' Ivo asked.

'That's him. He's worked for Dad since way back and does the late-night walk around with him. He has a caravan and unlocks the gate when he wakes up in the morning. Unless there's a delivery expected or one of us calls him to open up earlier, it's usually around ten.'

Jasmine made a note to check out Bertie Kelly. Then she had a thought. Something wasn't making sense. 'Was Badger Waites staying on the campsite?'

'Not while we're here, because he had a flat a few miles away. If he'd been kept on after we moved, he would have been given a tent.'

Another puzzle that wasn't making it any easier for Jeremy Quinn. The only way Badger could have come in early on the morning he was killed was for one of the family members with a key to let him in. So unless one of the Quinns was lying, the only one who might have done that was Jeremy. This was like one of those locked room mysteries in reverse. A man was murdered in a place that he didn't have access to. 'What time would Badger normally have started work?' she asked.

'Usually not until midday. They start up the rides for an hour before the afternoon show begins. The only reason for him to come any earlier would be if there was a problem with the machinery.'

'And had there been a problem that evening?'

'Not that I heard.'

Jasmine closed her notebook and sighed. Ivo had been very quiet, which usually meant he was about to come up with an impossible and unbelievable theory. 'Any questions?' she asked him.

'Which gate do they lock last?' he asked.

Jasmine wondered why that mattered.

'The service gate,' said Caitlyn. 'Dad closes and locks the box office after seeing off whoever was selling tickets. He collects up any cash that was taken and locks it in the safe in his caravan.'

'Then he goes round and locks the service gate?'

'No, Bertie locks it before he goes to his caravan.'

None of this was helping and it was time they left. Jasmine was tired, and she needed to think over what she'd learnt this evening and make notes ready for tomorrow's meeting. She thanked Caitlyn and Keavy again and stood up. She looked at her watch and realised it was later than she'd thought. Eleven-fifteen. Another fifteen minutes and Paddy would be on his rounds and he'd no doubt find her and Ivo and escort them off the premises. She thought she might hang about and see what happened but decided against it. They'd take a look at what was going on in the box office instead. When they arrived at the gate the kiosk was closed, although the gate was still unlocked. She remembered that Mike Stone had told them he'd be off to the pub because there would be no rides working that evening. She wondered who was usually there and if the box office had closed early the night before the murder. Because that would mean there was a short window of opportunity for someone to slip in unnoticed, in between Paddy completing his rounds and locking the main gate.

They walked back along the riverbank and Jasmine said good-night to Ivo at *Shady Willows*. She walked the short distance back to the café wondering if she'd learnt anything helpful and decided that she hadn't. Nothing that would help Jeremy; in fact, rather the opposite. Everything they'd discovered about security only supported the idea that the murder was an inside job, the finger of suspicion pointed ever more firmly in Jeremy's direction.

# 11

Jonny looked at the time on his computer screen. His back ached, his eyes were tired, and he was lonely and hungry. But he knew a lot more about the internal workings of carousels than he had when he sat down at his desk after breakfast. He'd learnt about drive gears, pulleys, horse hangers, electric motors, pinions and rotation transfers. He'd learnt that a horse carver worked for thirty-two hours before the horse was ready to be painted and that they were sometimes decorated with rhinestones, but only on the romance side, which is the outer side, the view that most people see, rather than the inside, which is on view only to whoever is manning the rides. What Jonny hadn't learnt was how to stash a body under the canopy above the carousel. There were plenty of diagrams of the inner workings of various designs, but nothing that told him about vacant roof space. He needed to see for himself. The Quinns' carousel was still a crime scene, covered with a stout canvas cover and tied up like a parcel with crime tape. There was no evidence of the police actually doing anything there, but Jonny supposed all they needed was a few more photographs to support the prosecution case. And since a trial date had yet to be set and it was an apparent cut and dried case, there was no hurry. At least no hurry for the police.

Cordelia was calling them daily. The circus was due to move on in a few days. She was already losing revenue from not being able to run the funfair, and she was damned if she was going to be charged rent for leaving it behind. Jonny was unsure which she cared more about – freeing her grandson or losing money.

He turned back to the computer and tapped *where can I see a carousel* into Google. He'd never imagined there were so many. They were not only in funfairs; several town centres and parks also had them. But Jonny doubted that he'd be able to inspect any of them closely enough to gather any useful information. Then he had an idea and tapped in the name of Jolyon Bywater, the man whose name Cordelia Quinn had scribbled down on a scrap of paper she'd handed to Jasmine at their meeting. The man who sold his carousel to Cordelia Quinn when his own steam fair had closed down. Bywater's fair had not survived the pandemic and hadn't reopened once lockdown was over. He'd been struggling for a few years, but that had finished him off and he sold the remaining rides and went to work for a friend who restored vintage cars, steam engines and locomotives. They worked in an old engine shed near Didcot. Jonny tapped in the number and called him. And yes, Jolyon Bywater was working today and would be more than happy to chat about the inner workings of carousels.

Jonny closed down the computer and went downstairs to the café, where he bought himself a sandwich and a takeaway coffee in a biodegradable cardboard cup.

'Off out?' Jasmine asked as she put his food into a paper carrier bag, and he tapped his card on the machine to pay for it.

'I'm going to talk to the man who sold Cordelia the carousel.'

Surprised, Jasmine handed him the bag. 'We know the body was probably up in the roof. What more do you think he can tell you?'

She obviously thought he was wasting his time. Perhaps she was right. What was this guy going to tell him that they didn't already know? Possibly nothing. But the body was *probably* hidden in the roof, not definitely. There could be other possible hiding places on a carousel. Although maybe not too many places from where the body could drop onto the ground at someone's feet. But it was still worth asking about. At least it would get him away from the computer screen and talking to an actual person who, from what Jonny had learnt from his phone call to Bywater, would be happy to talk about his fairground machinery for as long as Jonny had the patience to listen. It would also be a badly needed opportunity to stretch his legs – why had he still done nothing about getting a dog? That would take him for regular walks. He'd been much fitter when Harold was living with him and he'd walked him twice a day.

IT WAS an hour's drive to Didcot, a slightly dull town known mostly for its connection to the Great Western railway and its steam museum. The perfect home for someone who was keen on steam fairs and vintage carousels. He found the engine shed easily. All he had to do, Jolyon had told him, was follow the railway line out of town. Obvious, really. Siting an engine shed far from a track would be stupid.

It was an interesting place, full of engine parts, wheels, an old railway carriage that was being painted and machines that Jonny knew nothing about. There were four men working in the shed, which was hot and smelled of oil. But there was a relaxed feel to it. One man was whistling as he worked, and two others were chatting amicably as they painted. It all felt unpressured and like a place where people were contented with their work.

Jolyon Bywater was expecting Jonny and greeted him as he came through the door. 'I'm too oily to shake hands,' he said, wiping his own hands on a rag he'd pulled from the pocket of his overalls. 'Come through to the office. I'll put the kettle on, and we'll be able to hear ourselves think.'

It was the kind of office Jonny's father would have felt at home in. It had an ancient mahogany desk with scuffed legs and scratched drawers – *distressed,* Jonny thought was the term for its lived-in, bashed-about appearance. Next to the desk were two leather-covered swivel chairs, again well used. On the wall was a calendar with pictures of steam trains with some of the dates circled in red – weekend steam rallies, he saw on closer inspection. Next to the door there were job sheets hanging from a wire and fixed with bulldog clips. Even the telephone looked like a relic of the nineteen-fifties. Jonny half expected to see a grey-haired secretary with horn-rimmed spectacles tapping away at an Olivetti typewriter. The only concession to modernity was a computer with a bulky monitor. Even this had been banished to a small table in a dusty corner of the office. Not much used, if the layer of dust that covered it was anything to go by.

Jolyon made tea in a brown china pot and poured cups for Jonny and himself. 'Grab a seat,' he said, pushing one of the swivel chairs in Jonny's direction and seating himself on the other. 'You want to know about carousels?'

Jonny gave him a brief rundown of the murder; told him about the body that had fallen from the Quinns' carousel and explained that Cordelia had asked him and a group of colleagues to prove her grandson's innocence. 'You sold Cordelia the carousel. I thought you might be able to tell me how easy it would have been to hide a body in the mechanism.'

Jolyon leant back in his chair and took a gulp of his tea. 'Ah, yes,' he said. 'The carousel. I was sorry to see her go. She'd been with me for many years, but I've known Cordelia a long time and she'll give the old girl a good home. But you say the body was hidden in the roof? I'd have said that wasn't possible. Did someone spot it up there? Tell me exactly what happened.'

'It must have been fixed there with rope. It was tied to the man's ankles and wrists and had snapped in the middle. The body fell out onto the ground during the last ride before they closed down for the night.'

Jolyon shook his head. 'Not possible,' he said, reaching for a sheet of paper and a pencil and drawing a diagram. He turned it in Jonny's direction. 'I'm not saying it would be impossible to hide something, even somebody, up in the roof, but it would have been bloody difficult getting it up there. It would have had to be fixed to the roof struts, which would mean climbing up over the mechanism that makes the horses rise and fall.'

'You think one man couldn't have done it on his own? He couldn't have fixed up some kind of pulley to hoist it up?'

Jolyon stared at his diagram and thought about Jonny's question as he took another mouthful of his tea. 'It's possible, I suppose. But look at the angles. Even with the carousel at full speed it wouldn't have fallen from the roof onto the grass. It would have dropped down onto one of the horses or seats. It could have caused a very nasty accident. Was there anyone on the ride at the time?'

'There was hardly anyone left at the funfair. It was late and everything was closing. They were short-staffed that night because Badger, the guy who died, hadn't turned up. There were just the two of them running all the rides.'

'It runs on a timer,' said Jolyon. 'It only needs the click of a switch to start it up. Ideally someone keeps an eye on it because you get kids doing stupid things like trying to climb the poles. Basically, it runs on its own but that particular one could be a bit quirky. It sometimes stopped with a bit of a jolt. We spent a lot of time on it but never managed to get it running smoothly. Because of that, I designed and installed a safety system myself but, well, that might not have been such a good idea.'

'Why's that?' Jonny asked.

'It made people lazy. Why bother watching all the time when the system takes care of things? I doubt if the Quinns watched every ride. They probably just pressed the switch and left it on its own.'

'Just supposing someone did manage to get the body up into the roof. Would they need to know much about the design?'

Jolyon shrugged. 'Not much. They could probably see all they needed to from the ground.'

Jonny had probably learnt all he was going to, and decided he shouldn't keep Jolyon from his work. 'Can I keep this?' he asked, standing to leave and picking up the drawing.

Jolyon nodded. 'It's only a quick sketch. I can give you more precise measurements if you need them. But like I said, think about the angle of the fall. And if I were you, I'd take a good look at the rope. Look at the knots and if it had been cut or whether it just frayed and broke.'

'Thanks,' said Jonny. 'I will.' That was the kind of detail that would be in the police evidence and they'd have to disclose it to the defence team. But maybe Katya could smile sweetly at Lugs and get him to release it to her.

He drove home thinking about what Jolyon had said about angles. And when he arrived home, he sat down with a glass of cold beer and a pencil and did as Jolyon had suggested. He thought about the angles. He pencilled a cross where he knew from Jasmine's account the body had landed, and drew lines from there to a number of places on the carousel. Jolyon was right. If the body had dropped from the roof, it would have fallen onto one of the horses. It could have then rolled onto the ground, but it would have been noticed before that. Jasmine said that it seemed to come from nowhere, rolling off the step of the carousel and arriving at her feet. But where could it have been before that, if not in the roof? It might have fallen from one of the horses, but Badger died early in the morning. If the body had been placed on a horse someone would have spotted it. If only to comment that the same person had been sitting on the same horse all day. But that would account for Badger's condition after he landed, which Jasmine described as *folded up.* He could have been placed on the horse and rigor mortis had done the rest, so that he remained in a horse-riding position even after he fell. Perhaps he'd been wrapped in a cloak that had covered the rope and disguised the bruises around his neck. But there was no record in the report of a cloak, or any other garment having been found.

If they did discover that the body hadn't been in the roof at all, did that mean that Jeremy was less likely to be guilty? Jonny thought it might. It could mean that the murderer had set up a scenario that was leaving a message. Why would Jeremy do that? Could the murderer have meant the message *for* Jeremy? If so, they were going about this the wrong way. They should stop looking for a suspect who hated Badger and start looking for people with a grudge against Jeremy. In other words, it might be a set-up, or a warning.

He searched through the earlier notes he'd made about Quinn's haulage business and found something he'd overlooked in his earlier searching. A few years earlier, the company had been searched and a number of employees questioned about possible drug dealings. They'd all been cleared, but perhaps wrongly. Was the company still involved? And was there someone out there trying to avenge them? And the biggest question of all – would Katya take his idea seriously?

# 12

It was going to be a hot day and Katya wondered what she was going to wear. Deciding what to wear in winter was easy; just grab whatever was thickest and pile on the layers. It wasn't usually a big problem in the summer, either. Loose cotton trousers and a baggy shirt usually did the job. With sandals, because there was nothing worse in summer than hot feet. But today was different because Katya was having lunch with Cordelia Quinn. A sandwich in the office would have been fine, or a snack at the circus. Even an on-the-hoof box of something in the park or near the river would have been good. But today Cordelia had insisted on lunch at Olly's Orangery, part of an exclusive country club near Sunninghill, of which Katya assumed Cordelia was a member. Why, Katya wondered, when the Quinns lived half the year in Dublin? She googled it and discovered it was part of a chain of similar establishments that catered for *the well-connected businessperson on the move.* It also boasted a sauna, gym and health spa. Cordelia hadn't mentioned those, so Katya assumed the invitation was for lunch only. She hoped so. She found it hard to imagine discussing evidence of the innocence or otherwise of Jeremy Quinn while wearing nothing more than a towel. An upmarket one no doubt, made of dazzling white Turkish cotton, which before she used it might possibly have been folded into the shape of a swan, but even wrapped in one of those, Katya would feel exposed. Her ankles were too thick, and she'd not properly studied her shoulders in a mirror for many years. She looked at the website again to see if it mentioned a dress code and found that it didn't. But she was sure there would be one, even if only in the form of disapproving looks from the immaculately groomed clientele.

Katya got out of bed and shuffled into the kitchen to make a cup of tea. Having drunk the tea, she had a shower, dousing herself liberally in some shower gel that Jonny and Belinda had given her last Christmas. It smelt of lily of the valley, which Katya found quite pleasant, although it reminded her slightly of some old ladies she'd interviewed during a suspected case of embezzlement at a very expensive care home near Cliveden.

Once dry, she opened her wardrobe, hoping to find something suitable that she might have forgotten about. And to her surprise, she did. She pulled out a dress that she'd bought years ago for a reception held at the Guildhall to welcome a new police commissioner to the area. She'd hoped to make a good impression and speed her possible promotion to detective inspector. It hadn't worked. The wretched man had barely acknowledged her presence and she never did make it to inspector. Katya took the dress off its hanger and laid it on the bed, where it looked like one of the seed catalogues that dropped through her letter box now and then. She'd no idea why when she didn't have so much as a window box. The dress was bedecked with every flower known to whoever had designed the fabric and probably a few that they'd made up. It was bright with tulips, daisies, daffodils and roses, floribundas she thought, although she was no expert, and many more that she didn't know the names of. She wasn't sure if a full-length frock was suitable for lunch. But maxi dresses were back in fashion, weren't they? Anyway, it would have to do. The only alternative was her usual shapeless baggy trousers and oversize shirt combo. She dug out a pair of black flip-flops. A bit the worse for wear, but they'd not show with a long skirt. She brushed her hair, dabbed on some lipstick and set out.

Cordelia had errands in town and told Katya she would pick her up outside the NatWest bank opposite the parish church. Katya arrived a few minutes early, not wanting Cordelia to be moved on by one of her ex-colleagues for parking in a restricted area; any slowing down, never mind parking that close to the castle was dealt with in haste by the police, who enforced a rigid zero tolerance policy.

Cordelia arrived fifteen minutes late, but Katya had been happy enough to sit in the sun on a wall near the churchyard and watch the bustle of tourists heading towards the castle and the security people walking up and down with sniffer dogs, pretending to be common or garden dog walkers.

Katya was almost nodding off in the sun as a black Mercedes pulled up at the kerb. Paddy jumped out and held the door open for her. 'Just popping into the bank,' he said. 'I'll walk back. Have a nice lunch.' Katya climbed into the passenger seat and Paddy closed the door, slapped the roof of the car. Then he headed across the road and into the bank. After a quick nod of greeting, Cordelia pulled away from the kerb and headed down the hill, away from the town towards the Great Park. Katya watched her as she drove. Did the woman ever wear casual clothes? Jeans, perhaps, with a baggy jumper? Katya doubted it. Today she was wearing beige linen trousers with a gold belt, a cream silk blouse and gold sandals. Her white hair was expensively bobbed and the whole ensemble was finished off with an enormous pair of sunglasses. Katya felt plain and dumpy beside her. But what the hell. She'd given up on her appearance long ago. At least her dress was cool and comfortable and wouldn't show the dirt the way beige and cream might. But it was likely that Cordelia's lifestyle was a lot less messy than Katya's, even if she did work in a circus. She'd have people to do the dirty work. In both senses of the phrase, if what they had discovered about the family was correct.

They drove in silence, Cordelia saying only that she'd made notes after her visit to Jeremy in prison and they could probably both do with a drink inside them before talking through what she'd learnt.

Twenty minutes later, having skirted Ascot racecourse, Cordelia turned into the gravel drive of Olly's Orangery and parked at the end of a row of BMWs and Range Rovers. 'Looks busy,' said Cordelia. 'But I've booked a table in a quiet corner. We won't be overheard.'

They were escorted to their table in an alcove and Cordelia ordered a bottle of sparkling Pellegrino. 'Driving,' she said. 'But don't let me stop you ordering a G and T, or a glass of wine.'

'Water is fine,' said Katya, thinking it would be best to keep her head as clear as possible, although a gin and tonic was tempting. They ordered seafood salad and while they were waiting Cordelia opened a large leather satchel and spread out her notes on the table.

'How's Jeremy holding up?' Katya asked, remand prisons not being most people's residence of choice.

'Jeremy's fine. He can look after himself. He survived an Irish boarding school, didn't he?'

He'd actually been flung out of one, Katya remembered, but she thought it best not to bring that up.

'He's always been a tearaway and usually in some kind of trouble. But I honestly don't think he's capable of murder. He's a rogue but quite a lovable one. But, to answer your questions.' She picked up the sheet of paper Katya had given her with a list of things to ask Jeremy about. She pointed a red lacquered fingernail at the first item on the list. 'The quarrel, or argument, or whatever it was witnesses heard. Apparently, Badger had accused Jeremy of not taking safety seriously enough. Jeremy admitted to calling Badger a sycophantic little toerag and told him no one was going to take his word against that of a Quinn.'

'Nice,' said Katya. 'But hardly a motive for murder. He could have just sacked him, I suppose.'

'Not really. Or only if I agreed. I never trusted Jeremy to hire and fire people. Badger was a friend of Joseph's and I'd trust his judgement over Jeremy's any day.'

'Had there been tension between Jeremy and Badger on other occasions?'

'Probably, but not enough for it to come to my attention.'

'What about the other two who worked the fairground rides? Would they have taken sides?'

Cordelia sipped her drink. 'They're both long-term employees, so if it was a case of taking sides, I imagine they'd take Jeremy's. But I never heard any talk of it.'

'Okay,' said Katya, making notes on her own list. 'How did he explain the jacket?'

Cordelia smiled the smile of an indulgent parent explaining why their offspring had scribbled on a newly painted wall and suggesting that their child was probably a second Michelangelo. 'He'd been with a girl after the show on Friday night. They'd crawled under the carousel cover for a bit of... well, you know. Jeremy adores that jacket, and he didn't want to risk damaging it, so he took it off and hung it on a guy rope. He remembered the following morning that he'd left it there and went to pick it up.'

'So they didn't spend the night in the carousel?'

'No, Jeremy saw the girl home. He doesn't remember the precise time but says it was probably well after midnight, and he went straight to his caravan when he returned.'

'Do you know the name of the girl?'

'Something of an aristocrat,' Cordelia said proudly. 'Her name's Bella Trumpington. She was at the evening performance with friends. Jeremy bought her a drink after the show and they took it from there. He walked her back to the family home in the Lower Ward.'

'Very gentlemanly,' said Katya. She drained her drink and wondered if they were about to discover that a vital witness was the daughter of a high-ranking castle official, since they were the only people allowed grace and favour accommodation in the Lower Ward. That could be embarrassing. If they wanted to interview the girl at home, she'd have to get Lugs to clear it with castle security. It was an uneasy relationship at the best of times, and she couldn't see Lugs agreeing to clear it for her to go and ask questions.

Their food arrived and Cordelia pushed her papers to one side while they ate. When they'd finished their salads they were offered a dessert, which Cordelia refused without consulting Katya. *A pity,* Katya thought, eyeing the selection of sweet delicacies that were being wheeled around on a trolley by a girl in a very short skirt and frilly apron. But this probably wasn't the time to make a fuss. She could pick up a cream slice or a doughnut from *Jasmine's* on her way home.

Cordelia continued answering questions as they drank their coffee, having moved out into a garden where they sat on cane chairs and watched koi carp in a lily pond. Jeremy, Cordelia told her, had been unable to think of any reason why Badger should have been murdered; he was generally liked by the team as long as they kept him off the topic of music and bands. Even Jeremy quite liked him, or he did when Badger wasn't going on about health and safety. He categorically denied he'd killed Badger himself and had no idea why he had been tied up or how he had been hidden in the carousel. And he definitely hadn't noticed the body until it fell out onto the ground.

She'd not learnt very much, Katya reflected as Cordelia drove them back into town. The account of the jacket seemed believable, and she'd learnt that Jeremy had upmarket tastes in girlfriends. And not much else. But at least she'd had a good lunch, even if lacking in dessert. She asked Cordelia to drop her outside the Royal Station and made her way down the steps to *Jasmine's*, where she satisfied her sweet tooth, now thankfully free of pain, with a chocolate éclair and a glass of iced mint tea.

# 13

Ivo sat on the steps at the back entrance of *Jasmine's*. It was a hot day and Harold had gone inside to lie down on the cool stone floor near the freezer. *I've done an excellent job,* Ivo thought as he examined the work he'd just finished. He and Jasmine had bought two cast iron garden tables at a car boot sale near Staines, which Ivo had dismantled and driven to the café in his van. Originally white, they'd been unwanted and neglected and had turned a muddy grey. Ivo had spotted them under a collection of ugly glass vases, some dated costume jewellery and a pile of chipped porcelain dinner plates. 'You could use those tables on the pavement outside *Jasmine's*,' he'd said. 'People like to be al fresco in the summer.'

'They're a mess,' said Jasmine. 'And I'd have to get a licence to have tables and chairs on the pavement.'

'I can clean them up and paint them,' said Ivo. 'And if you don't want them, someone at *Shady Willows* will. Somewhere to sit with an evening glass of sherry.'

Ivo looked at them now; sanded and painted dark green, they looked as good as new. Jasmine appeared, still wearing her apron, and waved her phone at him. 'I've got the licence,' she said, showing him the email from the council.

'That was quick.' In Ivo's experience councils worked extremely slowly, but Jasmine had needed to pay a fee with her application, so he supposed for something that would bring in money, they sped up a bit. 'Shall I carry them round now?' he asked.

'I've still got breakfast customers, so you can't bring them through the dining room.'

'No problem. I can use the cut through.' There was a small alleyway between *Jasmine's* and the empty shop next door. He hefted one of the tables onto his shoulder. 'What about chairs?' he asked.

'I'll bring some of those wooden folding ones from the storeroom. They'll be a bit dusty, though.'

'Give me a brush and I'll clean them up.'

Twenty minutes later, he'd set up the two tables each with two chairs and placed them either side of the café door. They looked good. Ivo thought so, and so apparently did potential customers. A couple were strolling along the road, pausing to read Karim's blackboard, which today was offering maids of honour, made from a special recipe that Karim had found in a cookbook someone had produced for the coronation. Karim had chalked *Celebrate the Trooping of the Colour With Our Special Maids of Honour.*

'Can we sit here?' the man asked. The woman, who was wearing white jeans, sat down on one of the chairs and Ivo hoped he'd brushed away all the dust.

Ivo squatted on one of the steps and watched them, eavesdropping on their conversation. 'You'll need to go inside and order,' he said.

'You do that, darling,' said the woman. 'My feet are tired.' She sat down and kicked off her sandals. Ivo wondered if Jasmine should provide buckets of cold water for tourists with tired feet. There were already bowls of water for thirsty dogs. Harold frequently took advantage of them.

'Are we trying the maids of honour?' the man asked, reading from Karim's blackboard.

'Definitely,' she said, smiling up at him in a flirtatious way. 'I haven't had one of those since we went to Kew.'

'All of three days, then,' said the man, laughing. 'Coffee with them?'

'Do you suppose they have lemonade? I could do with something cold.'

'It's a speciality,' said Ivo. 'Homemade with sprigs of mint and ice.'

'Lovely,' said the woman, as the man headed inside to place the order. 'Mine's a large one.'

'You're not from around here, are you?' Ivo asked, intrigued by their accents.

'We're from Toronto,' she said. 'On a tour called The Royal Sights of Old England. We're in Windsor for three days. We did the castle yesterday and tomorrow it's Royal Ascot races. And this evening we've tickets for an old-fashioned circus.'

'Great,' said Ivo, thinking it best not to mention the murder.

Harold appeared refreshed by his cool nap. He sauntered down the steps, stopping for a refreshing drink out of one of Jasmine's metal bowls, lapping noisily and showering the pavement at the same time. Having quenched his thirst, he settled down under the unoccupied table, a hopeful eye on the tray the man was now carrying out of the café.

*I should go,* Ivo thought. He still had work to do and these two should be left to enjoy their snack without Harold drooling and begging for scraps. Then his phone pinged and he sat down again to read the message.

It was from Rosa, the car mechanic from the arches. She'd sent him a picture of a flyer for a band. *Why?* he wondered, and then remembered she'd promised to send him any info she had about the band Badger Waites played in. They were called The Waiters. Badger's idea, he guessed, and they'd probably need to change that now. The band was performing a warmup set for a much more famous band at an arts centre somewhere near Bracknell that night. He read the message Rosa had sent.

*They're making it a tribute to Badger. One of the guys in the band popped in with the flyer because he knew Badger had worked for me. A bit short notice but I think I'll go. Want to join me?*

Ivo liked the idea that someone was remembering Badger. Everything was skewed in favour of the Quinns, and whether or not Jeremy was guilty. It was time someone spared a thought for the victim. They knew nothing about Badger Waites and why anyone would have wanted to murder him. This could be a chance to find out a bit more and chat to people who knew him. He stood up, nodded at the Canadian couple, who looked as if they were enjoying the maids of honour, and calling Harold to follow him, he went inside.

'Fancy this?' he asked, showing Jasmine the flyer on his phone.

She took the phone from him and looked at it. 'I'd like to, but I'm meeting Teddy for a drink later.'

'He could come too,' Ivo suggested. 'Unless he's something different planned.'

'No, just a drink at the Oarsmen in Eton. I'll text him and suggest the band instead. He can drive us all there.'

'Okay. I've a few chores to do at *Shady Willows.* Let me know what he says.' He called to Harold and set off home, whistling. A night out listening to music would be fun, and if they learnt a bit more about Badger, then so much the better. And Bill would enjoy another evening dog-sitting Harold.

'VERY POSH,' Jasmine commented as Teddy turned into the arts centre drive. 'Was it once a family home?'

To her surprise, Teddy had leapt at the idea of Jasmine's change of plan. Jasmine guessed that he'd asked her out for a drink to get the latest on their case, and meeting Badger's musician colleagues would be even better. When he'd first suggested meeting for a drink, she'd warned him that she didn't have anything to tell him. Sadly, that wasn't just an excuse. It was true; they hadn't made a lot of progress yet, but even if they had, Jasmine was sure Katya wouldn't want it to appear in one of Teddy's stories. The details of the arrest would have to be kept out of the press until the trial began, and Jasmine could imagine the police fury if a journalist started suggesting anything like wrongful arrest before then. But there would be no problem with a touching story about a band paying tribute to one of their members who had died far too young.

'The house belonged to a family of grocers until the early seventies,' said Teddy. 'They went out of business when supermarkets took off. It was sold to a trust who developed it as an arts and crafts centre.' He pulled into a parking space, and they spotted a sign that said *Jazz concert this way.*

'I didn't know it was a jazz concert,' said Ivo.

'It's a jazz and ale evening,' said Rosa. 'One of the players knew Badger and suggested a tribute set by his band at the start of the evening. I don't know what kind of music they play. Probably cover stuff.'

They followed a path round to the back of the house and found an outdoor stage under an awning conveniently erected close to the bar. There were no seats, and groups of people were lounging in deckchairs and on rugs. Teddy had brought a rug from the boot of his car, which he spread out on the ground.

'You're well prepared,' said Jasmine.

'I've covered events like this before. Anyone fancy a pint? It's locally brewed.'

'Just lemonade for me,' said Jasmine.

'Me too,' said Ivo.

'I could handle a pint,' said Rosa.

While waiting for Teddy to return with the drinks, Jasmine watched the stage, which was lit with floodlights and raised a few feet off the ground. At the front of the stage, on an easel, was a picture of Badger – the kind that was taken from a photograph and manipulated to look like a painted portrait. Jasmine realised it was the first time she'd seen an image of him alive and it was very different from the bloated, discoloured face that had landed on the grass in front of her a few days ago. She turned to Rosa, who was the only one of them to have actually met Badger, alive that was. 'Is it a good likeness?' she asked.

'Not bad,' said Rosa. 'It was probably done from a photo the band used for publicity.'

Jasmine nudged Ivo. 'We should copy that,' she said.

'I'll take a photo,' said Ivo. 'Once they've finished playing and I can get closer.'

Teddy returned carrying a tray with two pint glasses of beer, two cans of lemonade and four packets of crisps. He eased himself down onto the rug and passed round the drinks. 'Help yourselves to crisps,' he said. 'Various flavours.'

'You were a long time,' said Jasmine, picking up a packet of ready salted. 'Was the bar very crowded?'

Teddy shook his head. 'I popped backstage to ask the guys if they'd like to do an interview after the show.'

Jasmine had been right. Teddy wasn't there for the pleasure of her company. He was after a story. Not that she minded. Teddy was okay, but she wouldn't want anything more than a casual friendship with him. He was right about the music, though. They started with *I Believe in Angels,* followed it with *Hallelujah* and ended with *Time to Say Goodbye.* All of which made Jasmine feel quite weepy. She suspected that Joseph was right; The Waiters were not very good. The vocalist was a bit wobbly, possibly because of the emotion of the occasion, and the bass guitarist was a little off the beat. The keyboard player was excellent, though, and as The Waiters finished their act and the jazz band took their place, she realised that it had been the jazz pianist who had taken Badger's place on keys. Because of that, it might well have been the band's best ever performance. If Badger was somewhere up there in the big beer garden in the sky, would he be pleased for the band, or jealous because they'd found a better player than him?

## 14

'How's the tooth?' Jonny asked, arriving in the office and putting a cup of clove tea down in front of Katya.

They were very thoughtful, this team of hers. 'It's fine, thank you. It was an abscess.'

'Nasty,' said Jonny.

'I had it lanced and now I'm on antibiotics. Root canal treatment to follow.' *Too much information,* she thought, watching Jonny turning pale. 'What the hell is this?' she asked, taking a sniff of her tea.

'It's an infusion of cloves,' said Jonny. 'Very good for toothache.'

The pain had gone. She'd forgotten all about it the following day and lunch with Cordelia had been unaffected. It would have been a very great pity if she'd had to cry off a posh lunch because of a bad tooth. She thanked Jonny for the tea, although she'd have preferred proper builders' tea, but it was kind of him to think of it, so she gulped some down. In fact, it was quite nice. It reminded her of Christmas.

It was time to get going. The case was moving forward at last. Not necessarily in the right direction, but they'd all been busy and they needed to collate the information they'd collected and decide how to move on.

'Were you helping out?' she asked Jonny. 'I hope Jasmine won't be long.'

'I was helping in the kitchen. It was Karim who recommended the clove tea, an old Persian recipe apparently. Cloves were grown in Indonesia and traded along the silk route.'

'Very interesting,' said Katya, but it didn't help their case at all. It was bad enough trying to work out what had been going on in Ireland, never mind Indonesia and Iran. The only Oriental connection so far was that Dara had worked in India, and that was unlikely to be relevant. 'Did Jasmine look like she'd be here soon?'

'She was nearly done. Just about to hand over to Stevie to get the lunches going. Ivo's down there as well, swallowing coffee like it's going out of fashion. They were both out late last night.'

'Partying?'

'Didn't they tell you? They went to a jazz concert because Badger's band had a tribute slot.'

Katya frowned. Why didn't she know about it?

'It was rather last minute. Ivo's car mechanic friend was sent a flyer and he and Jasmine went along to it. Teddy as well.'

'Teddy?'

'He was going for a drink with Jasmine anyway, and he joined them hoping for an interview with the band.'

They couldn't have told her? Sent a text to let her know what they were doing? Invited her to go along with them, even. But she'd been out with Cordelia for most of the day, and once home she'd turned her phone off so she could grab a bit of sleep. She was too old for late night concerts anyway. But she hoped Teddy wasn't about to write something that would compromise their case. She'd never really trusted his discretion. Had never really trusted journalists, full stop. But before she could muse over it any further, Jasmine arrived closely followed by Ivo and Harold. They looked tired, with dark shadows under their eyes. Not Harold, who was either asleep or wide awake; nothing in between.

'What time did you two get home last night?' she asked, sounding like a nagging parent.

'Around one, I think,' said Jasmine, looking at Ivo for confirmation.

'Something like that,' said Ivo, yawning.

'For God's sake, how long did Badger's band play for?'

'Only the first fifteen minutes,' said Ivo. 'After that it was the jazz band. They were really good.'

'I pity the neighbours,' said Katya.

'It was way out of town and I don't think anyone lives close by. But the band finished at around eleven. After that, Teddy took us to a late-night curry place and bought us all a meal.'

On expenses, no doubt. Katya absent-mindedly rubbed her cheek, inside of which was a gaping hole awaiting root treatment and a new crown.

'How's the tooth?' Jasmine asked.

'Much better, thanks. It was an abscess.' She was about to expand on her recent dental experience but noticed Jonny looking rather green. No stamina, these men. It was the same with the police. All macho on the surface, but confront them with a bit of gore and they go to pieces. 'But enough about me, let's get on with our meeting. Last time we met it wasn't looking too good for Jeremy. Anyone discovered anything to turn that around?'

Ivo fished out his notebook. 'Jasmine and I checked the security at the circus. We walked all around the outside. There are two gates, which are either manned or locked, and a long chain-link fence surrounding the site.' He passed round a plan that he'd drawn.

'The car park and campsite are outside all of that,' said Jasmine. 'We asked about people coming and going. It's easy enough during the day. Harder at night. The family all have keys to the gates. Everyone else has to go to the box office, where they call through to whoever they've come to see. There's a back gate manned by a bloke called Bertie Kelly, who lets in delivery vans and people who work there during the day.'

'And at night?'

'Paddy locks up every night and checks that there's no one on site who shouldn't be,' said Ivo.

'I'm not sure how reliable that is,' said Jasmine. 'There must be places people can hide. Paddy can't possibly check every nook and cranny. Even with his German sniffer dog.'

'What about someone coming in early in the morning?'

'Only the family have keys to the main gate, so if they're expecting anyone, they'd have to open up themselves. It's only left unlocked when there is someone in the box office, which is from late morning when people start to arrive for work. Deliveries would come through the service entrance at the back. Paddy has a key for that and so does Bertie Kelly. He's a bad-tempered bloke. He shouted at me and Ivo when we walked past, so we didn't get to ask him if he'd let anyone in early the morning of the murder.'

'We need to know that,' said Katya. 'I'll talk to him myself.' She made a note on the board. 'We need to know why Badger was on site so early. And how he got in. That would tell us if it was possible for the murderer to get in as well. And that might just help to get Jeremy off the hook.' There'd not been anything so far that would do that, but just the possibility that someone could get in unnoticed might help to weaken the case against him. It would take a lot more than that to get him off the charge, though.

'Did you get anything useful from Cordelia Quinn?' Jonny asked.

Katya opened her own notebook and read the notes she'd made when she got home after their lunch the previous day. 'She visited Jeremy in prison and asked him about the argument he and Badger had. Apparently, Badger didn't think a lot of Jeremy's safeguarding procedures and told him so. Jeremy called him a sycophantic little toerag.'

'Did Cordelia make any comment about that?'

'She hinted that Jeremy was a bit slapdash. That's why he was running the fairground and not involved in any circus equipment. But at the fairground he was with two long-term, experienced employees. I get the impression that she'd put him there deliberately. She suggested that things were probably safe with them around. Wrongly, as Badger's death proved.'

'Why do you suppose Badger didn't take his complaint to one of the more experienced blokes?' Ivo asked.

'Probably because Jeremy was a Quinn and essentially their boss,' Jonny suggested.

'Maybe,' said Katya. 'We'll probably never know.'

'What about the jacket?' Jasmine asked. 'Was he able to explain it?'

'That was interesting,' said Katya. 'Jeremy chummed up with a young lady called Bella Trumpington, who had been at the show with some friends. He bought her a few drinks and then they crawled under the carousel cover for a bit of privacy. He was very fond of his jacket, so he took it off in case he snagged it on the metal clips that hold the canvas cover in place. That would have been at around ten-thirty when the bar closed.'

'And he forgot to pick it up again when he left?' said Ivo. 'He can't have been that fond of it.'

'Other things on his mind, I suppose,' said Jonny, grinning.

'How long were they in there?' Jasmine asked.

'He walked Bella home in the small hours of the next morning. He didn't remember the exact time.'

'So he'd been inside the carousel cover and not discovered by Paddy when he did his rounds?'

'Looks like Paddy isn't all that thorough after all,' said Jonny.

'He probably didn't expect snogging couples in the carousel,' said Ivo.

'Or perhaps Jeremy was in the habit of taking girls in there and Paddy turned a blind eye.' Katya made a note to ask him. Not that she expected an honest answer. She was beginning to suspect that none of the Quinn sons knew much about an honest day's work. Paddy's so-called check was probably a quick scan around the site with a torch and then back to the caravan for a date with a whiskey bottle.

'If he walked Bella home, Jeremy must have used his key to open the main gate,' said Ivo. 'Perhaps he forgot to lock it again when he returned.'

'That could explain how Badger got in,' said Katya. 'But we still don't know why.' She'd leave that one hanging for now, she decided, and turned to Jonny. 'What did you find out about carousels?' she asked.

Jonny opened a folder and spread out some sheets of paper in front of them. 'I talked to the man who sold Cordelia the carousel.'

'Looks like you did a lot more than talking,' said Katya, eyeing the various diagrams and photos he'd laid on the table.

'He didn't go along with the theory that Badger had been up in the roof,' Jonny continued. 'He said it would have been pretty much impossible to tie him up there, and in any case, he would have fallen onto one of horses, not onto the ground. It's all to do with the angle and what happens when the carousel stops. It's always had a dodgy mechanism, he told me. It can stop very suddenly, throwing off anything that isn't securely attached.'

'That sounds really dangerous,' said Jasmine. 'What if there are children on the rides?'

'There are safety straps, a bit like the ones on treadmills in gyms, and the ride won't start unless they are secured. It stops if there is a sudden tug on the safety strap, which would happen if someone fell off. Jolyon, the guy I talked to, was very proud of the system. He'd invented it, apparently, and it's unique to that carousel.'

'So it isn't possible to ride on one of the horses without wearing a strap?' Ivo asked.

'They're not worn exactly. They get clipped to the rider's sleeve.'

'But if Badger had been on a horse, someone would have spotted him. He'd have been there all day.'

'He might have been in one of the seats,' said Jonny.

'Seats?'

Jonny pulled out a photo of the carousel. 'Most people ride on one of the horses that go up and down. But there are also a few fixed seats shaped like old-fashioned sleighs.' He pulled up another photo.

'And do they have safety harnesses as well?'

'Something like a car seat belt,' said Jonny. 'They are recommended but not enforced. Not wearing one doesn't stop the carousel from working.'

'He'd still have been seen,' said Jasmine.

'And there'd have been nothing to cut through the rope,' Ivo added. 'The police thought he must have been in the roof because of all the struts and things that have sharp edges.'

Katya sat back in her chair and sighed. 'Does anyone else feel like we're looking at an impossible situation?' She picked up a pen and wrote on the board:

*Motive – argument. Jeremy could have toned it down for Cordelia but even then, it's not much of a motive. Jeremy's job with his gran was secure. Even if Badger had a point about his safety processes, Jeremy could have had him sacked.*

*Opportunity – the evidence suggests that Badger was killed in or near the carousel. Could this be wrong? And how and why did Badger get onto the site early that morning? If Jeremy wasn't the murderer, could someone have killed Badger offsite and moved him to the carousel when there was no one about?*

*Means – we know he was strangled with old-style lighting flex. Is there any evidence to show Jeremy ever used, owned or bought any? Why was hemp rope used to tie him up? Why tie him up at all unless it was to fix him in the roof of the carousel, which Jonny's friend says is impossible. He couldn't have gone anywhere once he'd been strangled.*

'So, in Jeremy's favour,' said Jonny thoughtfully, 'he didn't have much of a motive, he had no way of knowing that Badger was on site that morning and there's nothing to show he's ever used plaited electrical wire for anything.'

'That about sums it up,' said Katya. 'Any suggestion about what we do next?'

'I don't know if it helps,' said Jasmine, 'but Teddy picked up some info about Badger when he interviewed the band last night.'

'Is he going to publish a story about the murder?' Jonny asked.

'He's not allowed to write about the details of the crime itself or the arrest until it comes to trial,' said Katya.

'This is just a tribute for the local paper,' said Jasmine. 'But we've got so little about Badger. There could be something about his life that would shed some light on a motive.'

'And Teddy passed his notes on to you?'

'He emailed them to me. It's all going to be in the paper in a day or two, but he said he had more detail than he will actually use.'

Jasmine clicked open her email and scrolled to the file Teddy had attached. 'Badger's mates described him as a bit of a loner, but very single-minded about the band. The guitarist is someone he knew at school, and they started the band together a few years ago, but Badger was the persistent one who went round pubs begging for open mic nights, finding busking opportunities, having flyers printed and fixing up rehearsals. He was also the one who persuaded the vocalist to join them. She'd already been singing with another band, but she said Badger pestered her until she caved in and joined them.'

'What did they think of him, as a person? Did he have enemies?'

'They said he was very serious, not someone they felt they could get close to. They also described him as high-minded and a stickler for rules.'

'That backs up his argument with Jeremy about safeguarding,' said Jonny. 'Perhaps he was threatening to complain to Cordelia about him.'

'Not really grounds for murder,' said Ivo. 'Jeremy is obviously Cordelia's blue-eyed boy. She'd have taken Jeremy's side and probably kicked Badger out.'

'There was a suggestion Badger might have been on the Asperger's spectrum. He could be irritatingly obsessive where the band was concerned, but they couldn't think of anyone who hated him. Certainly not enough to kill him. They actually spoke about him quite affectionately. He was quirky, but they were fond of him.'

'What about his family?' Katya asked. She hadn't followed that up with Lugs, who must have discovered who his next of kin was.

'He lived on his own in a bedsit in Slough,' said Jasmine, reading from Teddy's notes. 'Never mentioned family, but they thought he had a slight Midlands accent.'

'I'll ask Lugs about that,' said Katya. 'Perhaps there was a falling out with the family.'

'Has he ever been in any trouble?' Jonny asked. 'Someone from his past looking for revenge?'

'I'll ask Lugs about that as well,' said Katya. 'It might be useful to know if anyone called him or if he had anything in his pockets that might suggest he was meeting someone early that morning.'

'Will Lugs be allowed to tell you that?' Ivo asked.

'If they are using it as evidence, they'll have to disclose it to the defence. Another question for Cordelia, I think.'

'Have you got tasks for us?' Ivo asked.

Katya studied the list she'd been making. 'Jasmine, I think you need to go back to the circus. Ask around and try to find anyone who might be able to give Jeremy an alibi for that morning. And ask if anyone saw him going to his caravan in the small hours.'

Jasmine wrote that down. 'I'll have another chat to Keavy. She exercises the dogs early in the morning.'

'Ivo,' said Katya. 'Go and chat to Badger's neighbours in Slough.' She scribbled down the address and handed it to Ivo. 'Take some of your flyers. There may be people who need a handyman.'

'I'll take Harold,' he said. 'People are always chattier when there's a dog around.'

'Okay,' said Katya. 'Jonny, see what you can find out about Bella Trumpington. It would be useful to know exactly what time they left the circus that night. Also if they planned to meet again.'

'Okay,' said Jonny. 'Do you have an address for her?'

'She lives with her family in the Lower Ward. You'll need to ask around, but it's not very big. Someone will know her.'

Jonny wrote it down and then looked at Katya in surprise. 'Did you say Trumpington?'

Katya nodded.

'Not Major Clive Trumpington's daughter?'

'No idea,' said Katya. 'Do you know him?'

'Not personally,' said Jonny. 'But I've heard of him. If he lives in Lower Ward, he must be the Major Trumpington who works for the Royal Household. Belinda probably knows him.'

'Then take care,' said Katya. 'It's his daughter we're interested in.

We don't want to be embroiled in a confrontation with the castle staff.'

'Try Bella's socials,' Jasmine suggested. 'She's probably posted stuff about the circus, and you can message her rather than involving her father.'

Jonny smiled at her. 'Great idea,' he said. 'But I may need to get back to you if I get stuck. I'm not that into the kind of social media used by posh young girls.'

'I think that's about it,' said Katya. 'I'll get onto Lugs, and we'll meet again the day after tomorrow.' She bundled up her papers and headed home.

# 15

A clumsy bit of tree felling at the edge of *Shady Willows* had damaged part of the flagstone path between two of the chalets. Not massive damage but enough to trip up a resident who was a bit wobbly on their feet. Most of them were spry and energetic, and also fiercely independent. It would be more than Ivo's life was worth, not to mention his job, if he suggested they weren't. But there were one or two with poor eyesight or joint problems, and the last thing Ivo wanted was for them trip and fall on one of the cracked paving stones and need medical treatment. He knew they all lived in fear of being carted off to hospital simply because of their age, and not being able to get out again. There had been a lot in the newspapers and online about bed blocking because of a shortage of the kind of staff who could arrange help for them. The elderly were written off as a problem that no one had a solution to and it made them furious. It also made Ivo angry. His residents were friends and perfectly capable of making up their own minds about what they needed. Why were they treated like children? The least he could do was ensure that the paths were even and safe to walk on by everyone, and that included the sons, daughters and grandchildren who visited.

Having checked the on-site shed and made a list of what was

needed, Ivo and Harold set off on one of their regular trips to a builders' merchant on the Slough trading estate. Once there, he loaded up the van with two bags of cement, some stone slabs and a wire brush. He signed an invoice that would be sent to the owners of the site, Ivo not being expected to shell out for materials. Which was just as well, bearing in mind how little they paid him. But he couldn't and didn't complain. Why would he? He had free accommodation on the banks of the river. He and Harold were the lucky ones.

It was early afternoon and there was plenty of daylight left to complete his work on the path. He'd left it with a warning sign and blocked it with some planks balanced on milk crates. There was not much danger of anyone tripping over it and it would take an hour at most to repair it. Plenty of time to drive to the block of flats that had been Badger Waites' home.

The trading estate wasn't known for its eye-catching beauty. It was functional and boring. But compared to the depressing part of town Badger had inhabited, it was a haven of good design. It was clean with wide roads and grass verges. The street Ivo drove down to reach the block of flats Badger had lived in was shabby, run down and dirty. A terrace of nineteen-twenties shops and houses that hadn't seen a lick of paint, or even a bucket of soapy water and a mop, for years. Possibly never. Several windows were boarded up, the pavement was cracked and uneven – and Ivo had worried about a couple of chipped paving slabs – and the gutters were littered with fast food wrappers and crushed beer cans.

Ivo pulled the van into a parking space outside the row of shops; a newsagent, a dusty looking mini market with baskets of bruised fruit and veg lined up on the pavement, and a pharmacy protected by metal shutters. He looked across the road at a small, two-storey block of flats – eight in all, Ivo thought – with a grimy reinforced glass door that had a keypad entry system. A group of bored-looking teenage boys stood in a group at the end of the road and Ivo wondered if it was safe to leave the van unattended. He wanted to talk to Badger's neighbours and then return to a van that had its full complement of wheels and that still contained his tools. He could leave Harold to stand guard, but on the whole he would rather risk damage to the van than damage to his dog, so he fastened Harold to his lead and ostentatiously locked all the van doors.

They crossed the road and gazed through the glass doors. Badger had lived at number six, which Ivo guessed was on the first floor. He was just wondering how long he'd have to wait for someone to either enter or leave the building, hopefully admitting him at the same time, when a man appeared carrying a bunch of keys. Harold growled at him, and Ivo had to agree that this didn't look like the friendliest person he had ever met. Dressed in a grubby white vest that did nothing to conceal tattoos of a violent nature, jeans that displayed a large area of midriff, and workmen's boots, Ivo guessed he'd been working on a building site or possibly on the new railway track. Was this one of Badger's neighbours?

It appeared he wasn't. 'If you've come about the flat,' he said, 'you'll have to wait. Can't relet until it's empty.'

This was the landlord? Ivo was glad he wasn't a tenant of the private renting sector. 'Flat?' he asked.

'Yeah,' said the man, pulling a tin out of his pocket and starting to roll a cigarette with one hand, rattling a bunch of keys with the other. 'Number six. Tenant won't be needing it any more. Dead.'

Ivo adopted an expression of startled innocence and a distaste for moving into accommodation that someone might have died in. 'Sick, was he?'

'Nah, got himself killed, didn't he? Had the police round. Said not to let anyone in. Effing nuisance. His rent was due, and we need to get a paying tenant in as soon as.'

'Are you the landlord?'

'Nah, just work for the letting agent. A right mean bastard if you know what I mean. Nagging me to get the place emptied. I called some people to come and do it but they're haggling about the price.'

So the police had been round there, looking for a next of kin, Ivo supposed. 'Did he live here on his own?' Ivo asked.

'Yeah, and he didn't seem to have any mates. Never saw any, at any rate. Kept himself to himself.'

If all his neighbours were like this bloke, Ivo wasn't surprised. 'So you're waiting for someone to come and go through his stuff?'

'And take it away. Once the police give the go ahead, I'll be getting a skip round. It's cheaper than those man in van types. Poor bloke didn't have anything worth hanging on to, anyway. Might just as well get it to the tip.' He took a drag of his cigarette. 'Except one of them music keyboard things. I'll hang on to that. It might be worth a bit down the market.'

Was that legal? Ivo wondered. Shouldn't it go to his next of kin? Whoever that was. 'Do you live in one of the flats?' he asked.

'Number one, ground floor.'

'So did you know the dead guy well?'

'Only to pass the time of day. And collect the rent, of course.'

'So you know when he died?'

'Early Saturday morning, the police said. Funny that. I felt a bit bad about it.'

He hadn't struck Ivo as the *feeling bad* type. 'Why? You weren't involved with his death, were you?'

'In a way I might have been. I had to get the rat people in, see. I usually get the council to do it, but a mate said he knew someone who'd do it cheaper for cash. But he only works weekends. It meant clearing all the rooms, blocking up drains and putting down boxes of poison under the floorboards. All the tenants had to be out by six that morning and weren't allowed back in until late that night.'

That would account for Badger's early start at the circus. But not how he had got in. And why hadn't he stayed on the campsite for the night?

The man took another drag of his cigarette. 'Some of them kicked off. Said they needed more warning. I got to see most of them by early afternoon Friday, but Waites was out all day and I had to push a note though his letter box.'

That would explain it. Badger wouldn't have returned home until after the evening performance. Half an hour or so by bike, so he'd have been back there around midnight. He'd hardly want to cycle back to the circus then try to find an unoccupied tent. And after an argument with Jeremy, he probably didn't fancy being back there anyway.

'So, are you interested?' the man asked, stubbing his cigarette out and stamping it into the pavement.

'In what?'

'Taking the flat once it's been emptied. I'm okay with dogs as long as they behave. If you leave me your number, I can get back to you. There'll be plenty after it, though. You'll need to let me know quickly.'

'No, you're all right,' said Ivo, heading back to the van with Harold. Even if he'd still been homeless, and even if the man did put up with dogs, Ivo would not have been tempted to live in a miserable area with a bad-tempered landlord and rats. He climbed into the van and headed back to his comfortable home at *Shady Willows.*

# 16

Jonny didn't have to search very hard for Bella Trumpington. He found her in his dentist's waiting room. Katya's toothache reminded him that he was long overdue for a check-up. He looked back though his diary for over a year before he found the date of his last visit. Before covid, he'd gone every six months without fail. They usually sent him a reminder, but presumably that had got lost during his tussle with long covid. He wondered if Belinda was similarly behind, but now wasn't the time to ask her. She was too busy sorting out her post-council life and she'd never needed any kind of dental treatment for as long as he'd known her. She even managed to avoid the dreaded hygienist. But Jonny had no excuse for putting it off any longer, since he only lived four doors away from Sulieman Gupta's private dental practice. He called and made an appointment.

'You're in luck,' the receptionist told him. 'We've just had a cancellation. Can you get here in fifteen minutes?'

He assured her he could and thanked her profusely for fitting him in when it wasn't an emergency.

'No problem,' she said.

Jonny gave his teeth a good scrub and swilled some mouthwash around his gums. When had he last flossed his teeth? Not that long ago, was it? And while he didn't mind much what the dentist did to him, he dreaded having to visit the hygienist, who filled his mouth with cotton swabs and rubber suction tubes, while she attacked his teeth with metal prongs and an ultrasonic gadget that sent uncomfortable vibrations into the sensitive gaps between his teeth. She accused him of not cleaning his teeth properly and delivered lectures about how do it by showing him plaster casts of mouths full of teeth and a selection of weird looking toothbrushes, all of which he was expected to purchase from the receptionist on his way out.

He arrived exactly fifteen minutes after his call ended and was greeted by the extremely apologetic receptionist. 'I'm so sorry,' she said. 'We had to fit in an emergency. A nasty abscess. Mr Gupta will be about another twenty minutes if you don't mind waiting. Or I can rebook you. He has a slot three weeks from today.'

Better get it over and done with and sit it out for twenty minutes with the magazines in the waiting room. 'That's fine,' he said. 'I don't mind waiting.' He might have developed cold feet about the whole idea in three weeks and then be struck off for non-attendance.

'The waiting room is just across there,' she said, pointing to a room with plush sofas and a view of the garden. 'We'll call you when we're ready for you.'

Jonny made himself comfortable on one of the sofas and studied the selection of magazines fanned out in front of him on a glass-topped coffee table. They were all glossy, chunky and recent. He wasn't interested in society events or expensive ways of remodelling his home but settled for the nearest, which had a picture of one of the minor royals attending Ascot races on its front cover. A few pages in, his attention was caught by a photograph of a young woman in an elaborate ball gown that reminded him of the pink hydrangeas in his parents' garden. Hydrangeas had gone out of fashion now. Belinda wouldn't allow even a small one anywhere near her garden. And Jonny wasn't at all sure they came in small anyway. The caption read *Bella of the ball goes for head-to-toe pink.* He read on. *Bella Trumpington (19) celebrates with friends at the Stockberry Manor summer ball.* A charity event, apparently. The closest thing to the Queen Charlotte's Ball that used to be held every year for the daughters of the rich at the start of the London season, which they attended in order to find husbands. Bella had been at the ball with a group of friends and Jonny wondered if it was the same group that she had been to the circus with. *Probably not,* he thought. Bella would have a wide circle of friends. The article told him she was currently building a career as a model, having recently strutted the catwalks of fashion weeks in London, New York and Paris. It wasn't going to be easy to engineer a quiet chat over a cup of coffee to discuss Jeremy Quinn, and Jonny was beginning to think he'd have to go back to Katya and admit defeat when he discovered, at the end of the article, an invitation from Bella to *follow my Insta feed.* There was still no sign that Sulieman was going to see him any time soon, so he downloaded Instagram to his phone and typed in the link to Bella's page. There were hundreds of photos of Bella in ball gowns of every colour, swimwear, shorts worn with strappy tops, and sandals. All no doubt super expensive. He doubted that Bella knew her way around Primark. All of which was interesting but not helpful. And then he came to her most recent post, which she'd modestly captioned *Helping to boost trade in my local caff - Capoodle.* Jonny knew it. Recently opened near the gates of the castle, it served *exotic* coffee in thimble-sized bone china cups and charged exorbitant amounts for doing so. Bella, she claimed, was spending a couple of weeks slumming it behind the counter wearing minuscule shorts to attract customers. *I'm not popular with Daddy dearest,* she wrote. *But all in a good cause, right?*

Jonny could imagine Major Trumpington, highly respected member of His Majesty's household, not being best pleased by his daughter flaunting herself in skimpy shorts selling coffee, but at least he now knew where he could find her. Should he take Katya with him? he wondered. Probably not. He didn't know what delicacies Capoodle served with their coffee, but they were probably miniature works of culinary art and purchased in Katya-sized quantities, would likely bankrupt him.

. . .

JONNY LOOKED at his watch as he walked away from the surgery. Sulieman had declared his teeth in good order after twenty minutes of poking, scraping, taking x-rays and chatting about the luxury cruise he and his wife were about to take around the Greek islands. Jonny left the surgery seventy-five pounds worse off but with the satisfaction of not having to make an appointment with the hygienist and not having to come again for six months. His occasional sessions with dental floss had obviously paid off. But seventy-five pounds for twenty minutes' work? Sulieman must be raking it in. But then, staring into people's mouths all day probably wasn't a lot of fun. He no doubt deserved his expensive cruise, and Jonny could now walk into town and be at Capoodle by mid-afternoon, having hopefully avoided the lunch crowd.

He needn't have worried about any type of crowd. The place was empty apart from a skinny young man with long hair, who was standing behind a glass-topped counter polishing a brass coffee pot, and Bella, who was lounging in an easy chair, her long, suntanned legs balanced on a low table in front of her. She was playing with her hair, twisting it around her fingers while flicking though a glossy magazine, probably in search of photos of herself. She didn't strike Jonny as a reader of serious political periodicals. The man looked at Jonny. 'Bella,' he said. 'Customer.'

Bella yawned and put the magazine, still open, face down on the table. She stretched and made her way with an evident lack of enthusiasm to the service counter. Jonny followed her and looked through the glass at a selection of cakes that were, as he'd expected, tiny but beautifully decorated. It would be a shame to eat them, almost.

'What can I get you?' Bella drawled.

It was hardly surprising the place was empty of customers if this was the greeting they received. He studied the menu on a stiff white card with an embossed background of gold coffee beans. What to have? He could order Black Tie made with star anise and tamarind seeds, Caffe Gommosa, which was basically espresso stuffed to the brim with marshmallows and probably not a good idea after his recent visit to the dentist. Coffee Alamid didn't appeal since it was made from the excrement of civet cats. As had one of the first covid vaccines, he remembered, or was that monkeys? Either way, he preferred not to try it. Cheese coffee and Vietnamese egg coffee were only slightly less repulsive options. 'Turkish coffee,' he said. Even Bella looked relieved by his choice. She picked up a brass pot with a long handle, spooned out some coffee grounds and set it to boil in on a silver Primus stove.

'Anything to eat?' she asked.

He didn't ask what she recommended. She was whippet thin and probably survived on salad leaves, recoiling at the idea of letting anything with sugar pass her lips. He pointed to a tray of small, square cakes labelled Revani. They were unpriced and he could probably get a square meal at *Jasmine's* for whatever Bella was about to charge him. But it was all in the cause of freeing Jeremy, and he wasn't short of a bob or two. 'I'll have one of those,' he said. Bella picked one up with a pair of tongs and placed it on a small but highly decorated square plate. 'Where are you sitting?' she asked. 'I'll bring it over.'

He scanned the empty space that surrounded him. He had the whole café to choose from, but pointed to a small table tucked into a corner at the far side with couple of chairs and a miniature Tiffany lamp, and went to sit down.

'It's quiet in here,' he remarked as Bella set his coffee and cake in front of him a few moments later.

'Yeah,' said Bella. 'It'll probably pick up when the tourist trade kicks off. Or there's another royal funeral. But that won't happen for a while. Not if Charlie boy is as robust as his mum.'

'Or a wedding?' Jonny suggested.

Bella considered this for a moment. 'Nah, the important royals are already spoken for.'

She'd know, he supposed. But there must be a few single minor royals of suitable marrying age. Not famous enough, perhaps, to attract the royal watchers of Windsor or drive through the town in an open carriage, as Harry and Meghan had done a few years ago.

Anyway, he should be getting onto the topic of Jeremy Quinn, who was a long way from the upper-class bachelors that no doubt made up Bella's social circle. 'You're Bella Trumpington, aren't you?' he said.

She sat down suddenly on the chair next to him. 'How did you know that? Oh God, you're not one of Daddy's spies, are you?'

Hardly. If Major Trumpington wanted to spy on his daughter at work, he barely needed to step out of his front door. But she was now on the defensive, which could be in his favour. When he came in, she had been acting like the entitled rich girl she obviously was. Now she was more of a vulnerable teenager who was scared of her father. What was he likely to do? Ground her for the foreseeable future, Jonny guessed. It's what he would do if he'd had the misfortune to have bred a spoilt little madam like the one who was sitting next to him right now. But he wanted her on side, at least until she'd told him all she knew about Jeremy Quinn. 'No,' he said. 'I won't tell *Daddy* what you've been getting up to.' He didn't know what she'd been getting up to, but there was obviously something she didn't want her father to know. And it was quite possibly to do with being picked up by a good looking, possibly feckless young Irishman, and spending half the night with him under the cover of a carousel. It was highly unlikely that, successful as the Quinns were in their own field, this was the kind of match Major Trumpington had in mind for his daughter. 'I want to ask you some questions about Jeremy Quinn.'

'Who?' she asked, looking relieved and regaining some of her composure.

So that wasn't the secret she was trying to hide. If it was, she'd have at least recognised the name of the young man involved. He didn't know what she was playing at, but it didn't look like it had anything to do with Jeremy Quinn. He was happy to let other aspects of Bella's behaviour go and leave it for her father to sort out. Was it possible, he wondered, for two young people to spend several intimate hours together under a carousel without exchanging names? He supposed it might be, although Jeremy had remembered *her* name. 'Jeremy Quinn of Quinn's Circus,' he said. 'You were seen together last Friday night.'

'Oh, Jeremy,' she said. 'Soz, I'd forgotten all about the circus. I went with some chums. We thought it would be a laugh. You know, all those men in leotards, lion tamers and stuff. Such a hoot.'

'The Quinns don't have lions,' he said.

'No, mega disappoints.' Bella giggled. 'I just had to make do with Jeremy.'

'Had you met him before?'

She gave him a scornful look. 'You have to be joking. Of course I hadn't. Why do you want to know about him, anyway?'

'He's been arrested,' said Jonny. 'And charged with murder.'

'OMG,' she said. 'What frightfully bad luck. Poor Jeremy.'

'Worse luck for the bloke he allegedly killed.'

'I suppose. Who was he?'

'He was a mechanic called Badger Waites.'

'Never heard of him. But I don't really know any mechanics.'

Jonny believed her. 'You may have seen him around the fairground that evening. He had a distinctive white streak in his hair.'

Bella shrugged. 'Sounds cool. Sorry I missed him.'

Of all the impressions Jonny had of Badger Waites, cool came low on the list. The likes of Bella Trumpington would barely notice his existence, striking hair colour or not. 'So you didn't see him?'

'Not that I remember.' She stopped fidgeting with her hair, tossed it over her shoulder and stared at him. 'You don't look like police,' she said. 'Why do you want to know all this?'

'I'm working for Jeremy's grandmother. We're trying to prove he didn't do it.'

'I hope you do,' she said, with just a hint of sincerity. 'He was quite sweet.'

Sweet wasn't exactly the impression Jonny had of Jeremy from the various bits of information he'd discovered. If he was like the rest of the family, he'd be good-looking in a raffish kind of way. But it occurred to him that he didn't know what Jeremy looked like. 'I understand he walked you home that night. Can you confirm what time you left the circus?'

'Sure I can,' said Bella, grinning and looking pleased with herself.

She reached into the back pocket of her shorts and pulled out her phone. 'I took a selfie of us as we left. Look, it's time-stamped.' She scrolled through some photos and showed him one of the two of them standing cheek to cheek, with the circus in the background. The time was two-thirty am.

'Would you mind AirDropping it to me?' said Jonny, getting out his own phone.

'Sure,' she said, clicking on it. 'Will it be evidence?'

'You never know,' said Jonny. He wasn't sure how helpful it was going to be. It didn't give Jeremy an alibi. He could easily have seen Bella home and been back in plenty of time to kill Badger. 'Did you go straight home after that?' he asked.

Bella giggled. 'Tucked up in bed by three.'

'And you didn't invite Jeremy in for coffee or anything?'

She hesitated and looked down at her hands. Then she started playing with her hair again. 'More than my life's worth,' she said, not looking him in the eye. 'I can almost see Daddy standing at the top of the stairs with his shotgun.'

A pity. Not that Jonny wanted to see Jeremy with his backside peppered with lead shot, but it would at least have given him an alibi. 'Did you post this photo anywhere on social media?'

'No.' She pouted. 'Jeremy's sexy but he's hardly society page material, is he? I have my reputation to consider.'

'I wouldn't know, but you are probably right not to spread his picture around. He'll be notorious if it goes to trial and it's probably best if you don't share this right now. I'm guessing you won't want your father to know you've been consorting with a suspected murderer.'

'God, no. Daddy won't have to know, will he? Should I delete it from my phone?'

She was all or nothing, wasn't she? 'No, as you said, the police might want to see it. Discreetly, of course,' he added, noticing her alarmed expression. 'Just don't share it online.'

. . .

He paid for his coffee and cake, not quite the exorbitant amount he'd expected, and walked away down Peascod street thinking about what Bella had told him. Talking to her, for reasons he couldn't explain, had convinced him that Jeremy Quinn was innocent. Jeremy was a healthy, good-looking young man and it was no surprise that he'd hooked up with an attractive young woman. But she'd described him as sweet, and he'd walked her home in a delightfully old-fashioned, gentlemanly way. Had he then returned to murder Badger Waites? Jonny didn't think so. But someone had. Who the hell was it? And why?

# 17

It was harder to get onto the circus site than it had been a few days ago. Fair enough, there had been a murder, but Jasmine couldn't help the words stable doors and bolting horses floating through her mind. The gate was unlocked, but she arrived at the box office to be confronted with a man she hadn't met before, whose instructions, it seemed, were not to allow anyone in under any circumstances.

'Can't let you in until half an hour before the show and then only if you have a ticket. You'll have to wait in the queue.'

Jasmine looked around. There wasn't a queue. The afternoon show had ended, and it was over an hour before the start of the next one. She sighed impatiently. 'There isn't a queue.'

'You'd better start one, then. Over there.' He pointed to a bench near the gate.

'I've not come to watch the show,' she said. 'I've come to see Caitlyn.'

The man looked as if he didn't believe her. 'Expecting you, is she?'

'Not really.' She'd not called before she left home, but Caitlyn had told her she was welcome any time as long as she wasn't mid-performance. But she wasn't going to explain the ins and outs of her friendship with Caitlyn to this officious man who'd probably been hired from some security company – Rentabouncer? she wondered. She took out her phone, tapped Caitlyn's number and explained the situation.

'Let me speak to him,' said Caitlyn, and Jasmine handed her phone over.

'Okay, you can come in,' the bouncer bloke said grudgingly after listening for a moment to Caitlyn, who sounded like she was giving him an earful. He handed the phone back to her, opened the barrier a few inches and held it while starting to give her directions to Caitlyn's caravan.

'It's okay,' said Jasmine. 'I know where to go.' She pushed through the barrier, which, to her satisfaction, had probably left the man with bruised shins, and headed round the back of the big top to the caravans, where she found Caitlyn sitting on a step, drying her hair in the sun. Keavy was lying on the grass, earbuds firmly in place, listening to something on her phone and swaying in time to the music.

'Who's the bloke at the box office?' Jasmine asked.

'It should have been Tony Black, but he had to go to the walk-in place in Slough with a bad knee and they warned him there'd be a long wait. Mike's not working today so we had to hire someone in.'

'He's taking the job very seriously. I didn't think he'd let me in at all.'

'Granny told him to be strict. Everyone's a bit edgy right now.'

*Not surprising,* Jasmine thought. And if people were feeling vulnerable it meant that there was a consensus that Jeremy was innocent. They'd be afraid there was still a murderer on the loose somewhere.

'How's the case going?' Caitlyn asked.

'We're trying to build up an alibi for Jeremy. We know he left the site in the early hours of Saturday morning, but we don't know what time he returned. Jonny talked to the girl he was with, but she was a bit flaky about the time he'd left her. We don't know if he came straight back here or what he told the police about where he was. If he didn't come back until after eight and someone saw him, he might be in the clear.'

'Wouldn't he have told the police if he had an alibi?'

'You'd think so, wouldn't you? Perhaps he did but didn't have any way of backing it up. But someone could have seen him that he didn't notice. Can you think of anyone I should ask?'

'Keavy was up and about early. Did you see Jeremy?' she asked her sister. When there was no reply, she nudged her in the knee and yanked out one of the earbuds.

'What?' said Keavy, frowning as she looked up from her phone.

'Did you see Jeremy when you went to visit the dogs on Saturday morning?'

'Saturday?'

'The day after you arrived here, remember?'

'Yeah.'

'You saw him?'

'No, I remember which day Saturday was.'

'So did you see him or not?'

'Not,' said Keavy, shaking her head and plugging her earbuds in again.

'I wouldn't count on that,' said Caitlyn. 'She was probably still half asleep. I was surprised she wanted to get up early because she'd only arrived the night before and I expected her to sleep in, but she told me she wanted to see the dogs.

'You know what teenagers can be like,' said Jasmine. 'What time did she arrive on Friday?'

'It was just after the end of the show.'

'Was she on her own?'

'No, a friend of Mum's, Martyn Roberts, travelled with her on the flight from Dublin. He runs a circus school and has known Mum for years. When she heard he was coming over she asked him to look after Keavy. He picked up a hire car at Heathrow and dropped her off here.'

*Interesting,* Jasmine thought. Could this be a possible suspect? 'Why was he here?'

'Scouting for talent. He needs a couple of trapeze artistes to mentor some of his students, but the Hungarians that are over this summer weren't interested. They'll go home as soon as our season's ended. None of them fancied a winter in Ireland.'

'Did he stay here on Friday night?'

'Yes, Dad has a spare bunk in his caravan. I think they probably put away a bottle or two of whiskey.'

And perhaps with the prospect of a visitor and a sociable evening, Paddy hadn't been as thorough as he should have been with his rounds. 'Is he still here?'

'No, he left early on Saturday. Another couple of circuses to visit, apparently.'

'Paddy waved him off after breakfast, I suppose?'

'I doubt it. Knowing Dad, he'd have slept in with a hangover.'

'So how did he get off the site?'

'I hadn't thought about that,' said Caitlyn. 'He might have woken Bertie to let him out, or Dad could have lent him his key to the back gate and he slipped it back into the post box as he left.'

'Do you think anyone saw him leave?'

'Bertie might have, if he was up that early.'

Jasmine didn't fancy another meeting with Bertie Kelly, so she'd leave that for now. Katya wanted to question him herself, so she could ask about Martyn Roberts at the same time. They needed to know more about him. If Paddy slept late with a hangover, he probably wouldn't have heard Martyn creeping around early in the morning, making his way out. If no one was about, he could easily have gone through the fairground, killed Badger, hefted his body onto the carousel and then made his way to the car park and driven off. So Martyn Roberts was definitely a person of interest, possibly a suspect. Although she couldn't imagine what he could possibly have had against Badger. Had they even met before? 'Does Martyn come over very often?'

'Not as far as I know. He told me he'd rarely left Ireland.'

He could have been lying about that. 'You say he's a friend of your mother's. How long have you known him?'

'Since Mum moved to Galway just before Keavy was born. I'd have been about ten.' Caitlyn suddenly gasped as if she'd just realised what Jasmine had been thinking. 'But he'd never kill anyone. That's what you are thinking, isn't it?'

'Well, he was here at the crucial time. He was able to wander round the site without anyone asking questions. You've got to admit it looks a bit suspicious.'

'But why would he kill Badger? He'd never even met him before.'

'Are you sure he hadn't?'

'Of course. Well, only if Badger had spent time in Galway.'

*Could he have?* Jasmine wondered. No reason why not. There was a festival every year that attracted loads of buskers into the town. The other band members would know and Teddy would be able to give her contact details for them.

She left Caitlyn and Keavy to prepare for the show and walked home feeling quite pleased with herself. She was the only member of the team who had discovered an alternative suspect. Now all she had to do was find a link between Martyn Roberts and Badger Waites.

# 18

Lugs chose some interesting meeting places. In the old days, when she worked for him, Katya's meetings with him had always been in the office. Why go anywhere else when they worked together? Sometimes he took the team out for a drink, but that was to celebrate the successful end of a case. It would be a social occasion, not work. Since she had retired, they usually met in pubs, which Katya liked because they were warm, and their meetings more often than not involved food. There was plenty of variety. Some were in town and some well away from his usual patch. On one occasion they'd met for fish and chips from a van parked near the river. This evening they were sitting in deck chairs in Alexandra Gardens, eating spicy noodles out of cardboard trays. There was quite a crowd in the park, but most of them were at the far end, gathered around the bandstand and listening to the band of the Coldstream Guards. The Lilywhites, as they were known – although Katya had no idea why – were seen regularly in the town in their bright red coats, marching from the barracks to the castle and back for the Changing of the Guard. It was less usual to see them performing in the park, but tonight they were there raising money for Help for Heroes. It was a warm evening and Katya noticed they were not wearing their usual bearskin caps. She knew they didn't wear them when performing indoors and she assumed that, since the bandstand had a roof, it counted as inside. Just as well or they'd be passing out with heat-stroke before they got to the end of the first piece.

By the time Lugs and Katya had finished their noodles and disposed of the trays in a nearby bin, the band had come to the end of Nimrod and had launched into Land of Hope and Glory. Lugs lounged back in his deckchair, grinned and rubbed his stomach. 'Makes you proud to be British, doesn't it?'

'A lot of overdressed blokes blowing down pipes?'

'Come on, Katya, don't tell me something about that music doesn't make your heart beat just a little bit faster?'

'While my chest swells with pride?'

Lugs laughed. 'Always the cynic,' he said, not without a note of affection in his voice. He cracked open a can of lager.

Katya opened her own can and took a swig. 'You've not brought me here to discuss good old British traditions, have you?'

Lugs shook his head and reached under his chair for a plastic folder. 'We've handed back the carousel,' he said. 'It's no longer a crime scene, but I thought you might like to see a copy of the report.'

'Anything that lets Jeremy off the hook?'

'Inconclusive, I'd say. But take a look yourself. Seems we were wrong about the body being tied up in the roof.'

*Ahead of you there,* Katya thought. Jonny's research had told them that much. She opened the folder. The crime scene officers had concluded that the body had been hidden on one of the seats, covered with a tarpaulin and with a sign that told prospective riders that the seat was out of order.

'Funny that no one had spotted that when the body was first found,' said Katya.

'The tarpaulin was still on the seat. I suppose covering bits of rides and putting an out of order sign is fairly usual.'

*That could work,* Katya thought. The body could have been kept in place by looping the rope that was attached to Badger's wrists and ankles over the end of the seat. Maybe rubbing against something that weakened it until the carousel came to a jerky halt and it snapped, tossing the body onto the ground at Jasmine's feet. And then she read the next paragraph. The rope had indeed been knotted around his wrists and ankles, but it had not been weakened by friction. It had been cut in two. And there was nothing on the seat sharp enough to do that. The rope had been deliberately severed with a sharp knife. A clean cut, a single blow from a very sharp blade. Lengths of rope of various kinds were kept in premeasured lengths in one of the storage trailers. These were kept locked and on inspection all the ropes had been intact, with no sign that any had been cut or were shorter than their labels suggested.

Katya read the next paragraph. The tarpaulin was in fact one of the seat covers that was used when the carousel was dismantled for transporting on one of the circus trucks. It had been forensically examined and traces of Badger's DNA were found. No surprise there. There were also traces of DNA belonging to Jeremy, Tony Black and Mike Stone, who had given samples voluntarily, and of one other person as yet unidentified and not on any databases either in the UK or Ireland.

The wire that Badger was strangled with had been cut from a table lamp that had been thrown into a skip by the back gate, the contents of which would be collected when the circus moved out. Several of the caravans used plaited wire to connect table lamps via a cable to the generator used for lighting, but no one had reported throwing one away and none had been reported missing. There were no fingerprints on the lamp itself, which Katya thought suspicious. It meant that whoever had thrown it into the skip had wiped it clean or had worn gloves.

'Can I keep this?' Katya asked. She needed to read it again, slowly and with time to think about it. There was nothing that proved Jeremy's guilt but nor was there anything that indicated his innocence. Unless they could trace the unknown DNA, which might throw up another suspect.

'Sure,' said Lugs. 'The defence have a copy so there's nothing that hasn't been disclosed. Just don't publish it on social media or give it to anyone in the press. But it will all come out if it goes to trial.'

'If?' Katya asked. 'Is there any doubt about that?'

'It's possible Quinn could plead guilty.'

'Not if his grandmother has anything to do with it. She'd probably start shouting about police brutality if he did.'

'She's convinced of his innocence, is she? Not just hoping to get him off whether he is or isn't?'

Katya gave this some thought. 'I don't know,' she said. Could she see Cordelia going for some kind of whitewash? If she thought Jeremy was guilty, would she admit it? He'd been in trouble before. Did she leap to his defence then?

'She doesn't have any evidence, does she?' said Lugs. 'The defence haven't come up with anything.'

'She probably knows him better than anyone. I'm sensing some friction between Jeremy and his father, so possibly his grandmother is the one he's always turned to when he's been in trouble.'

'His father is Aidan Quinn, the haulage guy?'

'That's right.'

'The company's been on a Garda watchlist in the past, but they've never been able to prove anything. There was some suggestion they might have been smuggling drugs but that's way back in the past and nothing came of it.'

The band had come to the end of their set and were strolling around with cans of beer. Katya thought she wouldn't stay for the second half of the concert. Lugs didn't seem keen either, so they sauntered away from the park and back to the town centre together. 'It's a rum case,' said Katya. 'A man no one disliked, barely noticed most of the time, murdered for no reason. Then left to look like some macabre tableau.'

'Allegedly murdered by a man who, by all accounts, had no reason to harm him and who then drew attention to it, and to himself.'

Lugs walked with her as far as her flat, and as she rummaged in her bag for her keys, she turned to him and sighed. 'It feels like wading through mud,' she said.

Lugs patted her on the shoulder. 'Perhaps you are,' he said. 'Maybe it's time to accept that Jeremy is guilty.'

Katya had a lot of respect for Lugs, but in this case, although she couldn't put her finger on why, she was sure he was wrong.

After saying goodbye and letting herself into her flat, she made a cup of tea and sat down to think about the case. The key had to be the murder weapon. Most people didn't go around with a piece of flex in their pocket. Well, Ivo might because he needed it for work. And she herself had some odd stuff in her pockets.

Someone in one of the caravans had thrown out a table lamp. Did they cut off the flex and stuff it into a pocket on the off chance that it might come in handy? Which suggested a spur of the moment murder. Or had they cut off the flex and then wiped the lamp and thrown it away, which pointed to a premeditated crime. Either was possible, and since the lamp had been found in one of the skips, it looked like an inside job. Just, she hoped, not one done by Jeremy. She needed to find out more about the family dynamics. She went through them one at a time. She could probably rule out Cordelia. Unless she was trying some complicated double bluff, she was the one who wanted to prove Jeremy's innocence.

Paddy? He seemed affable enough. Could he be covering up a hatred for Badger? Not likely. There was no reason to think Badger had ever done him any harm.

Aidan? An unpleasant type, but with no evidence that he had it in for Badger, or even knew him very well.

Dara? She knew nothing about him. Could he be the one they were looking for? He hadn't come to their first meeting. Was that because he knew what had happened and didn't want to give himself away? She'd visit him and if nothing else, check the lighting in his caravan.

She wrote that down on her task list along with talking to Bertie Kelly and went to bed hoping a good night's sleep would clear her head.

## 19

Katya was on her own in the office, sitting at the computer typing up a list of questions raised by the crime scene report, and thoughts she had after her meeting with Lugs, when an email arrived from Teddy.

*Not sure if this helps with your enquiries,* he wrote, *but it's interesting.* He'd sent a link to a report in an Irish newspaper dated four weeks earlier. Katya clicked on it and read the headline.

*Release of Donal Maguire after serving a five-year sentence in Mountjoy Prison.*

That meant nothing to Katya. She googled Mountjoy and discovered it was in Dublin, but it still didn't ring any bells. She'd never had anything to do with crime in Ireland, so why was Teddy sending her this now? She read on.

*Maguire was sentenced five years ago following a conviction for drug trafficking. He was arrested at his home in Dundrum after a tip-off to Dublin police. He was found unpacking a consignment of class A drugs with an estimated street value of £50,000. Evidence was produced in court that showed payments into Maguire's bank account that he claimed he was unable to explain. Several burner phones were found hidden under floorboards at his home along with lists of details of known drug dealers.*

*Ten years earlier, Maguire had been cautioned by police for possession of cannabis but had no other previous convictions. In court, he claimed he had been framed but was unable to produce any evidence to support his claim.*

*Maguire maintained his innocence throughout his sentence and on release announced that he would leave no stone unturned until he cleared his name and avenged those who had caused his incarceration.*

Katya yawned. What was Teddy thinking sending her this? What possible interest could she have in the case, even if it turned out to be a gross miscarriage of justice? It wasn't a cause she would take up. She'd keep her cases local, thank you very much. She was about to close the website and get back to solving the murder at the circus, when the final paragraph caught her attention.

*For the two years leading up to his conviction, Maguire worked for Quinn Logistics in Dublin and he claimed that* 'they had it in for me' *after he'd reported some dubious financial records to the authorities. The company underwent thorough forensic searches of their finances and premises but were cleared of any suggestion of involvement in the crime. Quinn Logistics has refused to comment on Maguire's release, but it seems they are unlikely to re-employ him.*

Katya replied to Teddy's email and thanked him for sending her the link. The mention of Quinn was interesting, but she didn't see how it could relate to her case. But just to be sure, she searched for accounts of the court case that had sent Maguire to prison. Could Jeremy have been involved? He'd worked for his father, and if Maguire was right and he'd been framed, Jeremy could well have had something to do with it. But very few names were mentioned. She searched carefully but found no mention of Jeremy. In any case, it was Badger they were interested in, and from what she'd learned of him so far, she couldn't imagine him as the type to either be involved in drug dealing or setting someone up to take the blame if that was what he was doing. Badger, by all accounts, had lived an austere life in his small flat in Slough, interested only in his music. As far as they had discovered, his only link with the Quinn family was his friendship with Joseph Quinn. A connection to Paddy or

Aidan might have aroused her suspicion, but Joseph and his father Dara had had little to do with any of the family businesses until their return to the UK after the death of Safiya and two of the band members in 2013. She wondered how Joseph and Badger had met. Could that have been in Ireland? Had Badger lived and worked in Dublin and somehow crossed Maguire's path that in some way had led to Maguire blaming him for his arrest? It didn't seem likely, but that didn't mean it hadn't happened and everything should be checked. She reached for a sheet of paper and started making a list of questions.

Had Badger ever visited Dublin – would his family know? Ask Lugs what contact there had been with them. There must be a next of kin somewhere who might know a bit about his past.

Find out more about Donal Maguire – would it be in order to ask Lugs to trace Garda records of the case? Then she scratched that out. Lugs was not working on the Quinn case, which was now in the hands of the prosecution. She wouldn't want to risk his professional reputation.

They should talk to Joseph. Why hadn't they thought of that before? He would know more about Badger than anyone else at the circus. She flicked back through the notes of the first meeting with the family. Jasmine had carefully recorded his exact words. 'He was a friend of mine,' Joseph had said. 'I knew him a few years back. He tried to join a band I was involved with.'

Was it a band in Dublin, perhaps? What if Badger had worked for the Quinns at the same time and had discovered something that implicated them in the drugs deal? Something that had rapidly been covered up to put the Garda off the scent. Possibly with Cordelia's help. Could Badger have been blackmailing them?

Katya's head was beginning to spin again, and she was relieved when the rest of the team began to drift in for their meeting.

'You're looking thoughtful,' said Jonny as he switched on the coffee machine.

Katya sighed. 'I've put a possible scenario in place,' she said. 'But it's probably as daft as one of Ivo's ideas.'

'Some of my ideas have been good ones,' said Ivo as he settled Harold under the table and sat himself down.

Katya had to acknowledge that he'd been on the right track on several occasions in the past. 'The trouble is,' she said, accepting a cup of coffee from Jonny, 'if my theory is correct, I've just made things look a whole lot worse for Jeremy.'

'And your theory is?' Jonny asked, pulling up a chair and sitting next to her.

'That Jeremy was somehow mixed up in framing Maguire. Badger found out and was blackmailing him.' She turned the computer screen so he could read the article Teddy had sent. Then she showed him the list she'd made.

'You're not wrong,' said Jonny. 'It does make Jeremy look even more guilty.'

'But only if Badger was ever in Dublin,' said Ivo, squinting at the screen.

'Yes,' said Katya. 'One of us needs to go and talk to Joseph. I don't think there's much point in asking Aidan if Badger ever worked for him. He'd claim he couldn't possibly remember everyone who ever had. Plus he'd be incriminating Jeremy even further if he admitted it.'

Jasmine had been listening to their conversation with interest. 'What do we know about Badger's family?' she asked.

'Very little,' said Katya. 'And that's where we need to start asking questions. I'll have a chat to Lugs and ask who identified the body.'

'And then go and question them?' said Ivo. 'Won't that be a bit... well, upsetting for them? They are probably relieved that the murderer is behind bars. We can't really go storming in suggesting he didn't do it after all.'

'No one's going storming anywhere,' said Katya. 'But you are right. We need to be sensitive.'

'Perhaps,' suggested Jonny thoughtfully, 'we could say we think the motive is weak and we need to know more about any connection between Badger and Jeremy that might strengthen it.'

'*We* being...? We can hardly go along and say we're working for Cordelia, who wants to prove Jeremy's innocence.'

'That's a good point,' said Ivo. 'But we've worked alongside the police before – can't we say we're doing that again?'

'It wouldn't really be true, though, would it?' said Jasmine.

There was silence around the table while they tried to come up with a solution.

'Rosa,' said Ivo suddenly.

'Care to explain?' Katya asked.

'Badger used to work for Rosa. She was quite fond of him, I think. It was her idea to go and hear the band tribute. When we find out who the next of kin is, we could go and see them with Rosa, to offer our condolences. We could take some flowers.'

*Not a bad idea,* Katya thought. If it wasn't far away, they could go there now. She called Lugs, who gave her a name, address and phone number, which she wrote down on a scrap of paper. 'Lucy Waites, Badger's sister. Lives near Reading.' She handed the paper to Jasmine. It would be better for the two youngsters to go. If they took Rosa with them they would seem more like authentic mourners than nosy parker detectives. 'Can I leave that with you and Ivo?' she asked. 'See if Rosa's okay with it and then give Lucy Waites a call. We'll pay for the flowers out of Cordelia's budget.'

'Okay,' said Jasmine. 'I'll phone her, and Ivo can round up Rosa. I'll ask if we can go this afternoon.'

'Good,' said Katya. 'And while you're doing that, Jonny and I will go and talk to Joseph.'

# 20

Lucy Waites was happy to talk about her brother and Jasmine arranged for the three of them to call on her that afternoon. Rosa fed the address into her satnav and they arrived in a quiet street of small terraced houses. Rosa checked the house number and pulled her car onto a paved area outside. Lucy Waites opened the door promptly and Jasmine suspected she had been looking out for them from behind her lace curtains.

'I was a poor sister,' she said, inviting them into a small hallway. 'It's good of you to come.'

Rosa handed her the flowers. 'It's good of you to see us,' she said. 'We just wanted to say how sorry we are about your brother.'

'Did you know him well?' Lucy asked.

'I didn't know him all that well,' said Rosa. 'But we chatted a bit when he was in the workshop.'

'He used to work for you?' Lucy asked.

'Occasionally, after he lost his job. He was a good mechanic and I'll miss him.'

Lucy nodded. 'I'll make some coffee,' she said, wiping away a tear. 'Make yourselves comfortable,' she added before disappearing into the kitchen.

Rosa and Jasmine perched on a small sofa and Ivo sat on the floor, pulling Harold close. It was a small room, a crush with the four of them. Just as well Ivo had him under control, Jasmine thought. They didn't want Harold tripping Lucy over when she returned. She might be carrying a tray and not see him. She looked around at the bare, impersonal room, guessing that Lucy lived alone. There was no evidence of children, no toys or small shoes. The single coat hanging from a hook in the hall suggested there was no husband or boyfriend and there were no photographs on the walls. It looked as if Lucy was the solitary type. Just like her brother.

'Sorry about that,' said Lucy, coming back into the room with mugs of coffee, her eyes still red from crying.

'Don't be,' said Jasmine, taking a mug from her and offering her a seat on the sofa. 'It's so sad losing a member of the family.'

'We weren't close,' said Lucy. 'We should have been. He was my only brother, but he wasn't easy to get on with. He didn't let people get to know him and I didn't make enough of an effort.'

'Do your parents live nearby?' Ivo asked.

Lucy shook her head. 'They're both dead,' she told them. 'Killed in a motorway pile-up near Wolverhampton seven years ago.'

'I'm so sorry,' said Jasmine. Lucy and Badger had had more than their fair share of tragedy. It wasn't surprising that Badger had become a loner. He was probably scared of losing anyone he became close to.

'Badger was always solitary, even before that,' said Lucy. 'He'd been tested for autism when he was little, but that just suggested he was somewhere on the spectrum. It didn't really help him much.'

'But he loved his music?'

Lucy smiled. 'That was the only thing he cared about, so the band tribute was a lovely idea.'

'You were there?' Rosa asked, looking at her in surprise.

'Just at the start. It was kind of the jazz band to do that.'

'Did Badger's band travel much? Abroad, perhaps?' Jasmine asked, thinking she should bring the conversation around to the real reason they were there. Although she wasn't certain Ireland counted as abroad.

'Hardly,' said Lucy. 'It was all they could do to get themselves around Berkshire.'

'So Badger never visited Ireland?' Jasmine asked, thinking that was another theory flying out of the window.

'Never,' said Lucy. 'He hated public transport. He'd never have managed a plane, and trains and ferries were out of the question for him. Why do you want to know?'

'We know he was friendly with Joseph Quinn. Do you know him?'

Lucy shook her head. 'I didn't know any of his friends. Not that he had very many.'

'It was Joseph who got him the job at the circus. We just wondered how they knew each other.'

'Why?'

'Joseph is Irish. We thought they might have met there.'

'I don't know where he met people, but it wouldn't have been in Ireland. Wait a minute,' she said, putting her mug down on the table. 'Did you say Quinn?'

'Yes, I did,' said Jasmine, thinking she might have strayed into dangerous territory.

'Not the man who was arrested for his murder?'

'No,' said Jasmine. 'That was his cousin, Jeremy. I'm sure Joseph had nothing to do with it. But he might feel responsible for introducing them. I'm sure he feels very bad that it was one of his family and of course that he was the one to get him the job. The trouble is the police haven't really established a very strong motive. You wouldn't want the murderer to get away with it because his motive was weak and got the charge thrown out, would you?'

Lucy stared into her coffee cup for a moment. 'I suppose not, but I wouldn't want the wrong man convicted either,' she said.

It was a relief to know not everyone thought it was a cut and dried case; even the next of kin had some doubts. 'You think they might have arrested the wrong person?' Jasmine asked.

'I've had my doubts from the start. It was too quick. It seemed like the police just wanted the whole thing done and dusted and someone locked up,' said Lucy. 'This bloke, Jeremy Quinn, was Badger's boss. Why would he want to murder him and leave his body somewhere so obvious? I know Badger could be irritating, but...' She let her sentence hang in the air.

'So, do *you* know anyone who might want to kill him?' Ivo asked.

'No, absolutely not.' She looked at Ivo with a horrified expression. 'It's just, well, I'm not one of those people out for revenge at any cost. Sometimes it seems to me that the police just want a conviction, never mind if it's valid or not.'

Jasmine was unsure how to react to that. She took out her phone and tapped on the article Teddy had sent Katya. She let Lucy read it and then said, 'We wondered if Badger could have got himself involved with the other Quinns. Maybe something to do with drugs. That's why I asked if he'd ever been to Ireland.'

Lucy shook her head. 'Badger never had anything to do with drugs. He was too scared of becoming addicted and anyway he never broke any rules. We may not have been all that close, but I do know that much about him. And I know he never went to Ireland.'

Which ruled out blackmail and knocked Katya's theory on the head.

'Perhaps,' said Lucy, 'he discovered something while he was working at the circus, and someone decided he knew too much.'

'That's possible,' said Ivo. 'It would be more of a motive, wouldn't it?'

And it took them straight back again to Jeremy being guilty. Or one of the other Quinns. Jasmine was beginning to wonder if she could trust any of them.

'I'm not saying I think this Jeremy Quinn is innocent,' Lucy continued. 'I just don't know. And I'd hate to think it was someone else. Someone who could still be wandering around free and able to kill again.'

Jasmine could tell she was worried. If the police had arrested the wrong man, who knew where the real murderer might strike next? 'Look,' she said, 'we'll keep asking questions.'

'And if we find anything we'll let you know,' Ivo added.

'Thank you,' said Lucy. 'And thanks for coming. I do appreciate it.' She looked at her watch. 'I don't mean to rush you, but I have to be at work soon.'

'Of course,' said Jasmine. 'We should be getting back as well.'

Rosa shook Lucy's hand. 'If it's any comfort,' she said, 'I enjoyed working with Badger and I can't think of any reason anyone would want to hurt him.'

'Thank you,' said Lucy, wiping away a tear.

'What do you think?' Ivo asked as they climbed into Rosa's car. 'We just got a bit closer to condemning Jeremy, didn't we?'

'Not necessarily,' said Jasmine, although they certainly hadn't got any closer to clearing him. 'We know Badger was never in Ireland, so the blackmail idea only works if he discovered something about the Quinns over here. There could still be a non-circus link to the family. We'll just have to wait and see what Katya learns from Joseph.'

## 21

Jonny pulled his car up at the back gate to the circus and he and Katya climbed out. 'Why the back entrance?' he asked.

'I want a word with this Bertie Kelly,' said Katya.

'The scary bloke?' Jonny asked, laughing. 'The one who accused Jasmine and Ivo of being murder tourists?'

'I doubt he's that bad. In the past I've been tempted to tell anyone I thought might be a murder tourist to bugger off. Anyway, scary or not, I think I can probably handle him.'

Jonny didn't doubt it for a moment.

Bertie was sitting in his deckchair, reading a newspaper.

'Oi,' Katya shouted over the gate. 'Can we have a word?'

Bertie lowered the paper and scowled at her. 'Who the hell...?'

'We're working for Mrs Quinn,' said Katya. 'Would you like me to call her so she can vouch for us?' Allying oneself with the boss usually did wonders when it came to improving manners and loosening tongues.

Bertie put the paper down and ambled over to the gate. 'No, you're all right,' he said. 'What can I tell you?'

Katya waved her investigator pass at him. 'I'd like to know who you let through the gate early last Saturday morning. Shall we say between five and eight?'

'No one comes in that early. I don't bother getting out of bed before nine.'

'Supposing there's an early delivery?'

'They'd have to call me to come and let them in.'

'So nothing on Saturday morning, in or out?'

He shook his head. 'Not until after midday.'

So he hadn't seen Martyn Roberts leave. 'Anything after the gate was locked on Friday night?'

'I let one of the circus vans in. Bloke from the garage brought it back after a repair.'

'And what time was that?'

Bertie scratched his head. 'Around eleven-thirty, I think. I'd just locked the gate and was having a last smoke before going to my caravan.'

'Did you let anyone else in or out after the show? While you were having your smoke?'

He chuckled. 'Young Keavy. I didn't exactly let her in. She vaulted over the gate like a star.'

'Was she on her own?'

'No, she was with this bloke. Said he was a friend of her mum's and staying the night with Paddy. Came in a hire car.'

'So you opened the gate for him to drive in?'

'No, he left it in the car park and I had to open the gate for him. Just a crack, mind. He was a skinny bloke but not agile like Keavy.'

'Let me get this straight,' said Katya. 'The only time you opened the gate fully was for the van. That's very late for the return of a repair, isn't it?'

Bertie shrugged. 'Dunno. We don't usually send them out for repairs. Either one of the lads here can do it or we wait until we're back in Ireland.'

'So this could have been an emergency?'

'S'pose so.'

'And who would be able to tell me the name of the garage who did the repair?'

'Aidan, I suppose, or maybe Dara, because he does the accounts and that.'

'Okay,' said Katya. 'You've been very helpful. Now perhaps you could direct us to where we can find Joseph?'

'In his caravan, I expect. He's not much to do while the Romanians are here.' He pointed to where the caravans were parked in a circle, which reminded Katya of the way covered wagons huddled together looking, as Jasmine had noted, as if they were in an old film about the wild west.

She and Jonny made their way across the field towards them. Joseph, who she recognised from their meeting a few days ago, was sitting on the step of one of the caravans with an older man – Dara, she assumed – and a plump, middle-aged woman who was mending a tear in a sequin-encrusted leotard.

Joseph stood up and smiled at them. 'Good morning,' he said. 'Nice to see you again. Have you met my father and Norah?'

Jonny and Katya shook hands with both of them while Joseph unfolded a couple of camp chairs. 'Have a seat,' he said. 'Would you like coffee?'

'That would be very nice,' said Katya.

'I'll go and make it,' said Norah, folding up her sewing and disappearing into the caravan.

'How's the investigation going?' Joseph asked.

'We're making progress,' said Katya, hoping that he wouldn't ask how much progress they were making. 'We just have one or two questions for you. Things that might move it on a bit faster.'

'For me or Dad?' Joseph asked.

'Both of you, probably,' said Katya, worrying that the chair she was perching on was about to collapse. She could feel the canvas straining under her weight. 'First, can you tell me how long you've known Badger Waites and where you met him?'

'I met him at a gig quite near here about three years ago. We got talking about various makes of keyboard and which ones we preferred. He was thinking of buying a new one. I made a few suggestions, and he gave me his email so I could send him some links he might be interested in. We kept in touch, and he used to pop up whenever I was playing anywhere in the area.'

'And you got on well with him?'

'He was okay, rather intense but that was fine. I only saw him now and then and he'd go on a bit.'

'Go on a bit?'

'It's like he had a one-track mind. He only ever wanted to talk about music and how he could get more work on keys. But I heard him play once and he wasn't very good, so I made all kinds of excuses and told him it was a tough world to get into and I'd only done it because of my dad's connection to the music business. Badger could be quite hard to get away from, but I didn't want to upset him so I usually let him talk himself out. He'd kind of latched onto me because I guess I was the only pro musician he knew. But, well, you know... it's easy enough to tune that kind of thing out and I didn't want to offend the guy.'

'And you say you only ever saw him when you were around here?'

'That's right. I don't think he travelled much.'

'So you don't know if he was ever in Dublin?'

Joseph laughed. 'I told you, he was very single minded, obsessive almost. If he'd been in Dublin when I was there, he'd have tracked me down.'

'And when you arrived here this summer, he found you and asked you if you could give him a job?'

'He did, yes. But this year we've got the Romanians and they're more or less self-sufficient. I occasionally fill in on keyboards, but it's an easy season for me. When we don't have a visiting band, I get freelance players in, but as I said, Badger wasn't nearly good enough. I felt sorry for him, though. He told me he'd been laid off from his job so I asked Aidan if he could work with Jeremy on the funfair stuff.'

'Why are you asking about Dublin?' Dara asked, speaking for the first time.

'It's just one lead we're following up,' said Katya. 'We read an article about a man called Donal Maguire and it mentioned he'd been employed by Quinn Logistics.'

'You think that had something to do with the murder?' Dara asked, looking surprised.

'We're just looking for background,' said Jonny.

'That'll not clear Jeremy's name,' said Dara. 'If anything, it could incriminate him even more.'

'Why do you say that?' Katya asked as Norah arrived with a tray of coffee.

Dara didn't answer immediately. He waited until Norah had handed round mugs of coffee and placed a plate of home-baked biscuits on a small camping table. 'I remember the Donal Maguire case,' he said at last. 'It was a nasty business. I know they were cleared, but I'm fairly certain Quinn Logistics was involved somehow. Our mother would have known all the right people to get them off any kind of charge.'

Dara didn't seem to have a high opinion of his brothers, or their mother.

'Is there any chance Badger could have been involved as well?' Katya asked, helping herself to a biscuit.

'Nah,' said Dara. 'I'm pretty sure he hadn't met either Aidan or Jeremy before he started working here. In any case, from what I saw of him, he was obsessively law-abiding.'

'That's what the argument was about,' said Joseph. 'He told Jeremy he wasn't sticking to safety procedures. Jeremy wouldn't have responded well to that, but it's hardly a motive for murder, is it?'

'That's what we're working on,' said Katya.

'I can see what you're getting at,' said Joseph. 'You're trying to find something that links Badger to some kind of revenge murder, and Donal Maguire's claim of wrongful imprisonment could be a motive. But I think it's unlikely that Badger had anything to do with it.'

Katya was beginning to think so too. 'How much time does Aidan spend in Dublin?' she asked.

'Enough to stay in control. He tours with the circus, but he's always flitting back and forth between wherever we are and Dublin.'

In other words, perfect cover to organise drug smuggling. 'So he's not fully employed backstage?' Katya asked.

'When he's here, yes. When he's away I stand in for him.'

'What's your role in the circus?' Jonny asked. 'Apart from covering for Aidan when he's away.'

'I don't have one really,' he said, grinning. 'I'm just a hippy layabout.'

His long hair, colourful beads and baggy patchwork trousers certainly backed this up as far as Katya was concerned. Stereotype hippy. Probably hadn't changed his look since he was a teenager.

'Dad's retired,' said Joseph. 'He's enough money from stuff the band sold to keep ticking over.'

And spend his days sitting around meditating, Katya assumed.

'And I enjoy life in the circus,' said Dara. 'Helping out where I can, odd jobs and that. And it's good to spend time with my son.'

'And me,' said Norah, feeding him a biscuit and nudging him playfully.

*She could do better,* Katya thought. A bonny-looking woman who could sew and bake biscuits. Quite a catch in the right circles. This was an interesting and very likely one-sided relationship. She noticed that Dara pretty much ignored Norah. As far as anyone could when having their mouth stuffed with biscuit. 'I also wanted to ask you about the van,' she said.

'Van?' asked Dara.

'Yes, the one that was out for repair and returned on Friday night.'

Dara shook his head. 'Who told you that?' he asked.

'Bertie Kelly, on the back gate. He told me he'd let someone through on Friday night returning the van from a repair garage.'

'Then he got it wrong. We do all the maintenance here on site. It's only ever minor repairs. All the vehicles are serviced before we leave Dublin at the start of the season.'

'And Bertie would have known that?' Katya asked, wondering if they should be treating Bertie as a suspect.

'He's a dozy old lad,' said Joseph. 'He was probably half asleep and misheard what the driver told him.'

'Or he'd had a few pints too many and made it up,' said his father.

'But there are vans kept here? Rather than in the car park?'

'We've just got the two vans,' said Dara. 'We use them to transport odds and ends between showgrounds, and sometimes for errands like getting in extra feed for the horses. Mostly they stay in the car park for the duration. Occasionally they stay on site if there's been a late drop-off or they're going to be loaded up for an early start in the morning. But like I said, we don't use them very much while we're camped up in one spot.'

*Where are they both now?* Katya wondered.

'Who has the keys?' Jonny asked, taking the words out of her mouth. He was more wide awake than she'd given him credit for.

'In a small trailer with Aidan's tools. It's parked at the back of the circus tent and the keys are on a hook just inside the door.'

'So anyone could take them?'

'They'd be expected to clear it with Aidan first, but yes.'

'Could Badger have driven one of them?'

'I doubt it,' said Joseph. 'Only our regular employees are insured.'

And by all accounts Badger was way too law-abiding to drive an uninsured van. Katya watched as Jonny drained his coffee cup and helped himself to another biscuit. She almost expected him to ask Norah for the recipe. She wished he had. They'd make a welcome addition to the office snacks, delicious though Karim's pastries were. 'Well,' she said, standing up, 'you've been very helpful. We'll leave you to your...' Her sentence trailed away as it wasn't obvious that Dara, Norah and Joseph were doing anything much to be left to get on with. She looked around. Their caravan had an air that suggested *holiday,* the three of them lounging in camping chairs in the sun. Norah's sewing was the only circus-related activity she could see.

~

Jonny and Katya made their way back to the gate, which was now locked, Bertie having deserted his post. 'What do you think?' Katya asked. 'Vault it like Keavy, or walk round to the main entrance?'

Jonny studied the gate. A five-barred, farm type gate and he'd have given it a go. This one was made of iron, a series of upright struts with horizontal bars top and bottom.

'Only if you go first,' he said, fairly sure that Katya would not take up his challenge.

'Main gate it is, then,' she said, setting off purposefully round the side of the big top towards the box office. 'Mind you, I might never have been as athletic as Keavy, but I'd have given it a go when I was a few years younger. We did stuff like that when I was training.'

Jonny tried to visualise Katya vaulting and couldn't. She didn't have the right build for it. Comfort rather than agility, that was Katya. He tried to remember if he'd ever been able to do it. Probably at school, on cross country runs, perhaps. 'How old would you have been then?' he asked.

'In my twenties, I suppose. Why?'

'Badger was in his twenties. Do we know if he was at all athletic?'

'No idea. It's not the kind of info you get in post-mortem reports. Might be worth finding out, though.'

They walked through the main gate and round to where Jonny had parked his car near the back gate. Before unlocking the car, he walked over for a closer look at the gate. 'I don't suppose anyone in the police checked it for fingerprints, did they?'

'Shouldn't think so. Why would they? They had their suspect, and he was already on the inside.'

'And it would be no use suggesting it now.'

'Not unless we can produce evidence that the murderer wasn't Jeremy.'

Jonny noticed something lying on the ground at the side of the gate. He reached through the bars and picked up a small piece of fabric with a button attached. 'Remind me how you do a gate vault,' he said.

'You pull yourself up on your arms, lean over as far as you can reach with one arm while hanging onto the top rail with the other. Then it's a kind of body twist over the top. You have to stay very close to the gate.'

'So it might be possible to catch a cuff and rip it?' He handed the scrap to Katya.

She took it from him, studied it and then reached into her pocket for one of the small ziplock bags she carried around with her. She placed the scrap of fabric inside and stared at it through the plastic. 'There's some hair twisted around the button,' she said.

'Badger's?'

'No idea, but it would be worth getting a DNA test done on it. If it does turn out to be Badger's, it could explain how he got in that morning. I'll pass it on to Lugs.'

'Will he get it tested for us? I thought things like that cost money.'

'They do, but it could strengthen the case against Jeremy, so he'd probably be willing to do it.'

'That's not going to help us. We're trying to prove he was innocent.'

'But not at the expense of the truth.'

She was right, of course, but she didn't look too downhearted about it, and he wondered why. They climbed into his car and set off back into town. Katya was quiet as he drove, but as he was pulling up outside her flat she said, 'The van.'

Jonny had been miles away, thinking about gate vaulting. 'Which van?' he asked.

'The one Bertie Kelly let in that night.'

'The one that was being returned from repair?'

'But it wasn't, was it? We need to know if anyone else saw it and who was driving it. And another thing. Did you see two vans parked out in the car park?'

'No,' said Jonny. 'I didn't. I checked, particularly after what Dara said about them. There was only one there when we left.'

'Hmm,' said Katya. 'I'm beginning to think the Quinns are rather more lax about the comings and goings than they'd led us to believe. All that stuff about Paddy checking that no one's there who shouldn't be every night. I should think it's just a quick flash around with a torch then a quiet night in his caravan with a bottle of whiskey.'

IT WAS ONLY when Jonny had driven off and Katya let herself into her flat that she realised how tired she was. This case seemed to be going nowhere. Everything they discovered just made Jeremy look more guilty. Was it time to throw in the towel? Tell Cordelia Quinn they'd done all they could? She slumped down in an armchair and eased off her shoes. Hot weather always made her feet swell and that did nothing to improve her temper, or her optimism. She padded into the bathroom in her bare feet, sat on the edge of the bath and turned on the cold tap. Bliss. She'd read somewhere that chilling socks in a freezer and wearing them at night was a way of keeping cool, but Katya didn't suffer from hot feet at night. It was during the day that they ached and burned. Had anyone invented ice-pack socks for wearing inside comfortable shoes during the day? Her feet still soaking, she got out her phone and started to search Google.

Before she'd found the answer to her problem, the phone rang with a number she didn't recognise. She clicked to reply. It was Joseph Quinn.

'Hope I'm not disturbing you,' he said.

'Not at all,' said Katya. 'Have you remembered something?'

'Not exactly, but after your questions about the vans, Dad and I went to check up on them. We found one where we'd expected in the car park. The other one was parked round the back of the kennels. It's the one we use to transport the dogs. It has a cage inside and a ventilator in the roof to keep the dogs cool. The thing is that no one has taken the dogs anywhere recently, so it had no reason to be parked there. We asked around and no one admitted to using the van while we've been on this site.'

'Interesting,' said Katya. 'Do you have any idea why it might be there?'

'We did wonder if someone was using it to sleep in.'

'Why would they do that?'

'For a bit of privacy, perhaps. One of the acrobats or a band member who wanted somewhere quiet to go for a bit of... well, you know. A place to take a girlfriend or boyfriend.'

'I suppose it is a bit public on the campsite. Everyone knowing what you're up to all the time.'

'I'll have a chat to some of the musicians. They might have heard rumours. There's no harm in it, but...'

'But?'

'Well, maybe someone sneaked in from outside and used it as a hideaway.'

Katya began to see where this was going. 'And waited for an opportunity to kill Badger?'

'That's what Dad and I wondered.'

'But they'd hardly stay there once they'd done it, would they?'

'No, they'd have left. But if you'd just killed someone your first thoughts wouldn't be to move the van to a different parking place. Not if you'd only used it to keep watch from.'

In an odd way, that made sense to Katya. Camp out in a van and wait for an opportunity to kill Badger. They knew someone had driven the van onto the site the night of the murder and Badger had arrived early the next morning, possibly vaulting the gate to get in.

'There's more,' Joseph continued. 'Dad and I thought we'd take a look inside the van to see if anything had been left behind. Like we told you, the keys are kept on hooks in Aidan's trailer. There are four keyrings, each with keys for both vans. But only three were there.'

'So one set was missing,' said Katya. 'Perhaps someone wanted to use the other van and forgot to return them.'

'I could get Aidan to ask around, but it's more than my life's worth to interfere with his workforce. He'd probably be furious if he knew Dad and I had looked inside the van.'

'Best leave it then,' said Katya. 'Did you find anything in the van?'

'Just a couple of old blankets.'

'So someone might have slept there?'

'More likely they were for the dogs. They could have been there since the vans left Ireland.'

'Who would have driven them then?'

'Jeremy would probably have driven one of them. Mike or Tony the other.'

'And will you move the van back to the car park now?'

'That's up to Aidan, but probably not. We'll be moving out in a day or two and we'd only have to bring it in again to load up the dogs.'

'Right,' said Katya. 'Thanks for letting me know.'

'Anything to help Jeremy,' said Joseph, although in Katya's opinion, not without a note of cynicism. She suspected this family were not as close knit as Cordelia liked to make out.

She ended the call and dried her feet. Could this be what they were looking for? A murderer hanging out in the van waiting for his opportunity was more likely than someone parking it there and using it for a bit of nooky on a heap of smelly dog blankets. And she didn't really think that Romanian musicians and Hungarian acrobats were particularly prudish about on-tour hookups. The campsite was probably a hotbed of casual affairs. No one would think twice about couples carrying on in tents.

But whatever she thought, there was not enough there to take to Lugs. And removing Jeremy as a suspect also removed any kind of motive. Badger sounded quite irritating – well, very irritating. Katya had worked with obsessives in her time but had never wanted to kill any of them. Well, not seriously. She may have expressed it at times, but everyone did that, didn't they? People got murdered for various reasons, more often than not connected to money or affairs of the heart. She'd never come across irritation as a motive. She thought of the people they'd discovered who had known Badger: Rosa; Joseph; musicians in his band. They had all spoken of him with a degree of affection, so what could he have done that made someone hate him enough to kill him?

Katya's thought of giving up the case now forgotten, she wondered how Ivo and Jasmine had got on with Badger's sister. She'd call a meeting for tomorrow afternoon and they could compare notes.

# 22

It was seven in the morning and the café hadn't opened yet, when Flora Green's number flashed up on Jasmine's phone. She put down the cake stand she was carrying and clicked to answer the call. She'd not seen Flora since last Saturday at the circus. She and Teddy had gone to the police station to give statements, but they were done by a couple of on-duty constables. The lack of police presence was usually a good sign. It meant, even though the tourist season was well underway, there had been very little criminal activity. Jasmine hoped that wasn't about to change. It was possible that Flora was going to warn of a need for vigilance; watch out for forged bank notes, suspicious credit cards and pickpockets. But that was usually done by community officers, not detective sergeants. Flora was more likely to be dealing with burglary or violent attacks and Jasmine really hoped this wasn't about one of those. She hated the idea that someone she knew had been the victim of a serious crime.

'Jasmine,' said Flora. 'Glad you're there. We need your help.'

'Okay. What kind of help?'

'We've a young girl here called Keavy. She won't tell us her full name and says she will only speak to you. Do you know anything about her?'

'Keavy?' said Jasmine. 'Caitlyn Quinn's half-sister?'

'Ah,' said Flora. 'She didn't tell us that. All she told us was her name and that she'd been kidnapped.'

'Kidnapped?' Jasmine gasped. 'I don't understand. Wouldn't it have been reported? Caitlyn must have missed her.'

'You know as much as I do. We can't question her without a responsible adult and since she's only prepared to talk if you're there, you would seem the obvious person to ask. Is there any chance you could get round here now?'

Of course she could. She'd explain to her dad and give her friend Stevie a call. He was never busy first thing in the morning, and he knew his way around *Jasmine's* almost as well as she did herself. 'I can be there in fifteen minutes. Is Keavy okay? Does she need anything?'

Flora assured her they were looking after Keavy and the best way to help her would be to get her talking about what had happened.

IT WAS a short walk from *Jasmine's* to the police station. Flora met Jasmine at the entrance and briefly explained what she knew about Keavy's abduction. They'd taken a call from a man who had been waved down on the slip road to the M4 at Langley by a girl with bare feet, wearing only shorts and a tank top. Her arms and legs were bruised, and she was clearly in shock. He asked if she needed help and offered her a lift. The girl turned down the offer of a lift and also refused to wait with him in his car but asked him to call the police and to wait at the side of the road until they came. Which he did. 'We have his details,' said Flora. 'And he's coming in to make a statement later, but he's obviously an innocent driver who just happened to be passing. We had our doctor come in and check Keavy over. She refused to talk to her apart from answering the purely medical questions, but the doc said she was fine. She's had a cup of tea and a cheese sandwich followed by a bar of chocolate. I took that as confirmation that she's okay, at least physically. She's been very well-behaved and polite but refused to say any more until we called you.'

'And no one has reported her missing? Not even Caitlyn?'

Flora shook her head. 'Believe me, any report of a missing teenage girl and we'd have been out in force looking for her straight away.'

Jasmine looked at her watch. It was still only seven-thirty in the morning, so it was possible Keavy hadn't yet been missed. She knew they were not early risers, but if someone had broken into the caravan and abducted Keavy, surely Caitlyn would have woken up.

'I'll take you to see her,' said Flora, leading Jasmine to a room they used for witnesses and victims of attacks. Keavy was sitting on a sofa hugging her knees. Her bare feet had been bandaged and were perched on the edge of the seat. She was wearing a large navy-blue jumper, the property, Jasmine imagined, of one of the CID team. Keavy looked relieved when she saw Jasmine and smiled at her.

Jasmine sat on the sofa next to her and put an arm around her shoulder. 'Are you okay?' she asked.

Keavy nodded.

'We need to let your family know you where you are. Shall I ask Flora to call Caitlyn? Wouldn't you like her to come and take you home?'

'I can't go home yet. Everyone's away.'

It took Jasmine a moment or two to realise that home to Keavy was Galway, not the circus. 'We can at least let Caitlyn know you're okay.'

'She won't be awake yet,' said Keavy. 'She doesn't get up until after nine and she'll think I'm with the dogs.'

Jasmine looked up at Flora with a *What do we do?* expression.

'Let's hear Keavy's story first. Then I'll give Caitlyn a call to let her know she's fine.'

'Take your time, Keavy,' said Jasmine.

Keavy pulled the jumper closely around her. 'I was kidnapped,' she said.

'Last night?'

'No, this morning. I never sleep very late. I like to get up early and do some work in the ring with the dogs while it's quiet and no one is watching.'

'So you came out of Caitlyn's caravan, collected the dogs from the kennels and took them to the ring?'

Keavy nodded. 'I worked with them for about an hour, then I let them run about for a bit. They were chasing around near the stables, and I stood and watched them. There was someone else there.'

'Do you know who it was?'

'I didn't see him, but I could hear him talking on his phone.'

'Could you hear what he was saying?'

'Not really, but he sounded cross. I whistled for the dogs and took them back to the kennels. He must have followed me because as I left to go back to the caravan, he grabbed me. He put his hand over my mouth and carried me under his other arm. I tried to bite him, but I couldn't get my mouth open. I was wriggling and trying to shout, but he told me to shut up or he'd kill one of the dogs.'

'How did you get from there to the Honda roundabout where you were found?'

'One of the vans, the one they use for the dogs, was parked at the back of the kennels. He stuffed a rag into my mouth and pushed me into the dog cage in the back. He knocked my head against the side of the van when he threw me in, so I was a bit dizzy and by the time I pulled myself together we were driving away. The main gate must have been open. I heard him shout to someone, but we didn't stop.'

'How did you escape?'

'It took a while. I had to get rid of the gag, but my throat was quite sore so even when it had gone, I couldn't shout for help. I banged on the side of the cage, but no one would have heard me. Even the man who was driving. The cage isn't locked. It doesn't need to be because there are bolts and the dogs can't undo those. And the back doors of the van are easy to open from the inside. I saw a YouTube about it.'

'And this man didn't see what you were doing?'

'There's a partition. It was put in so the driver wouldn't be distracted by the dogs when they bark. The back of the van is sealed off. I got the door open a crack and I could see the road. I could tell it was a proper road, not one of the tracks that go through the fields. I knew if it was a proper road there would be cars that I could wave down and ask for help. But we were going quite fast, and I had wait until the van slowed down before I could jump out.'

Jasmine was impressed. 'That was very brave,' she said.

'It was a bit scary, but we learn to jump off moving horses and a van isn't so different. I was afraid the man would notice I wasn't there any more and come and look for me.'

'Do you have any idea who he was? Had you ever seen him before?' Flora asked.

'I didn't really get a proper look at him. He was Irish.'

That wasn't going to be a lot of help in a circus where most of the workforce was Irish. 'Keavy,' Jasmine said gently, 'are you scared to go back to the circus because you think it was one of the family?'

Keavy shook her head. 'Aidan can be a bit frightening, but I'm sure it wasn't him. Anyway, why would he kidnap me?'

A good point. Jasmine couldn't think of any reason why he would. It was more likely to be a discontented worker seeing an unexpected way to demand a ransom from Cordelia.

'I'm scared to go back in case the man is still there. I don't think he was anyone in the family but... I want my mam.' She dissolved into tears and Jasmine could hardly blame her. She'd been very brave and had done all the right things, not getting into a strange man's car and asking him to call the police and wait with her. But she was only fourteen. She must have been terrified.

'Come home with me,' said Jasmine. 'You'll be safe in our flat and we can call your mum.'

Jasmine looked up at Flora, who nodded. 'I'll get a car to drive you back,' she said. 'And I'll call Keavy's mother and explain what's happened.'

'Will you call Caitlyn as well?' Jasmine asked. 'She must be worried about Keavy, or she will be when she wakes up and finds her missing.'

'Leave it all to me,' said Flora. 'I'll need to get a team out to the circus to look for evidence. We have to catch whoever did this.'

# 23

'She's staying with you?' Ivo asked, taking a bite of the sardine and dill sandwich Jasmine had made him, while gazing thoughtfully out of the office window, wondering if any kidnappers were lurking outside. There was no one looking suspicious enough to be any kind of criminal, so he turned his attention back to Jasmine. 'In your flat?'

'Well, I'd hardly let her sleep in the kitchen,' said Jasmine, removing the paper from an avocado wrap. 'She's not Cinderella. More Sleeping Beauty, as she's fast asleep in my room right now. She was exhausted when we got back here, poor thing, and all she was wearing was a pair of shorts and a T-shirt, and some flip flops someone at the police station lent her. I lent her some of my clothes. She had a shower and then she just crashed out on my bed.'

'But why is she staying here? Why not with Caitlyn?'

'She says she's scared and won't go back to the circus.'

Ivo was inclined to think she'd made the right choice. The Quinns en masse were decidedly scary. Never mind all the other people at the circus; Irish workmen, burly Romanian Gypsy musicians and even the Hungarian acrobats didn't look too trustworthy. People said circuses were romantic, but to Ivo they were plain frightening. Caitlyn was okay but hardly a match if the rest of the family ganged up against her.

'The police agree,' Jasmine continued. 'It's not the safest place for Keavy, even with Caitlyn to keep an eye on her. Not with a kidnapper on the loose. They called her mother to come over and fetch her, but until she gets here everyone agreed that this was the safest place.'

'Everyone?'

'Keavy's mum, Caitlyn, the police, social services...'

'They called in social services?'

'They had to. Keavy's only fourteen. There was talk of her going to a foster home, but they're thin on the ground at the moment and she got very upset at the thought of a children's home, even for a night or two.'

'What about Caitlyn?'

'I think she agreed with the police that the circus might not be safe for Keavy right now.'

'Do they think there is any connection to the murder?'

'No one's saying. Katya's going to see what she can get out of Lugs. But there doesn't seem to be any link to Badger. She's trying to persuade him to look at the possibility of Badger somehow being involved with the drugs bust that the Quinns were suspected of being part of.'

'She's going with the blackmail theory?'

'Reluctantly, because that would mean Jeremy is definitely guilty.'

Ivo thought that it was most likely that Jeremy *was* implicated in some way. Everything they'd discovered up to now just showed more evidence stacking up against him. It was possible that this would be the Breakfast Club Detectives' first failure. At least as far as the Quinns were concerned. The prosecution would probably think they were doing a splendid job. He glanced up at the board and the Quinn family tree. Jasmine had added photos of Keavy and Caitlyn. Jonny had downloaded a picture of Cordelia from the circus website. There were out-of-date photos of Aidan, Dara and Joseph, and the selfie Bella had taken of herself and Jeremy. They should have one of the victim as well, shouldn't they? And Ivo had one on his phone. He scrolled through his photos, AirDropped the picture of Badger that the band had on the easel at the concert the other night to the computer and printed it. Then he pinned it to the board next to the others. He stared at it, scratching his head. Suddenly he jumped up and grabbed Jasmine's arm excitedly.

'You okay?' Jasmine asked.

'I think I've got a new theory,' he said.

'One that Katya will think is barmy?'

'Probably. She thinks most of my theories are daft.' And yet several of them had turned out not to be so mad after all.

'Go on then,' said Jasmine. 'Tell me about it.'

Ivo moved the picture of Jeremy and pinned it next to the printout of Badger. 'Notice anything?' he asked.

'Not really,' said Jasmine.

Ivo turned back to the computer and clicked on Badger's picture. 'You're clever with this sort of thing,' he said. 'Can you edit out Badger's glasses and remove the white streak in his hair?'

Jasmine did as he asked and turned towards him, grinning excitedly. 'You just could be onto something,' she said. 'Although we don't know how tall Jeremy is.'

'The other Quinns are stocky rather than tall. I'd say around five ten. What about Badger?'

'Hard to say when the only time I saw him he was lying dead on the ground, but he didn't look particularly tall or short, kind of average, I suppose. But I wouldn't have called him stocky.'

'Average build though?'

'Maybe. Go on, tell me what you think happened.'

'It was a case of mistaken identity. Jeremy wasn't the murderer – he was the intended victim. The killer saw Jeremy's jacket hanging on the rail outside the carousel, crept under the awning and found Badger, probably lurking in the shadows and not easily recognised. But similar enough. He strangled him and fixed him in one of the sleigh seats, covered it and pinned on the out of order sign.'

'Hmm,' said Jasmine. 'You are right about the likeness, but why would anyone want to kill Jeremy any more than someone wanted to kill Badger?'

'Jeremy was a bit of a Jack the Lad, wasn't he? Perhaps it was an angry boyfriend.'

It wasn't a completely unlikely theory, Jasmine thought. Perhaps if they knew more about Jeremy's love life, it was an angle they could work on. She wondered if someone had seen Jeremy and Bella Trumpington together. One of the friends she came to the show with, possibly, who had been overcome with jealousy and waited for Jeremy to return from her house, only to mistake Badger for him. And it wouldn't be the first time Jeremy had made out with someone else's girlfriend. 'I suppose that had happened before,' she said. 'But that time it only led to a punch-up.' And she couldn't see Katya treating it as a viable theory.

Jonny and Katya arrived together. Jasmine had called Katya once she and Keavy were back from the police station, and Jonny had driven her there so she could catch up with what had now become a police case. 'Sorry I'm late, folks,' she said, putting her bag down on the table with a thump and sinking into one of the chairs.

'Any news of the man who took Keavy?' Jasmine asked.

'No sign of him yet,' said Katya. 'The main gate has been open earlier for the last day or two and the man in the box office saw the van leave. He shouted to the driver to slow down.'

'Did he get a look at the driver?' Jonny asked.

'Not really. He sounded like a nondescript kind of guy wearing a black t-shirt. He couldn't even say for sure whether he'd recognised someone working for the circus or if it was a stranger.'

'Not helpful,' said Jonny.

'They found the van abandoned in a car park in Langley.'

'That was quick,' said Jasmine.

'Wouldn't have been difficult,' said Katya. 'It's very distinctive with the circus logo and they knew the registration number.'

'Did anyone see him?' Ivo asked. 'He would have had a shock

when he discovered Keavy had gone. He probably legged it. Someone must have noticed that.'

'They've a team out looking for witnesses who might have seen him parking and who noticed the direction he went from there.'

'Keavy said he sounded Irish. He was probably headed for Heathrow and a flight to Dublin,' Ivo suggested.

'He couldn't have been if he'd planned to have Keavy with him. He must have had somewhere in mind where he could keep her while he waited for the ransom money.'

'We don't know if he was going to demand a ransom,' said Katya. 'We don't know what he had planned for Keavy. It's something I'd rather not think about. It's better left to the police.'

'But it doesn't change what we're doing, does it?' Jonny asked. 'We still want to prove Jeremy's innocence.'

'As far as I know, it's what Cordelia wants. And we'll carry on until she tells us otherwise. If we can show the kidnap was linked to the murder in some way, it could help Jeremy. There's no way he could have kidnapped Keavy when he's banged up on remand.'

'He might have paid someone to do it,' Ivo suggested.

'Kidnap his own niece? Why?'

'She's not actually his niece,' said Ivo. 'She's…' He paused as if trying to work it out. 'She's Paddy's ex-wife's daughter. Does that make Paddy her stepfather?'

'Not sure,' said Jonny. 'But she's Caitlyn's half-sister with a long-time connection to the circus. I can't see why Jeremy would do something like that. It would just alienate him from the rest of the family.'

'We'll leave that to the police,' said Katya. 'We need to go over what we've learnt about Badger. Jasmine and Ivo, did you pick up anything useful from Badger's sister?'

'Nothing new,' said Jasmine. 'Lucy just confirmed that Badger was a quiet, law-abiding type and while he didn't have a lot of friends, no one actually hated him. She said he travelled very little and had never been to Ireland.'

'So we can rule him out of the drugs case,' said Jonny.

Katya drummed her fingers on the desk, looking thoughtful. 'Unless he was working for them over here. A receiver, perhaps. If someone had framed Donal Maguire as he suggests, Badger might have got wind of it. And that would make him dangerous as far as they were concerned.'

'So you think Jeremy might have killed him to shut him up?' said Ivo. 'But like we've said before, why do it in a way that draws attention to himself as a suspect? It feels like a set-up to me.'

Jasmine looked at the notes she'd made. 'It was interesting that Lucy thought the same.'

'Lucy thinks Jeremy was framed?'

'Not exactly, but she did say she thought the arrest had been too quick and that she didn't want to see an innocent man sent down.'

'Hmm,' said Katya. 'That's unusual for a relative. They're normally out for revenge and want someone to be banged up as soon as possible. I don't suppose she had any useful ideas about who might have done it?'

Jasmine shook her head. ''Fraid not.'

'How did you get on at the circus yesterday?' Ivo asked.

'It was very useful,' said Katya. 'We talked to Bertie Kelly. The only people he let in late on the Friday night of the murder were Keavy and the bloke who came with her from Dublin, Martyn someone. Keavy vaulted over the gate and Bertie opened it for Martyn. And a while later he opened the gate again to let in a van. The driver told him it was being returned from a repair.'

'But Dara told us they don't send the vans out for repairs. They are serviced in Ireland and the mechanics on site can do minor repairs if necessary,' Jonny added.

'And he didn't let the man out again?'

'Apparently not.'

'So some unidentified person spent the night on site, possibly in the back of a van,' said Ivo.

'Looks like it,' said Katya. 'We checked on the way out and there was only one van in the car park. I was thinking I should go back for another look when Joseph called me. He and his dad had decided to check the van on their own. They discovered a set of keys was missing and the van had been parked behind the kennels.'

'With someone living in it?'

'Possibly, although they didn't find anything inside that suggested it.'

'And that was the van that was used to kidnap Keavy?' Jasmine asked. 'So the kidnapper could be whoever was living in it.'

'We'll have a better idea when Lugs gets the forensics report on it. That should be any time now. They don't hang about in cases of child abduction.'

'We think we know how Badger got in that morning,' said Jonny. 'A reasonably agile, youngish person can vault over the gate easily enough. Bertie saw Keavy do it and Badger wasn't a lot older.'

'No way of proving it, though,' said Ivo.

'We found a scrap of fabric with a button and a twist of hair. Katya's given it to Lugs to see if it could have been Badger's.'

'He's going to check the evidence bags for missing bits of shirt and if he finds some, he'll get it checked for DNA.'

'Do we think the murderer and the kidnapper were the same person?' Jonny asked.

'No reason to think so,' said Katya. 'If you murder someone you don't hang around on the off chance you might be able to throw in a bit of kidnapping. Just because we want to find a link doesn't mean there is one.'

'It is a bit of a coincidence, though,' said Jonny. 'Why didn't the murderer drive off in the van? Why leave it?'

'Because the main gate might still have been locked. It doesn't always open as early as it did the day of the kidnap. He could get away by vaulting over the back gate.'

'So someone comes along and finds a van strategically parked for an easy getaway and a victim practically tripping over him to be kidnapped?'

'Well, put like that...' said Katya. This wasn't getting them anywhere.

'Ivo has a theory,' said Jasmine.

'Of course he has,' said Katya with a tired sigh. 'Go on then, Ivo. Spit it out.'

Ivo frowned at Katya. 'You'll probably think it's rubbish.'

*Probably,* thought Katya, but they didn't have many ideas right now. 'Tell us anyway.'

'Mistaken identity,' said Ivo, pointing at the two photos on the board. 'See how alike they are? Jasmine edited Badger's photo a bit but under the carousel cover it would have been quite dark.'

This was a typical bit of off-the-wall Ivo fantasy. 'So you are saying that the murderer really wanted to kill Jeremy? Why?'

'I haven't quite worked that out yet,' said Ivo. 'But Jeremy's more likely to have enemies than Badger, isn't he?'

Another crazy idea? It raised far more questions than it answered. She tapped her pen on the table and gazed vacantly out of the window. Then, suddenly, it came to her. The light bulb moment she'd been hoping for. She slapped Ivo on the back. 'That's it,' she said. 'We've been looking at it all the wrong way.'

'You're losing me,' said Jonny. 'Are you saying Ivo's right?'

'Almost.' She laughed. 'I don't agree with the mistaken identity theory, though.'

'Then which bit do you agree with?' asked Jasmine, looking as puzzled as Jonny.

'Don't you see?' said Katya. 'The murderer didn't give a toss about who he killed. It was all staged. We shouldn't be looking at why Jeremy hated Badger. We should be searching for someone who hated Jeremy.'

'You think Jeremy was framed?' said Jasmine.

'Possibly,' said Katya.

'Someone hated him enough to get him framed for murder?' said Jonny. 'That would be one desperate man, wouldn't it?'

'Depends what Jeremy had done to him, I suppose,' said Katya.

Jasmine turned on the computer and found the notes Jonny made about Jeremy. She clicked on the folder read them out. 'He's not exactly a model of blameless innocence, is he?' she said.

'He's been in trouble,' said Jonny. 'But it's mostly fairly minor stuff. A few fights, a brush with drugs while he was at school. Nothing that would motivate the kind of vengeance you're suggesting.'

They were probably right. Katya wondered if they had enough to take to Lugs. It might get the prosecution to rethink. But Lugs was off the case. And even if he thought she was onto something, the prosecutors probably wouldn't take it seriously. Lugs could be in trouble for trying to throw a spanner into a case that was done and dusted as far as they were concerned. No, there were still questions to be answered before she took the idea to him. 'Why the rope?' she asked.

'It's a message,' said Ivo. 'Do you remember what kind of rope it was?'

Katya shook her head.

'Hemp,' said Ivo.

They all looked at him blankly.

'So?' Katya asked.

'Think about it. Hemp comes from the same plant as cannabis. It's a message about drugs.'

It was a bit far-fetched, but something started niggling in Katya's brain. 'So do we agree the murderer could be the guy in the article Teddy found?'

'Who was sent to prison for five years when by all accounts it should have been one of the Quinns.'

'Donal Maguire,' said Jasmine excitedly. 'We might just have a workable theory.'

'I've had another idea,' said Ivo. 'A way to tie it all together with the kidnapping.' He sat at the table and fondled Harold's ears, apparently reluctant to speak.

'Are you going to tell us what it is?' said Katya.

'Not if you're just going to treat it as a joke,' said Ivo.

Is that what she did? Ivo's theories could be over-imaginative, but she should be patient with the lad. He was no fool. 'I promise not to laugh,' said Katya, wearily. 'We need to hear all the ideas we can, however...' She stopped before the word *barmy* slipped out.

'Go on, Ivo,' said Jonny. 'We need to hear this.'

'I'm going back to my mistaken identity idea,' he said stubbornly.

'The killer sees Jeremy's jacket hanging on the rope outside the carousel, creeps under the awning and finds Badger, probably lurking in the shadows and not easily recognised but similar enough to Jeremy.' He unpinned the two photos from the board and put them on the table in front of them, then continued with his possible scenario. 'He strangles Badger and fixes him in one of the sleigh seats, covers it and pins on the out of order sign. He hides in the van, waiting for the main gate to open. Then perhaps he sees Jeremy picking up his jacket and realises he'd got the wrong man. Okay, he'd killed the wrong guy, but he could have another go. He lies low in the van for a few days, waiting for an opportunity to try again, but then he sees Keavy and decides blackmail might be a better idea. He plans to demand a ransom in return for keeping quiet about the Quinns' roles in the drug thing.'

'You think it was a mistaken identity revenge killing rather than framing,' said Jasmine. 'But I really think you're onto something. It ties in with the kidnap.'

Katya patted Ivo on the back. It made sense and he could be right, she admitted to herself grudgingly. But how were they going to prove it? She sat in silence for a moment thinking about it.

'Where do we go with this?' Jonny asked.

A good question. Katya suspected Lugs might now be interested, and the police would take over and they would lose their case. But that would be worth it, wouldn't it? If it meant an innocent man going free? 'I'll sit on it for an hour or two,' she said. 'Lugs will be in touch about the kidnapping. I'll talk to him then.'

## 24

Jasmine had forgotten what teenage appetites were like. Keavy was sitting in the kitchen while Karim plied her with food. She'd started with a full English breakfast with a double helping of sausages. Then she'd moved on to pancakes with fresh strawberries and cream. Now she was eyeing a tray of chocolate cupcakes. Karim smiled fondly at her. 'I remember when you were like this,' he said to Jasmine. 'Growing teenage girl, full of energy and always hungry.'

Keavy had recovered well from her ordeal but missed the dogs. Jasmine had offered to take her to the circus to see them, but Keavy shook her head, her eyes filling with tears. 'Caitlyn could bring them here,' she suggested timidly.

So whoever Keavy was scared of, it wasn't Caitlyn. Flora had done her best to persuade Keavy to tell her what she was frightened of, but Keavy had remained tight-lipped. Flora had left it. 'Once she's back with her mum, she might open up.'

Cathy, Paddy's ex and Caitlyn and Keavy's mother, was due to arrive later that afternoon. Flora had arranged a car to pick her up at Heathrow. She wanted to talk to her before bringing her round to

*Jasmine's* to be reunited with her daughter – both her daughters, if Caitlyn was going to be there as well.

'Why don't we all go to the park?' Jasmine suggested. Would that be safe? There was, after all, a kidnapper still on the loose. 'I'll just call Flora and check it's okay,' she said, picking up her phone and explaining her plan.

'Fine,' said Flora. 'We can't keep the poor girl cooped up all day. I'll just get a couple of uniforms to keep an eye on things.'

Jasmine wasn't sure if a couple of uniforms would make her feel safer or remind her that danger still lurked out there somewhere. But Keavy thought it was a great idea. Dogs and police protection. She'd definitely have something to impress her friends with when she got home. Jasmine had washed her clothes and Keavy changed out of the baggy tracksuit she had borrowed and arranged her hair in a plait over one shoulder. Then Jasmine noticed her bare feet. 'What happened to your shoes?' she asked.

'I wasn't wearing any,' said Keavy. 'I always go barefoot in the summer.'

'Well, you can't walk to the park in bare feet,' said Jasmine. 'You'd better wear the flip flops they lent you at the police station.'

Keavy gave her a sulky look. 'They're gross,' she said.

'You can take them off once we get to the grass. I'll call Caitlyn and ask her to bring your shoes with her.'

Keavy sighed and tossed her hair over her shoulder.

FLORA'S two uniforms met them at the door of *Jasmine's* and they walked to the park together. Caitlyn was there before them, ready to greet Keavy with a hug. Keavy wriggled free and gathered the dogs into her arms, letting them slobber all over her in excitement. The two police constables stationed themselves at the entrance to the park and Jasmine and Caitlyn sat on a bench to talk.

'I feel dreadful,' said Caitlyn. 'I didn't even know she was gone. Not until the police called me.'

'She didn't wake you up when she left the caravan?'

'No, I was dead to the world. Granny called after the show the night before. She wanted to talk about moving on to the next site. We had a drink together. Something Granny had been given by one of the players in the band. I've no idea what it was, but it tasted kind of fruity and I didn't realise how strong it was. I was out like a light the moment I got back to the caravan, and I didn't wake up until Sergeant Green called me. She said Keavy was safe but that it was best for her to stay with you until Mammy gets here.'

'Did she say why?'

'She just told me it would be safer for Keavy not to be back at the circus. She said she'd arrange a safe place for us to meet.'

'Does she think someone in the circus kidnapped Keavy?'

'I'm not sure. I think she was just being careful.'

Jasmine agreed. 'No one knew what the kidnapper would do when he found out Keavy wasn't in the van. He might still be looking for her.'

'That's why those two policemen are watching us, I suppose.'

Jasmine nodded. 'What did Cordelia say?'

'I haven't seen her. She'd gone out by the time I woke up.'

That was strange. Why hadn't she woken Caitlyn up before she went out? 'Do you know where she went?'

Caitlyn shrugged. 'I asked Dad and all he knew was that she'd gone off in the Merc with Aidan at about half past eight.'

'And they weren't back by the time you left with the dogs?'

'No. But there could be some problem with the new site, I suppose.'

'Does that happen a lot?'

'Hardly ever.'

'Perhaps they're visiting Jeremy.'

'Yeah, maybe.'

An odd coincidence, though, that Cordelia and Aidan had left shortly after Keavy had been abducted.

Any further thoughts were interrupted by the arrival of Flora. She pulled her car up at the entrance to the park, had a word with one of the constables and then made her way to where Jasmine and Caitlyn were sitting. She was accompanied by an attractive woman in her forties. Caitlyn and Keavy's mother, Jasmine guessed, seeing a likeness; shoulder-length dark hair and an athletic build. Keavy was cartwheeling with the dogs and didn't immediately notice her arrival until Caitlyn called her over.

'Mammy,' she shouted, spotting her mother and running towards her, four dogs in her wake.

Cathy hugged both her daughters. 'So you've been having an adventure,' she said. 'Can't let you out of my sight for a moment, can I?'

Flora looked around anxiously. 'We need to get you all back to *Jasmine's*,' she said.

'You think this man is still hanging around?' asked Cathy, looking worried.

'The two uniforms haven't seen anything, but I'm not taking any chances. We'll go back to *Jasmine's* for a cup of tea and then we've booked you all on a flight to Dublin this evening. You'll be safe there. But we've alerted the Garda to keep an eye on you just in case.'

'I can't go,' said Caitlyn. 'I can't just leave the horses.'

'And I've got my dog act this evening,' said Keavy.

'Well, unless you're prepared to perform with an armed guard, I'm afraid that's off for the moment,' said Flora. 'We can't get hold of Mrs Quinn so I'm thinking we should cancel tonight's show.'

'That would be a disaster,' said Caitlyn. 'It's our last show here, so we can't put on an extra one like we did earlier in the week. We'd have to refund everyone, and it was fully booked.'

'I'll talk to my DI,' said Flora. 'We can't force you to close.'

'If my daughters are with me in Galway, would that make a difference?' Cathy asked.

'I think it would,' said Flora. 'Perhaps we can suggest they run the show without the dogs or the horses.'

'I think that would be okay,' said Caitlyn. 'Keavy's safety is more important. Tina, one of the trapeze girls, can stand in for me with the horses. There's a simpler act she knows. She'll jump at the chance of performing it. The dogs will just have to take the night off.'

'Then we'll talk to Paddy,' said Cathy. 'I'm sure he can look after the horses for one night. The dogs as well.'

THEY WALKED BACK to the café, where Jasmine checked that everything was running smoothly without her and then she made tea for all of them. Cathy called Paddy, and Flora checked in with Lugs, who agreed the final show could run as long as Keavy was safely on the flight to Dublin. 'He's arranging a police presence for tonight,' said Flora, ending the call.

Keavy was looking pale and scared. 'It's all right, darling,' said her mother, noticing her distress. 'Paddy will take care of the dogs. He won't let anything happen to them.'

'It's not that,' said Keavy. 'I just remembered something.'

They all stared at her. Was she about to identify her abductor?

'Something about the kidnapping?' Flora asked.

'Kind of. I... I just remembered something I said. After we'd picked up the hire car at Heathrow.'

'Something you told Martyn?' Cathy asked. 'While you were driving to Windsor?'

Keavy shook her head miserably. 'No, well, yes. Martyn was there but it was the other man.'

'Other man?' Flora asked, with a warning glance in Jasmine's direction.

'We met him just after we landed. He'd been on the same flight as us. Martyn knew him, I think. Anyway, he told him we were on our way to Quinn's Circus and we had a car to pick up.'

'There was someone else in the car with you?'

'He'd asked Martyn for a lift, or maybe Martyn just offered. I don't remember, sorry.'

'It's fine, Keavy,' said Flora. 'Just tell us about the man. Did you drop him off somewhere?'

'In town. He didn't come to the gate with us.'

'And you talked to him?'

'Yes,' she said in a whisper. 'He was asking about the circus and I told him about the dogs. I was excited because I hadn't seen them since they left for the tour, and I told him about my act with them and how I was going to be allowed to be in the show when I'd practised with Caitlyn.'

'And he frightened you?'

'Not then. He asked what the dogs were called, and I told him. But I said the big one, Brody, was called BrooBroo. It was my silly name for him, and it slipped out by mistake. I never use it any more.'

She was trembling and crying. Cathy put her arms around her, trying to comfort her. 'Don't worry, sweetie. We all have silly names for the animals sometimes. You don't need to fret about anyone making fun of you.'

Keavy shook herself free. 'It's not that. It's the kidnapper. After he grabbed me and I was struggling, he said, "Keep still or I'll kill the dogs, starting with BrooBroo".'

'But the dogs will be fine. The police will be there, and Paddy will take care of them tonight.'

'That's not what's worrying her,' said Flora with a frown, kneeling at Keavy's side. 'Do you know the man's name?'

Keavy shook her head. 'But Martyn will know, won't he? If they'd met before.'

'Oh my God, the kidnapper,' said Cathy, as she suddenly realised why Keavy was so frightened. She turned to Flora. 'Should I call Martyn?' she asked.

'Do you know where he is?' Flora asked.

'He's in Galway. He arrived back last night and I called him this morning when I knew I was flying over to be with Keavy. He said he'd take care of everything until I got back with her.'

'Call him now,' said Flora. 'And then let me speak to him.'

AN HOUR later Jasmine sank into a chair, exhausted. It had been a real roller coaster of a day. Keavy kidnapped and rescued, Martyn Roberts becoming a suspect and then almost immediately not one any more. Flora had returned to the police station, having seen Keavy, Caitlyn and their mother off to Heathrow with an armed driver and the promise of a police escort onto the plane. And then the police were searching the local countryside for the suspected kidnapper. The man Keavy told them travelled in the car from Heathrow to Windsor town centre, identified by Martyn Roberts as Donal Maguire. The man in Teddy's press story, who had been sent to prison for five years for something he swore he hadn't done. He was there to get his revenge on whichever Quinn was to blame for his incarceration.

*Enough for one day,* Jasmine thought, as Karim joined her, having closed down the café for the day. 'You look as if you need a quiet evening in front of the telly,' he said. 'Want to see if there's something weepy on Netflix?'

'I'm fine, Dad,' she said, pulling herself together. She needed to talk to Katya and the rest of the team. 'You watch your cricket. I'll just make a couple of calls.'

She talked to Katya first, recounting the events of the day. 'You've had quite a time,' said Katya, not without a note of envy.

'We need to make plans, don't we?' said Jasmine.

'Absolutely. But it can wait. Let Lugs' team go after Maguire first. If his DNA matches what they found on the carousel, I don't see how they can refuse to take another look at the murder.'

'I should let Jonny and Ivo know what's going on, shouldn't I?'

'Yeah,' said Katya. 'Keep them in the picture. We don't want them to feel left out.'

'It looks like Ivo's theory was right, doesn't it? Donal Maguire mistook Badger for Jeremy and when he found out, he got his revenge by kidnapping Keavy.'

'Maybe,' said Katya. 'But let's see what Lugs says.'

Jasmine ended the call, feeling rather flat. Why wasn't Katya more excited? Hadn't they almost proved Jeremy's innocence? If it was Donal Maguire's DNA on the carousel, they'd have to let Jeremy go, wouldn't they?

But it had been a long day and Jasmine was tired. She called Ivo and then Jonny and reported everything that had happened since that morning. Then she went down to the café kitchen and arranged an assortment of leftovers onto two dinner plates, poured two glasses of lemonade, and carried them up to where Karim was engrossed in the cricket.

# 25

Katya was enjoying a late afternoon snooze with the tennis on the TV when her phone rang.

'We've got him,' said Lugs.

'Got who?' Katya asked sleepily.

'Not interrupting anything, am I?' Lugs asked as she yawned down the phone.

'No, no, just watching the tennis,' she said, hoping he couldn't hear her yawning over the phone. She turned down the sound on the TV and, noticing it was no longer tennis but some kids' film, turned it off.

'Sleeping in front of the tennis, more like.'

'Might have nodded off for a second or two,' Katya admitted. 'What were you saying?'

'We've got the kidnapper. Arrested him this morning after some useful info from that friend of the victim's mum.'

Katya was wide awake now. 'Martyn Roberts?'

'That's the chappie.'

'Tell me more,' said Katya.

'Well,' said Lugs. 'Where to start?' He paused and Katya drummed her fingers on the chair. 'Roberts had got talking to a man at Dublin airport. Turns out they both knew the Quinn family, although in Roberts' case it was an ex Quinn.'

'Cathy Connor. Used to be married to Patrick.'

'That's right. Well, they got chatting about why they were both travelling to England. Roberts explained he was talent scouting, starting off at Quinn's Circus near Windsor. The bloke he met said he knew the people who ran the circus. Then Roberts mentioned that he was taking a friend's daughter to stay with her sister, er...'

'Caitlyn Quinn,' Katya filled in.

'Exactly. Well, it seemed this bloke was planning a camping trip in Swinley Forest. He had a big rucksack, so Roberts had no reason to question what he'd been told. Roberts offered him a lift and dropped him off in Windsor where he could, so he said, catch an early morning bus to the forest.'

'A bus?' said Katya. 'You must be joking. Buses are like hens' teeth these days.'

'I know that,' said Lugs. 'But Roberts isn't familiar with the area and it seemed a reasonable enough idea to him. Of course, the man he gave a lift to knew that perfectly well. He nicked a car from the long-term car park near the station.'

'Was he lying about Swinley Forest?'

'No, that bit was true. That's where we picked him up early this morning. He'd rigged up a basic kind of camp site for himself. Took a bit of finding – we had dogs and drones and God knows what out looking for him.'

'And you arrested him for kidnapping Keavy?'

'Yup. Aren't you going to ask his name?'

'Donal Maguire.'

'How did you know that?'

'I'm a good detective,' said Katya. 'Have you had a chance to interview him yet?'

'We have. At first, he denied anything to do with it. He was just an innocent holidaymaker, he said. Just after a bit of peace and quiet. But then we suggested, in view of his interest in the Quinns, he might know something about the death of Badger Waites. We'd done a bit of a background check on him by then and knew he'd been inside for drug dealing.'

'Did he have a solicitor with him?'

'No, he said he didn't want one. We can't force it on people.'

'Do you have evidence that he was the kidnapper?'

'No need. As soon as we brought up his criminal record and mentioned a murder, he admitted it. He told us the Quinns had set him up and planted evidence that led to his conviction and imprisonment five years ago. He didn't care what happened to him as long as he cleared his name. He was going to use Keavy to force a confession that they'd planted the evidence in his house.'

'Parcels of drugs, packages of money...'

'How did you know that?' Lugs asked.

'Read an article about the case. Our theory was that he was there to kill Jeremy in revenge but killed Badger Waites instead. They do look a bit alike.'

'Nice idea, but you're wrong.'

'How can you be sure? What about the DNA that you found on the carousel? Have you checked Maguire's?'

'We sent off a sample, but actually that will only be for confirmation. Maguire's DNA is already on the Irish database of offenders. It's not a match for what we found on the carousel.'

'Oh,' said Katya, disappointed.

'But...' said Lugs, with a pause for dramatic effect. 'We made a very interesting discovery.'

'I'm all ears,' said Katya.

'Our local forensic technician took an interest. We knew who all but one of the samples belonged to, but no one had thought to cross check them against each other.'

'And?'

'The unknown DNA was a match with Jeremy.'

Katya didn't understand. 'One person can't have two DNA results, can they?'

'Only if they've had a bone marrow transplant.'

'Has Jeremy had one?' This was becoming intriguing. No one had mentioned Jeremy ever having been seriously ill.

'No. Nothing like that. This was a family match that indicates a cousin or uncle, possibly a half-sibling.'

Katya was trying to get her head around that. The only half-sibling in the family, to her knowledge, was Keavy. She'd be a match of that kind with Caitlyn but not with Jeremy. What were they, step-cousins? The only other cousin was Joseph. Did that mean Jeremy and Joseph were in this together? No, Joseph was in London for the weekend. But could still be an accessory. 'Will you be testing Joseph?'

'We'll have to. But we've checked his background. By all accounts he and Badger were friends. Not particularly close ones and we can't find anything to suggest a motive. And even finding his DNA on the carousel wouldn't be conclusive. He could have been helping out there at some time. So right now, we aren't considering him as a suspect.'

Katya was glad about that. Clearing one of Cordelia's grandsons was difficult enough. Two of them would be impossible. And besides, she'd liked Joseph. He struck her as straightforward and honest. Her instinct was usually right about such things. But it still looked bleak for Jeremy. 'So Donal Maguire is definitely off the hook?'

'Looks like it for the murder at least, but he's now asked for legal representation. I suspect he has some kind of deal in mind.'

'A deal? Does that mean he has something to bargain with?'

'He hinted as much before he clammed up. He admitted to using the circus van as a hideout while he planned his abduction of Keavy. He slept in it the night before the murder and claims he was still there for most of the next three days, watching and planning.'

'Did he see Badger fall out of the carousel?'

'The van was parked too far away for that. He did notice the police presence though, so he left the site for a day or two, hoping it would die down.'

'Interesting.' Katya was piecing things together. 'Donal Maguire could have been planning some kind of hit on someone as revenge for his prison sentence. Then he discovered Keavy and decided that kidnapping her would give him greater leverage. He would be able to trade her for an admission that one of the Quinns had set him up. He probably planned to take Keavy on the Saturday night after the show, but by then the site was crawling with police so he put it off for a few days, using the van as an occasional base.' She assumed he had some evidence to support his claim and that he was planning to use it as a bargaining chip to reduce the charge of kidnapping.

'There's another thing,' said Lugs.

'About the murder or the kidnapping?'

'It's about the scrap of fabric you found on the gate. It definitely came from Badger's shirt cuff.'

'Which doesn't help much,' said Katya. 'Except that we now know how he got in. And we already knew he was inside, because his body was found there.'

'If anything,' said Lugs, 'it helps confirm that the murderer was someone on the inside. The only alternative being that he was killed outside and then carried in and left on the carousel as some kind of message. And that was discounted from the start. Forensics were sure he was killed on or near the carousel.'

'And it all points towards one or more of Cordelia Quinn's grandsons being guilty,' Katya said glumly. This was a roller coaster of a case. The moment alternative suspects appeared, something turned up to clear them.

'Don't feel too bad about it,' said Lugs. 'When this is all over, I'll take you out for a heavy evening's drinking.'

'Thanks,' said Katya, probably never having felt less like an evening out than she did at that moment.

Katya put the phone down and turned her thoughts to food. She could usually rely on that to cheer her up. But then she was interrupted by the phone again. This time it was Jasmine.

## 26

'Well,' said Jasmine, after Katya had repeated everything Lugs had told her. 'It's good news, isn't it? It means it's safe for Caitlyn and Keavy to come back now.'

'I suppose so. But they may not want to, not just yet anyway. We don't know how upset Keavy was by it.'

'Will that affect the sentencing?'

'Looks like there's some kind of deal in the pipeline. Maguire hinted he had evidence about the drugs case. He might use that to bargain for a lighter sentence.'

'Can he do that?'

'It's out of our hands now. I'm not sure even Lugs has any influence. It will probably all be left to the lawyers to sort out.'

'Tough on Keavy if he walks free.'

'I shouldn't think it will come to that. Like I said, it depends what information and evidence he has on offer.'

'I suppose we just have to wait and see. But I called you about something Teddy uncovered. I'm not sure if it makes any difference to our case, but it would be good if you came and looked over it.'

'I can come round now. I'm getting fed up on my own thinking we're getting nowhere.'

. . .

Half an hour later, Katya and Jasmine were in the office with cups of tea and some orange brioche buns that Karim wanted Katya's opinion on. 'He values your judgement,' said Jasmine.

'They're good,' she said, taking a bite. 'But I've not yet tasted anything made by your father that hasn't been delicious.' She reached for a second one as Jasmine pulled up a web page on the computer screen.

'Teddy found this. He said you'd want to see it. It was in a magazine that runs a monthly column on mid-life career changes and claims to publish "in depth, no holds barred" interviews.'

Katya leant forward and read:

*Rosemarie says goodbye to the circus*

*An interview by Connie Smucks*

The article was headed with an image of, in Katya's opinion, an excessively skinny woman wearing an all-in-one bodysuit in bright purple, decorated with a pattern of silver sequins. Katya stared at the picture, trying to understand her position. She had her chin resting on the floor with feet either side of her ears, toes pointing outwards. 'How on earth does she do that?' Katya asked.

'Can't imagine,' said Jasmine, laughing. 'You'd think she'd get stuck, wouldn't you?'

'Perhaps they have people to unpeel her.' She scrolled down from the picture and read the rest of the article.

*Well-known contortionist and escapologist Rosemarie Quinn is to retire. I spoke to her in her immaculate, if isolated, home on the Cork coast where she has lived on her own, when not travelling, for the last fifteen years. She gave me the impression that she was not a* people person. *'I'm hell to live with,' she told me. 'I retreat here to get away from the common herd.'*

*For the last two decades, after long and rigorous training in Ulan Bator, Rosemarie has wowed audiences with her exotic brand of Mongolian contortionism known as Uran Nugaralt. When asked why she chose to retire now, Rosemarie (49) replied, 'I have no wish to spend the rest of my life folding myself up into ever more outrageous positions in front of audiences. I prefer to quit before cellulite and arthritis take over.'*

*Rosemarie has travelled the world appearing with circuses in Russia, China and South America. She now plans to devote her life to rainforest conservation in Borneo.*

*Interestingly, although connected to the well-known Quinn's Circus through her marriage to Aidan Quinn, Rosemarie has never performed with them. 'I left Aidan many years ago,' she commented. 'It is an episode in my life that I prefer to forget, and I have no wish to discuss it further.'*

*She was equally dismissive when asked about the recent arrest of her son on a murder charge. 'I have no son,' was her only comment. So much for maternal forgiveness!*

'Fascinating,' said Katya. 'But I don't see how it helps our case.'

'Read Teddy's email.' Jasmine clicked it open for her. 'He's headed it, "Share with Katya if of interest".'

*Among the online comments,* Teddy wrote, *were many that criticised Rosemarie's lack of feeling for her son. There were heated arguments about what was the appropriate way for a mother to react when discovering her son could be a killer. Opinion was divided, but I had a sudden thought that perhaps Rosemarie was not disowning him at all. I dug around in the archives – not easy in Ireland, but the records are there if you know where to look. I already knew Jeremy's date of birth from the press conference and then it was easy to find the birth certificate. Hold on to your hats. Jeremy's parents were not Aidan and Rosemarie Quinn as you'd expect. There was no father's name recorded and his mother was called Lorinda Cinque. So Rosemarie was speaking literally. She has no son.*

*I've searched the internet and so far, I can't find Lorinda Cinque. Sounds French, doesn't it? Or perhaps Canadian. There must be adoption papers somewhere, but I don't know how to access them. Let me know if you'd like me to make enquiries about that.*

*Good luck with the case.*

*Teddy*

'What do you think?' Jasmine asked. 'Shall I ask him to see what he can find out?'

Katya drummed her fingers on the table, thinking. 'I don't know,' she said. 'Let me sleep on it.'

'It probably isn't relevant, is it?'

Things were tying themselves in knots in Katya's brain. She needed time to sort them out. 'The Quinns move on tomorrow, don't they?'

Jasmine nodded. 'Down to Blackbushe.'

'We should call round in the morning and update them on the kidnap arrest, and discuss how we're going to take things forward.'

'Okay,' said Jasmine. 'Do you want us all there?'

'I think so. Meet at the back gate at twelve. They should be around then. I'll probably suggest we all talk to different people. I'll get a list of questions together.'

'Okay,' said Jasmine. 'You look tired. I'll call Jonny and Ivo if you like.'

'You're a good girl,' said Katya, patting her on the shoulder. 'Forward that article to me, would you?'

Katya walked slowly home, an idea forming in her head. She'd go to the circus early, get Jonny to drive her. They would be busy packing up and she'd be able to snoop around without being noticed.

# 27

Jonny had never imagined what packing up a circus and moving it to a new location would be like. 'I'd better park at the far end of the car park,' he said, looking at the activity near the back gate, which was open to allow an endless stream of trucks, lorries, horse boxes and vans on and off the site. On one side of the gate, tents were being taken down and loaded onto the back of a flatbed truck. Inside the gate, he watched as the roof of the big top, released from its scaffold of poles and ropes, floated to the ground to be rolled up and loaded onto one of a fleet of lorries. The tiers of seating, he supposed, had already gone.

'We bring in a specialist team,' said a voice behind him.

'Good morning, Paddy,' said Jonny, turning to greet him. 'I hope we're not going to be in your way. Katya thought we should touch base before you move on.' He looked round but Katya was nowhere in sight.

'Like I said, we've a specialist team. Come over to my caravan and we can think about how to proceed once we've moved. Any progress on the case?'

'Not as much as we'd like. We've identified likely suspects, only to have our hopes dashed.' Feeling it might be best to keep off the topic of Jeremy for now, he decided to change the subject. 'You know they've arrested Keavy's kidnapper?'

'I heard. Nothing to do with Badger's murder though?'

'That's what the police are saying, but I think there's stuff they're not telling us.'

Paddy nodded. 'The defence lawyers are saying the same. I called them this morning.'

'Don't give up hope,' said Jonny. 'There are still a few leads to follow.' He wished he was as confident as he sounded.

'You on your own?'

'Katya was with me. We're meeting the others in the car park at twelve. They both have to work this morning. I'm not sure where Katya is now.'

'She probably popped in to talk to Mother. She'll be tidying paperwork before the move.' He looked at his watch. 'She's planning to go into town for a hairdo, but she might not have left yet. Then she usually takes herself out for lunch and leaves the rest of us to get on with it. We move the caravans last so we can check the site before we hand it back to the owner. Watch it,' he said, pulling Jonny to one side as a horse box drove past. 'It's hard work without either Caitlyn or Jeremy here to help. I had to load the horses myself and Aidan's got to supervise packing up the funfair as well as all the other backstage stuff.'

'Will Caitlyn be back soon?'

'She's hoping to rejoin us in a day or two. I've got someone to tow her caravan down to the new site. I'm hoping Keavy will be back as well now they've arrested the kidnapper. We've missed her – the dogs are very popular with audiences.'

Where the hell had Katya got to? She'd muttered something about table lamps and disappeared into the jumble of vans, trucks and the burly-looking people loading them. As Paddy unlocked his caravan, Jonny found his phone and sent her a quick text: *With Paddy in his caravan, call me if you need anything.*

They went inside and Paddy made coffee while they talked through the set-up on the new site, and how they might proceed with the problem of proving Jeremy's innocence when the circus was no longer on their doorstep.

'You won't be far from here,' said Jonny. 'I could drive us over for a meeting once you're settled.'

'Good idea. Mother's visiting Jeremy again tomorrow and then talking to the new solicitor, an English guy that our Irish lawyers dug up. Mother and Aidan went to see him yesterday, but she needs to consult Jeremy before they engage him. There may be stuff you can do after that. I'll call you.'

Jonny thought he should probably go and find Katya, but he didn't want to get in the way of all the work outside, and Paddy didn't seem in any hurry to get rid of him. Katya would text or call him if she needed anything.

It was very pleasant sitting in the caravan, traditional Gypsy style on the outside with a thoroughly modern interior. State-of-the-art capsule kitchen, small walk-in shower, a MacBook Pro attached to a laser printer. Even double glazing, Jonny suspected, since he was unaware of any of the noise outside. 'Nice setup,' he said. 'Did you modernize it yourself?'

'We all did our own designs for the interiors and worked through the same outfitting company, who did us a deal. Mother insisted we kept to the original exteriors but using the circus colours. We had a free hand with the interiors. We spend a lot of time on the road, so we need to be comfortable inside and keep up our corporate image outside.'

'Advertising while on the move,' said Jonny. He was familiar with that, having been involved with the design of his own company's fleet of lorries in the days before he'd become a detective. 'Do you have WiFi?'

Paddy laughed. 'People used to ask about electricity and drains. Now WiFi is nearly always the first thing they want to know. And yes, we do. GPS routers.' He pointed to a box with winking lights under a countertop that Jonny had failed to notice.

'I suppose I should go and see where Katya has got to,' he said, looking at his watch.

'No rush,' said Paddy. 'She'll call you when she needs you. Have another coffee and I've got some cake that Norah made.'

*Why not?* He'd done what Katya had asked and talked to Paddy. He'd only get in the way wandering around outside and he was sure Norah baked excellent cakes. Her biscuits had been delicious.

THE PREVIOUS EVENING, Katya had walked home from *Jasmine's* with her brain spinning. As soon as she got back to the flat, she poured herself a gin and tonic and opened up Google on her phone. She should have stayed in the office, she realised as she squinted at the tiny text on her screen. But she wasn't going back there now, and with some judicious pinching and zooming she found what she wanted. It was something they'd all overlooked. She grabbed some paper and made notes. Then she read what she had written several times and tapped the pencil against her teeth while she made plans. Having read Teddy's email while with Jasmine, she now clicked the link and read it again. And suddenly it hit her between the eyes. With this last bit of research and a reread of the crime scene report, she'd stumbled on a solution. She'd found the final link in the chain. She knew who the murderer was. But how to prove it? She was fairly sure she knew where to find what she was looking for, but she'd need more than a suspicion. She had to get actual evidence, even a confession if she was clever.

She was meeting Jonny at the circus the next day. Better, she'd thought, if it was just the two of them. Ivo and Jasmine had to work in the morning, so she arranged for Jonny to pick her up early and for the other two to meet them there later.

Arriving on site, she was pleased to see it was every bit as chaotic as she'd hoped. Moving a circus and all its bits and pieces was a huge job. Everyone was occupied and no one was too concerned about what she was doing or where she was going. She gave Jonny a list of things to discuss with Paddy, which would keep them both out of the way for what she needed to do. She did a quick check around the rest of the family. Dara and Joseph were busy loading up music stands, lights and boxes of band music. Aidan was shouting instructions to the fairground crew, who were dismantling rides and loading them onto lorries. Cordelia, she learned, had gone to get her hair done in Windsor. Katya was not surprised. Mrs Quinn was hardly the lorry-loading type. She'd probably go for the full works beauty-wise, linger over an expensive lunch – no shortage of places she could do that in Windsor – and then take a leisurely drive to Blackbushe, where the circus had rented three fields adjoining the airfield and where someone would have her caravan all set up for her.

Amid all the activity, it was easy to give Jonny the slip. She wondered if she should have told him what she planned to do, but he would either have told her she was mad to even think about it, or he'd have wanted to go with her. This was something she had to do alone, because what she planned could be dangerous and illegal if she was discovered. And in any case, it would be faster on her own. A quick look around, a few photos taken on her phone and a rapid getaway, all hopefully without being seen. 'Just going to check a table lamp,' she said, moving away into the crowd before she knew whether or not he'd heard her. She hoped he hadn't, because she didn't want to go into details.

She knew which caravan it was; the only one not in the circle with the others, Caitlyn had explained, although she hadn't explained why. Just not wanting to be part of the group, Katya supposed, and right now that suited her very well. This caravan was parked close to the back fence where there was no one about. Everyone was too busy packing up, fully occupied on the other side of the site.

As she approached the caravan, Katya glanced over her shoulder to make doubly sure no one had followed her. Satisfied no one had, she climbed the two steps and knocked on the door. No one answered, so she waited a moment and knocked again. Still no answer. It was just as she'd expected. She had an excuse prepared just in case anyone was in, but it was a rather woolly one and she was glad she'd not needed it. She tried the door handle and found it locked, which again was what she'd expected. She left the door and did a quick walk round the caravan just to make sure no one had left a window open. They hadn't, and even if they had, Katya doubted she would have been able to squeeze through. She returned to the door and, after another quick check that no one was about, she reached into her pocket and pulled out a leather pouch engraved with a name: Dodger Hodges.

Katya had arrested Dodger following a series of burglaries around the town. As burglars went, Dodger was among the more charming she'd dealt with. 'A real gent,' Lugs had commented wryly, as he watched Dodger being loaded into the paddy wagon that would take him on an already familiar trip to the remand prison. 'Old school, your good-mannered, non-violent type of felon.' Katya had agreed. Dodger had, after all, doffed his hat to her as he was carted off. He'd been sent down for four years and let out after three. He called in at the police station on his release to deliver the news that his most recent stint in prison had done him the world of good. He was retiring, hanging up his housebreaking kit and flying off to sunny Spain to live with his son. He'd given his set of lock pickers in their smart leather case to Katya. 'To remember me by,' he told her as he left the police station to embark on his new, but in Lugs' words probably not entirely crime-free life abroad. Katya appreciated the gesture and put them away safely in her jumper drawer where they had remained. She'd never needed to pick a lock. Until today. They'd not been taught how to do it at police training college. They were more into pry bars and battering rams, so Katya had no idea how to use the kit. But what was Google for if not to teach one how to do stuff? Half an hour of close online study and she knew exactly what to do.

She opened the case and chose a tool that reminded her of her recent visit to the dentist. She had the door open in a matter of seconds and, after another furtive look around, went inside, closing the door behind her.

First things first. The table lamp. There wasn't one, which supported her theory. Even better, the resident wasn't a regular doer of housework and there was a clear, dust-free circle on the small table on which the lamp would have stood. Katya took a photo of it. Then she turned to her more serious search. It took her a while and she was beginning to think it had been a wild goose chase. And then she spotted it. The edge of a green cardboard folder poking out from under a pillow on one of the bunks. She pulled it out and flicked through the contents. Perfect. Exactly what she'd expected. She spent a few moments taking photos on her phone and then tucked the folder back under the pillow and returned the phone to her pocket. It was time to leave. She headed for the door, but before she got there it opened and she found herself staring into the barrel of a gun.

JONNY LOOKED AT HIS WATCH. There was still no sign of Katya and it was nearly time to meet up with Jasmine and Ivo. He'd enjoyed talking to Paddy and they'd made a sizeable dent in Norah's cake. He looked out of the window. While he'd been in there, the site had changed from a chaotic mass of ropes and poles, sheets of canvas and disjointed bits of fairground rides, into a more or less empty field with areas of dead grass. 'Quite a difference,' he commented.

'All on its way to the Blackbushe site,' said Paddy. 'The family caravans stay behind so we can do a final check and handover to the owner, or in this case to the owner's agent.' Across the field Jonny spotted four skips, all full to the brim with litter. And on the far side of the gate, he could see Jasmine and Ivo throwing sticks for Harold, who was enjoying the freedom of the now deserted campsite.

'I'd better be going,' he said. 'Thanks for the cake.'

Paddy slapped him on the back. 'We'll meet up again after the move,' he said. 'Make it a dram of whiskey next time. Although to be honest, I'll be glad to get back to a pint or two of good old Dublin Guinness.'

'I've never really been a Guinness drinker.'

'That's because you've never tasted the real thing. Now, if you ever come to Dublin, we'll make a night of it.'

Jonny didn't doubt it. Paddy looked like someone who knew his way around the pubs of Dublin. They'd be the real deal, dark décor, old furniture and stained-glass windows. And there would be live Irish music, singing and even dancing. It would be rowdy, the fun punctuated with the occasional street punch-up. Perhaps he'd make Dublin their next holiday destination. It would probably be free of the forty-degree temperatures and forest fires that were going to bring a halt to Mediterranean holidays any time now. 'You're on,' said Jonny. 'Next time I'm in Dublin. But give one of us a call once you're settled at Blackbushe.'

'Will do,' said Paddy, opening the door for him.

Jonny stepped out into the field, which had somehow shrunk now it was empty of circus paraphernalia. He looked around but there was still no sign of Katya and, looking at his phone, no message from her either. He strolled across the field to join the others.

'Hi,' Jasmine shouted, waving when she saw him. Harold bounded up to him, wagging his tail.

'Any of you seen Katya?' he asked.

'We thought she was with you,' said Ivo.

'She's not called you or sent a text?'

They both looked at their phones and shook their heads. Jonny tapped her number but it went straight to her voicemail. She must have turned it off. But why would she do that? They stared at the empty field. All they could see were three remaining caravans huddled together, another one parked by the fence at the far side of the field.

'Did she say she was leaving the site?' Ivo asked. 'Could she have gone home?'

'The plan was to meet here, update Cordelia on the arrest of the kidnapper and plan where we go from here,' said Jasmine. 'Teddy sent us a strange news article about Jeremy's mother.'

'What sort of article?' Ivo asked.

Jasmine opened it on her phone and handed it to him. 'Nothing that alters the case, I don't think.'

Ivo read it and handed the phone to Jonny. 'Can't see how that changes anything,' he said.

'Did Katya say where she was going when you last saw her?' Jasmine asked.

Jonny tried to remember. Katya had said something to him but then he'd caught sight of Paddy and hurried over before he disappeared. 'She was going to see Cordelia, I think. Something about a table lamp?' It hadn't meant much to him at the time, but now Ivo had turned pale. 'You okay?' he asked. It was a hot day; perhaps he'd been running around too energetically with Harold. He offered Ivo his bottle of water.

'Table lamp?' said Ivo. 'You sure?'

'Fairly,' said Jonny. 'I remember thinking it was odd and wondering if I'd misheard her.'

Ivo grabbed his arm. 'Jonny, you really can be slow at times. Think about it. Table lamp.'

Jonny thought. 'No, sorry. I don't get it.'

Jasmine sighed. 'For goodness' sake, Jonny. Table lamp – plaited flex?'

'The kind that Badger was strangled with,' Ivo added.

'Oh, God,' said Jonny as the penny dropped. 'The murder weapon.'

'You don't think Cordelia was the murderer, do you?' Ivo asked. 'She's quite tall, and strong.'

'Just two things wrong with that idea,' said Jasmine. 'She was the one who wanted us to get Jeremy out of jail and find a different suspect. Plus, what motive could she have had?'

'We should check out Cordelia's caravan,' said Jonny. 'Katya's probably just chatting with her over coffee.' That was, after all, what he'd been doing himself for most of the morning. 'Do you know which is her caravan?'

'I'm not sure. It looks different when there are only three.'

'Well, the one closest to us is Paddy's,' he said. 'It's where I've been for the last hour.'

'Caitlyn's is the one next to Paddy, so Cordelia's must be the other one.'

'Unless it's that one over by the fence,' said Ivo.

'No, that's Aidan's,' said Jasmine. 'He likes to be on his own. Let's try the nearest ones first.'

They walked across the field and knocked on the door. No reply.

Ivo peered in through the window. 'Looks like it's all packed up ready to go,' he said. He squinted for a moment longer. 'I can see a table lamp,' he said. 'It's lying on one of the bunks with the flex curled round it and a plug on the end.'

'They unplug all the electrics from the generator for the move,' said Jonny. 'No need to unplug a lamp, but I suppose it's less likely to roll onto the floor and break.'

'The point is,' said Ivo impatiently, 'the lamp is still there with its flex, so it can't have been used to kill Badger.'

'A good point,' said Jonny. 'But we still don't know where Katya is, or Cordelia.'

A man walked past, trundling bags of dog food in a wheelbarrow. 'If you're looking for Mrs Quinn,' he said, 'she's gone to the hairdressers. Her caravan will be going soon and all. Not to the hairdressers.' He laughed at his own joke. 'She never stays for the clean-up. She'll be driving herself to the next site when she knows it's all set up waiting for her.'

'So what now?' Ivo asked as they watched the man walk away.

'Check out the other caravans,' said Jasmine.

They looked through the windows of the other two, which were packed up ready to go just as the first one was.

'What about that one over there?' Ivo asked. He and Harold bounded across the field without waiting for an answer. He looked through one of the windows and then hunkered down on the grass, gesturing to Jasmine and Jonny to be quiet. 'She's in there,' he whispered as soon as they were close enough to hear. 'With Aidan.'

Katya took a step back. She bumped into the edge of the bunk with the back of her knees and sat down abruptly. The muzzle of the gun followed her. 'Going to shoot me, are you?'

'You're trespassing.'

'Guilty as charged, but it's hardly a capital offence.'

'Matter of opinion.'

*Keep him talking.* Her training was clicking into action. A suicide situation? You kept talking. People don't tend to jump off tall buildings or bridges mid-sentence. Even someone else's sentence. She'd only been in that situation once, but it worked then. A hostage? Again, keep talking. She'd never experienced that. And this was neither a suicide nor a hostage. But the principle was the same. At least, Katya hoped it was, and anyway, she wasn't going to sit there in silence waiting for the fatal shot. She might as well go out in full flow. 'So,' she said conversationally. 'Why did you kill Badger Waites?'

'What makes you think I did?'

'Because your table is missing its lamp, or more to the point, its flex. Which, like those in the other caravans, is plaited flex of the kind used to strangle Badger.' She didn't know for sure that all the caravans had the same lights, but she'd taken a quick look inside Dara's caravan and noted that he a similar lamp.

'So what?' said Aidan. 'Like you just said, other caravans have the same lamps. I don't see you accusing Dara. Or my mother.'

'Dara has an alibi. And your mother, well...' She wasn't going any further with that right now. 'And besides, an innocent man would hardly be standing there pointing a gun at me. So one more time, why did you kill Badger Waites?'

Aidan shrugged. 'Had my reasons.'

What a pity she'd forgotten to turn her phone voice recorder on. But recorded confessions didn't go down well in court. If she survived this, it would be her word against his, and of the two of them she'd be the more believable. And if he killed her, he'd still be done for murder. A win-win situation, one might say. Not for herself, obviously, but justice would be done.

'No doubt you did have your reasons. But can you explain why you are prepared to see your son serve a life sentence for something he didn't do?' Did she detect a slight shake of his wrist? Probably not a very good sign, although it could mean his aim wasn't all it should be, and he'd hit her in the leg or shoulder rather than her head.

'Huh?' he said with a frown.

'Perhaps I should have said your adopted son?'

He steadied his hand on the gun and scowled at her. 'What do you know about that?'

'I keep my ear to the ground, and I have a few useful contacts.' One of whom had provided her with details of Jeremy's parentage. At least she could be sure that Teddy Strang would write her a humdinger of an obituary.

'Collateral damage,' said Aidan. 'Jeremy's always been a trouble-maker. Nearly got me arrested over that drugs business. He and Donal Maguire thought they could shop me to the Garda. But I've got loyal mates in Dublin and we stopped that in its tracks. I'm damned if I'm going to let it happen again.'

And he would no doubt have done the same to Jeremy if necessary – plant stuff in his house and get him incarcerated as well. 'You set Donal Maguire up. Twice, in fact. First by planting evidence in his house and again by killing Badger and setting it up to look like a revenge killing. A pity they arrested Jeremy instead of Maguire. How did you plan to get around that?'

'No need. They've got Maguire for kidnapping Keavy. Could be twelve years for that.'

'So you get rid of them both. And if you kill me there'll be no one to tell the truth.'

'You're not quite as dumb as you look.' He steadied his shaking right arm by grabbing it with his left. Then he took aim.

'Of course,' said Katya, 'you'll have the problem of getting rid of my body.'

'Let me tell you something,' he said with a smirk. 'You chose the wrong day to come snooping. You'll have noticed all the toilets just over the fence? Three weeks here and the tanks will be full to bursting. And today they get collected. It's a good system. They're winched onto trucks just as they are. No need to drain them so no one gets their hands dirty, and the stink is minimal. It all goes off to the treatment centre where I'd imagine it sits around for a while. That lets the solid matter disintegrate, see.'

She did see. Not a lot left of Katya Roscoff after a few days in a slurry tank. And by the time what was left of her was discovered, Aidan Quinn would be a long way away. Somewhere that had no extradition arrangements with the UK or Ireland. 'And what do you intend to do with that folder of stuff you've hidden under your pillow? Waiting for the tooth fairy, are you?'

That wiped the grin off his face. 'What do you know about that?'

'I know that Donal Maguire planned to give it to Jeremy. He'd arranged to meet him, but for some reason Jeremy didn't turn up. I suspect he was delayed in a certain young lady's bedroom. But that didn't matter. Donal gave it to Badger Waites, who was avoiding a spot of rat disposal at his own home and came to work early. Why Donal trusted Badger to hand it over I don't know. Except that Badger Waites, according to everyone who knew him, was the epitome of honesty. Perhaps that shone out of him like some saintly halo. I wouldn't know. I never met the guy. But I suspect that folder has enough evidence tucked inside it to prove that both he and Jeremy were entirely innocent of drug dealing and point the finger firmly at your good self.' Katya had had just enough time to scan through the folder and knew its contents. It was Donal's bargaining chip and no doubt he had kept a copy. But just in case, Katya had uploaded it to her cloud storage as soon as she'd taken the photo and just before she turned her phone off. Why had she turned her phone off? So that Jonny couldn't pester her, wanting to know what she was up to. It was possibly not the best decision she could have made. The suggestion that Donal had given the evidence to Badger was pure guesswork on her part. But it obviously rang true with Aidan, which was a mixed blessing given that he was now about to shoot her.

'It's easy to get rid of. Just needs a box of matches.'

'I expect you're right. Just remember not to set fire to that ticket to Buenos Aires that's tucked inside it.'

Katya had run out of words. She'd kept talking for as long as she could, but other than enquire about the weather in Argentina, she could think of nothing else to say. She might as well close her eyes and wait for the inevitable. *Well,* she thought philosophically, *it will save me from a cold and miserable old age.* But as she was about to shut her eyes, something caught her attention. Movement at the window that was partly blocked by Aidan's shoulder. No matter. There was enough uncovered for her to see the top of Ivo's head appear and then disappear again almost at once. Katya was both touched by the fact that they had come to rescue her and terrified of what they were about to walk into. But she had no time to think about that as the door burst open and Jonny rushed into the caravan, followed by Jasmine and then Ivo and Harold. *Stupid, stupid,* Katya thought, watching in horror as Aidan swung around. But there was safety in numbers. In the split second that Aidan hesitated in his choice of who to shoot first, Harold charged forward and bit him on the leg. Your average dog would probably hang on and shake it like a rat he was trying to kill, and get itself shot in the process. But Harold was no average dog and Katya had to admire his tactics. He let go of Aidan's leg and leapt up at him, tackling him in the groin. Katya, having been trained in the disarming of suspects, launched herself at Aidan, grabbed his wrist and forced him to let go of the gun. She pulled his arms behind his back and handcuffed him. People, notably Lugs Lomax, laughed at her for keeping handcuffs in her pocket. 'If you'd wanted to go around cuffing people,' he told her, 'you shouldn't have retired.' Well, thank you Lugs. She'd just proved him wrong.

The gun had skittered across the floor and come to a halt at Jonny's feet. He picked it up gingerly and slipped it into his pocket. Then he pulled out his phone and called for police help.

# 28

It was an awkward meeting, but no worse than Katya had expected. They had done as Cordelia asked and proved Jeremy's innocence. Unfortunately, it was at the expense of her son Aidan, who had now been arrested and charged, not only with the murder of Badger Waites but also of organising a gang of drug smugglers. And of course, the attempted murder of Katya.

Maguire, it emerged, had not wasted a second of his time while in prison. He had used it to build a case for himself. He'd lobbied other prisoners, who knew people who knew other people who knew a great deal about Aidan Quinn and his methods. He'd collected written and recorded statements. He'd also trawled the internet – a surprise to Katya because she'd always assumed prisoners weren't allowed to do that – and dug up more evidence from social media sites. None of which did him any good at all. On his release he'd taken all his information to the police, who told him none of it was evidence and enquired who he thought would take the word of a load of convicted prisoners. Maguire then raised every penny he could by borrowing from friends and relations, and took it all to a lawyer, who told him much the same. He had one last hope. Jeremy Quinn. Jeremy had not come forward at the time of Maguire's trial. He would have been intimidated by his father in some way and forced to keep quiet. But whatever, it could be worth another attempt. Previous experience told him Jeremy might be unwilling to cooperate, in which case he would need a plan B. He'd no idea what this was going to be until at the last moment, a plan came into his head. It was while he was travelling from Heathrow to Windsor. He was being given a lift in a hire car by a man who was driving a friend's daughter to stay with her sister at Quinn's Circus. His original plan had been to find a car from somewhere near Heathrow and borrow it. He'd drive himself to Quinn's, where he would confront Jeremy with the evidence and hope that he would then do the right thing and go to the police to back him up. That might not happen, and if it didn't, his second plan could work just as well. His meeting with Martyn Roberts, a man he'd met before but didn't know well, was a stroke of luck. And it was during the drive with him that the new plan came into his head. He had a free ride to the circus and if Jeremy failed to help him, he'd pick a car from the car park, find a quiet place to camp well away from any kind of civilisation and make his way back to the circus when he was ready to put his plan B into action. He already had a place in mind having googled *wild camping Berkshire* before he left Ireland. Not wanting to leave a trail, he asked Martyn to drop him and his rucksack in town, where he quickly found an anonymous car to break into and *borrow*. He drove it to the circus and parked in the car park, but then realised he hadn't allowed for the security that was in place at night. Stealing one of the circus vans was genius. He could get through the gate and have somewhere to sleep without raising any suspicion.

From the van he sent Jeremy a text: *Meet me at the carousel at seven tomorrow morning*. He added a few kisses. Jeremy was one for the girls, and with luck he'd assume this was from the lady of his dreams. He used a SIM card he'd bought specially and fitted into his own phone. Once he'd sent the message, he replaced his own SIM and dropped the other into a drain. His plan was to hand the folder to Jeremy in the hope that he would support him, and then take his own copy to the police.

But Jeremy didn't turn up. Instead, he met an odd-looking bloke with a strange streak of white in his hair, who asked him what he was doing there when the public weren't allowed in until much later in the day. What could he do? This guy worked for Jeremy, so the obvious solution was to give him the folder and ask him to pass it on. Then he returned to the campsite to await developments. It was while scrolling through some news sites on his phone the next day that he learnt of Badger Waites' death and of Jeremy's arrest for his murder. The disappointment was shattering. Jeremy was not going to do anything to help him. Had he even got the folder? Even if he had, showing it to either his father or the police would be the last thing on his mind. And if it was discovered he was there, Donal himself could become the prime suspect. Plan B could still work, though. No one need know he was at the carousel that morning, and he had no motive for killing a stranger. He could still use the girl, but he'd be communicating with Aidan rather than Jeremy.

It was never his intention to hurt her. Once he had the confession he wanted from Aidan Quinn, he'd take her back unharmed. He'd even bought bags of sweets and some teen magazines to keep her happy while they waited. The day before the kidnap, he drove the car to Slough and parked it in a supermarket car park. He then hitched back to the circus, walking the final half-mile from the town, and hunkered down in the van until the young lady gave the dogs their morning exercise. He'd discovered a set of keys for the van in a shed and taken them, so that he could keep the van locked and wouldn't need to keep hot-wiring it when he wanted to drive it.

But then it all went pear-shaped. The girl escaped and all Donal could do was abandon the van, return to the campsite and plan his own getaway. He thought he was safe there. It was miles from anywhere and no one knew that he was the kidnapper. But as luck would have it, the girl recognised him as the man Martyn had given a lift to. And Martyn himself knew where he'd planned to camp. Donal had kicked himself for being stupid enough to tell him, but at the time he'd assumed he'd be well on his way back to Dublin as soon as his job was done.

He was found and arrested within hours of arriving at his improvised camp. But all was not lost. He could still negotiate with the police. He had the evidence that would bring down Aidan Quinn. And they could hardly imprison Donal himself when he'd just proved he should never have been locked up the first time.

KATYA HAD PIECED ALL of this together from Donal Maguire's statements to the police, and she was now with Cordelia Quinn, explaining it to her. Cordelia poured them both a stiff gin and sat back in her chair. Considering another of her close relations had been charged with murder, she looked in good form. At least Jeremy was now free. *Quid pro quo* in a way, Katya thought.

Cordelia took a swig of her gin. 'Will they let Maguire go?' she asked. 'If he was wrongfully imprisoned the first time?'

'I have absolutely no idea,' said Katya. 'I'm happy to let the police and lawyers slug that one out.'

'I should congratulate you for catching the real murderer, I suppose.'

'No need,' said Katya modestly. 'I'm just sorry for... well, you know.'

'I've always had my doubts about Aidan,' she said. 'He takes after his father. Ruthless and violent. Very different from Paddy, who is like me.'

'Charming?'

'If you say so. I should probably add devious, but there's no harm in him, or me. And then there is Jeremy. I'm happy to have him back.'

Jeremy had been released the day Aidan was arrested. There was no need to detain him in the light of Aidan's confession and his attempt on Katya's life. 'We were about to release him anyway,' Lugs had told her. 'Someone gave him an alibi.'

'If he had an alibi, why didn't he use it sooner?'

'Turns out he was a real gent after all. Not only did he walk his lady friend home that night, he kept schtum about the fact that he'd not sneaked out of the house until her father had left for work the next morning. The young lady in question was terrified of what her father would do if he discovered his daughter had spent the night under his roof with a circus hand, and Jeremy agreed not to tell anyone.'

'Her father would have turned a blind eye if it had been an officer in the Royal Guards?'

'Probably,' said Lugs with a laugh.

'She was a bit slow coming forward, wasn't she?'

'She didn't think she'd be believed, apparently. But it could also have had something to do with the fact that her parents have now departed for a holiday in the south of France for a month and she's home alone.'

'I'm still amazed Jeremy didn't tell you himself.'

'Oh, he would have done once he realised it really was going to trial. Someone,' said Lugs, beginning a close study of his feet, 'tipped off his solicitor, who persuaded Jeremy to admit it.'

'And the alibi checks out?'

'It does. We questioned them both separately and there's no way they could have been in touch with each other after Jeremy's arrest.'

KATYA SWALLOWED a mouthful of her own gin. How was she going to put this? Lost one son and gained another? She was still pondering it when Cordelia said, 'When did you realise it was Aidan?'

'Just the evening before I tackled him. When I realised it was a premeditated murder.'

'Because of the flex?'

'Partly, but by then I'd ruled out everyone else. Jeremy's motive was always weak, and once Lugs confirmed what was in Maguire's folder, it was even weaker. But really it fell into place when I worked out the anagram.'

Cordelia gave her an inscrutable look.

'I'm not as dumb as I look,' said Katya, as Aidan had pointed out when about to shoot her. 'I'm a big crossword fan.'

'Ah,' said Cordelia. 'Lorinda Cinque. Cleverly worked out.'

'Google's a wonderful thing,' she said. 'Very educational. Once I'd worked out your little puzzle, I looked more closely at DNA family matches. The DNA had to be Aidan's. Everyone assumed he was out of the picture. He might have had a motive and plenty of opportunity, but he wasn't a DNA match. Well, he was, but no one thought to test him. The police found two samples. One was Jeremy's. The other they later identified as a family match of twenty-five percent. So a half-brother or uncle. Aidan was out of the picture. As Jeremy's father he would have been a fifty percent match. As far as the police knew, Jeremy didn't have a half-brother, so suspicion fell on Paddy, Dara and Joseph. There wasn't enough evidence for any of them to be brought in and questioned, because at that point they were sure Jeremy was guilty. And they had alibis. Martyn Roberts was with Paddy in his caravan until nine that morning. Joseph was in London for the weekend and Dara was with Norah all night. And even when we discovered Aidan wasn't Jeremy's father, no one thought it could be his DNA. He wasn't an uncle or a cousin but he could be...' Katya looked at Cordelia, wondering how she was going to react.

'A half-brother,' said Cordelia. 'Well worked out.' She remained stony-faced.

'I'm thinking that should you offer your own DNA, it will show a fifty percent match. You're his mother, aren't you?'

Cordelia nodded slowly. 'A bad one,' she said. 'But I did what I thought best at the time.'

'You could have had him adopted, but you wanted to keep him close.' In other words, she'd loved him. He was a tearaway but she couldn't bear the thought that he'd be sentenced to life in prison.

'He'd have been better growing up thinking Paddy was his father. But Paddy had Caitlyn and Dara had Joseph. Aidan and Rosemarie couldn't have children. It seemed like the perfect solution. But Rosemarie and Jeremy never got on, and once she left, Aidan blamed Jeremy and couldn't forgive him. But Jeremy and I bonded. I tried to be the perfect granny. I rescued him when he was in trouble, paid for his schooling, gave him a role in the circus.'

'And Jeremy's real father?'

'A good friend of mine, but long dead. He left Ireland before I knew I was pregnant, and I never told him. I was forty-six. I thought I was past all that, so it came as a shock.'

'And you were sure this man was the father?'

'Completely. Oliver was away on business much of the time, and by then we were more like business partners than husband and wife. He'd have killed me if he'd ever found out.'

'He didn't notice you were pregnant?'

'I said I was suffering from nervous exhaustion and went to stay with an old friend in the north until Jeremy was born. It was easy to falsify the birth certificate. A little money goes a long way with rural bureaucrats. I simply said I had lost my ID and handed over a handful of banknotes. My husband never suspected anything. Aidan was never close to his father, so Oliver barely noticed the arrival of another baby in the family.'

'Does Jeremy know?'

Cordelia sighed, and for the first time Katya thought she noticed an expression of regret. 'No. I should tell him, but it will be a shock on top of everything else.'

'Maybe less of a shock than you think. You say you've always been close. He probably already thinks of you as the nearest person he's got to a mother. And I would imagine discovering his supposed father was a murderer will have been a worse shock.'

'I must tell him about his real father. I should have told him years ago. He was a good man and Jeremy could have been like him if I hadn't left it to Aidan to bring him up.'

But had she really had any alternative? Admitting it to Oliver would have broken the family up. Have the baby adopted and she'd never see him again.

Katya couldn't offer anything of any comfort, so decided it was best to leave Cordelia to finish her drink and mull over how she was going to break the news to Jeremy. As she left, Cordelia handed her an envelope, which Katya stuffed into her handbag and went in search of Jonny, who was waiting for her in his car at the entrance to Blackbushe airfield. This was a secret that was not hers to reveal, and

Jonny was just the person to be with right now. A quiet, comforting presence that she could trust not to ask too many questions.

'Where to?' he asked as she climbed into his car.

They'd solved the case and now it was time to put it all behind her and let the Quinns sort themselves out. That was no role for a detective. Her job was done. 'Back to the office. We'll tidy up the case files.' She patted the pocket that contained Cordelia's fee. 'Then I'm going to take you all out for a slap-up meal.'

'That sounds good,' said Jonny. 'We should celebrate the case that looked impossible.'

'Three out of three's a good score,' said Katya. 'But I always thought Jeremy was innocent.'

'Really?' said Jonny.

'No,' said Katya. 'I was ready to chuck it in several times.'

Jonny laughed. 'You never said.'

'Couldn't disappoint you all, could I?'

# 29

Ivo kicked off his shoes and ran into the sea. Harold was all set to follow him, but found that Jonny had him securely fastened to his lead and was holding tight. 'You wouldn't like it,' said Jonny. 'Dogs are not allowed on the beach, and anyway you hate water.'

Harold snorted and lay down with his head between his paws, watching Ivo.

'Silly dog,' said Jasmine. 'Ivo's coming back. The water's too cold for him to stay in for long.'

'He's probably forgotten that Ivo left him with me once before but always came back for him,' said Jonny, leaning back in a deckchair to enjoy the sun on his face.

Jonny had chosen the spot. They used to go there with his son Marcus when he was little, and more recently with his grandson. It was the closest seaside to Windsor – a stretch of grass with picnic tables and easy access to a sandy beach.

Jasmine opened the picnic hamper and started unpacking it. Karim had done them proud, and Katya gazed hungrily at the food. Jasmine covered the table with a linen cloth, one that Belinda had brought back from a holiday in Provence some years ago and never used. She unpacked bowls of fresh tomatoes, roasted chicken wings, crispy Persian rice, minty lamb kebabs, garlic bread wrapped in foil to keep it warm, and a green salad with asparagus tips and Greek olives. It would feed way more than the five detectives, even if one of them was Katya and another was a dog with an insatiable appetite.

The last things to emerge from the hamper were a flask of iced rose petal lemonade, which Jasmine poured into four pink, flower-embossed tumblers, and a bottle of water, which she tipped into an enamel bowl for Harold.

Ivo ran across the beach to join them, sitting on the grass and rubbing his feet dry on a towel that Jonny had kept in his car since the days when he'd walked Harold regularly.

'You should have brought swimming things and gone in properly,' said Katya, looking at children running in and out of the sea, swimming out ready to ride back on the breaking waves.

'Paddling's fine,' said Ivo, wiping sand from between his toes. 'And the water's cold. I'll wait until we go to Greece.'

'You're going to Greece?' Jasmine asked, looking at him in surprise. As far as she knew, Ivo had never been further than the Tower of London, and that was on a school trip.

'Beginning of September,' said Ivo. 'Brian gets discounted tickets. The sea's warm in Greece.'

'Anyone else going on holiday?' Katya asked. 'I might pop up to Yorkshire for a day or two, revisit some old haunts and look up a couple of contacts.'

'Dad and I thought we'd go away for a few days in the autumn. We haven't been anywhere together since I was little. We fancy a cottage by the sea, somewhere windy.'

'You'll close *Jasmine's*?'

She shook her head and grinned at Jonny. 'Can I tell them?'

'It's not a secret,' he said.

'Belinda and Jonny are going to be in charge while we're away.'

'We'll move in for a few days,' said Jonny. 'Belinda's decided she's going to open a second breakfast club. In High Wycombe this time. She's already found a café willing to be part of it. We'll work together while Karim and Jasmine are away so she'll get the experience she needs.'

'So you two won't have a holiday?' Ivo asked.

Jonny fished into his pocket and pulled out a leaflet. 'Just a short break at the beginning of September,' he said. 'We're going to this. Belinda's idea again.'

They crowded round to read it.

'Tents?' said Ivo. 'You're going camping?'

'Glamping,' said Jonny. 'You won't catch me pitching a tent and cooking on a primus.'

Jasmine grabbed the leaflet from Ivo and read it. 'It's a festival,' she said. 'I can't really see you wading through mud to listen to bands, even if you do have the use of a luxury tent.'

'It's a festival of ideas,' said Jonny. 'Writers and philosophers, a couple of politicians.'

'You sit around listening to lectures all day?' Ivo asked.

'There are some bands as well, and stand-up comedians.'

'Let's hope there are no dead bodies,' said Katya, as she helped herself to the last chicken wing.

BUT *WILL* there be a dead body? Find out by reading *Death at the Festival.*

The Breakfast Club Detectives' fourth case.

Pre order your copy here:

**https://books2read.com/u/mB8DNZ**

## ACKNOWLEDGMENTS

I would like to thank you so much for reading **Death on the Carousel** If you have a few moments to spare a short review would be very much appreciated. Reviews really help me and will help other people who might consider reading my books.

I would also like to thank my editor, Sally Silvester-Wood at *Black Sheep Books*, my cover designer, Anthony O'Brien and all my fellow writers at *Quite Write* who have patiently listened to extracts and offered suggestions.


Discover more about Hilary Pugh and download the Breakfast Club Detectives prequel novella **Crime about Town** FREE at www.hilary-pugh.com

## ALSO BY HILARY PUGH

<u>The Ian Skair: Private Investigator series</u>

**Finding Lottie – series prequel**

**<u>Free</u> when you join my mailing list:**

https://storyoriginapp.com/giveaways/61799962-7dc3-11eb-b5c8-7b3702734d0c

**The Laird of Drumlychtoun**

https://books2read.com/u/bwrEky

**Postcards from Jamie**

https://books2read.com/u/4X28Ae

**Mystery at Murriemuir**

https://books2read.com/u/mgj8Bx

**The Diva of Dundas Farm**

https://books2read.com/u/bMYMJA

**The Man in the Red Overcoat**

https://books2read.com/u/4DJRge

❀ Created with Vellum

Printed in Great Britain
by Amazon